ALAA AL ASWANY is the bestselling author of three previous books published in Arabic. He is a journalist who writes a monthly opposition newspaper column, and he makes his living as a dentist in Cairo, Egypt, where his first office was in the Yacoubian Building.

Praise for *The Yacoubian Building*

"Captivating and controversial ... An amazing glimpse of modern Egyptian society and culture."　　　　*New York Review of Books*

"With its interlocking vignettes and intertwining characters, Alaa Al Aswany's hip and racy novel creates a complex narrative of contemporary Egyptian life."
　　　　　　　　KAELEN WILSON-GOLDIE, *The Daily Star* (Beirut)

"Richly peppered with complex characters ... A provocative survey of the social and political pressures of the present that has many Egyptians looking too nostalgically to their more tolerant and hopeful past."　　　　DONNA BRYSON, Associated Press

"The publication of *The Yacoubian Building* has enriched the art of the Egyptian novel." GAMAL AL-GHITANI, author of *Zayni Barakat*

"Delves into a mix of power, corruption, sex, exploitation, poverty, and extremism ... [*The Yacoubian Building*] lucidly captures the varied aspects of Egyptian life: straight, gay, rich, poor, powerful, and powerless."　　　　　　　　　　　　　　*Egypt Today*

"The novel's elegant prose touches sensitive nerves in its look at the country's corruption and religious fanaticism ... No other Egyptian, or Arab writer for that matter, has so boldly broken through the literary stagnation of the last fifty years by addressing these themes. Except perhaps Naguib Mahfouz, the Nobel laureate who penned *The Cairo Trilogy* in the 1950s."
　　　　　　　　SAAD EDDIN IBRAHIM, *Foreign Policy* magazine

THE YACOUBIAN BUILDING

ALAA AL ASWANY

Translated by
HUMPHREY DAVIES

FOURTH ESTATE · London

First published in Great Britain in 2007 by
Fourth Estate
An imprint of HarperCollins*Publishers*
77–85 Fulham Palace Road
London W6 8JB
www.4thestate.co.uk

First published in Arabic in 2002 under the title *'Imarat Ya'qubyan*

1

A catalogue record for this book is
available from the British Library

ISBN-13 978-0-00-724361-7
ISBN-10 0-00-724361-8

Printed in Great Britain by Clays Ltd, St Ives plc

Recommended by pen

This book has been selected to receive financial assistance from English
PEN's Writers in Translation programme supported by Bloomberg.
English PEN exists to promote literature and its understanding, uphold
writers' freedoms around the world, campaign against the persecution
and imprisonment of writers for stating their views, and promote the
friendly co-operation of writers and free exchange of ideas.

This book is proudly printed on paper which contains wood
from well managed forests, certified in accordance with
the rules of the Forest Stewardship Council.
For more information about FSC,
please visit www.fsc-uk.org

Mixed Sources
Product group from well-managed
forests and other controlled sources
www.fsc.org Cert no. SW-COC-1806
© 1996 Forest Stewardship Council

FSC

To My Guardian Angel—Iman Taymur

Cast of Characters

Abaskharon: Zaki Bey's servant and the brother of Malak. His right leg was amputated when he was younger.

Abd Rabbuh: A police officer from northern Egypt doing military service in Cairo. He has a wife and a son, but is the love interest of Hatim Rasheed.

Busayna: The oldest daughter of a poor family that lives in the shacks on the roof of the Yacoubian Building. When her father died, she began earning money for her family by working at a clothing shop. She is Taha's childhood sweetheart and wonders if their relationship will last.

Dawlat el Dessouki: Zaki Bey's older sister, with whom he lives. While Zaki Bey loves her, they fight constantly. She has been married three times and has two children.

Fikri Abd el Shaheed: A lawyer and agent for the Yacoubian Building.

Hagg Muhammad Azzam: An extremely wealthy and successful businessman who started out as an immigrant shining shoes on the street. His business is located in the Yacoubian Building, and he aspires to hold a political office. He has a wife and three sons — Fawzi, Qadri, and Hamdi.

Hatim Rasheed: The editor in chief of *Le Caire*, a French language newspaper in Cairo. He is the son of aristocrats and his mother was French. He is a closeted homosexual who frequents Chez Nous, a gay bar in Cairo, and is in love with Abd Rabbuh. He lives in an apartment in the Yacoubian Building.

Kamal el Fouli: He is a secretary of the Patriotic Party; although he grew up in poverty, he has become a corrupt politician with major power over Egyptian elections.

Malak: A Christian shirtmaker and tailor, he longs to have a shop in the Yacoubian Building. Abaskharon is his brother.

Souad Gaber: She is a secretary from Alexandria with a son, Tamir, and has no husband. She catches the eye of Hagg Azzam and becomes his second wife.

Taha el Shazli: The son of the Yacoubian Building doorkeeper, who lives in shacks on the roof. He is a very devout Muslim who aspires to be a police officer and is in love with Busayna.

Zaki Bey el Dessouki: An aging playboy with inherited wealth, but is a failed engineer. He is the youngest son of Abd el Aal Basha Dessouki, who was a former prime minister and one of the richest men in Egypt before the revolution. He lives with his sister Dawlat, and has an office in the Yacoubian Building.

Acknowledgments

This novel would not have seen the light without the help of many friends, first among whom is my friend and teacher Alaa el Deeb, to whom I owe the credit for anything I have achieved in the field of literature. Next are Gamal al-Ghitani, who courageously undertook the publication of the novel in *Akhbar al-adab*, and Dr. Galal Amin, who adopted it enthusiastically and recommended it to the publishers. Likewise, I cannot forget the kindness of Bilal Fadl, Khalid al Sirgani, Ragab Hassan, Makkawi Sa'id, Mahmoud el Wardani, and Muhammad Ibraheem Mabruk, to all of whom I extend my thanks and gratitude.

Translator's Note

Alaa Al Aswany, born in 1957 and a dentist by profession, has written from an early age. His published works include novels, short stories, and a novella, as well as prolific contributions on literature, politics, and social issues to newspapers and magazines covering the political spectrum. *The Yacoubian Building* is his second published novel. Since appearing in 2002, it has gone through several editions and was the bestselling Arabic novel for the years 2002 and 2003. It was voted Best Novel for 2003 by listeners to Egypt's Middle East Broadcasting service. In 2004 Al Aswany published a novella and nine short stories in Arabic in a collection called *Niran Sadiqa* (*Friendly Fire*). He is at work on a novel entitled *Chicago*.

The Yacoubian Building exists, at the address given in the novel. Indeed, it was there that the author's father (Abbas Al Aswany, himself a noted author and winner of the State Prize for Literature for 1974) maintained an office, and there that the author opened his first dental clinic. However, a wanderer on Cairo's Suleiman Basha Street will notice that the real Yacoubian Building does not match its literary namesake in every detail: rather than being in the "high European style" and boasting "balconies decorated with Greek faces carved from stone," it is a restrained albeit elegant exercise in art deco, innocent of balconies. Similarly, the real Halegian's Bar is situated on Abd el Khaliq Sarwat Street, rather than Antikkhana Street. The same logic applies to the characters: while many Egyptian readers believe they know who a given character "really" is, few are portraits from life and in most cases a number of originals have contributed aspects to them. Likewise, the reader need not pay too much heed to the fact that the events described nominally take place before and during Iraq's 1990 invasion of Kuwait: the novel reflects the Egypt of the present.

It would be a mistake, in other words, to assume that everything mentioned in *The Yacoubian Building* is an exact portrait of an identifiable existing original. While the world of the book is undeniably that of today's Egypt, the author achieves this sense of verisimilitude by taking recognizable features from multiple known originals to form new creations. That these collages are so convincing is a measure of the novel's genius and explains in part its appeal.

Inevitably, the book contains numerous references to people and events that are likely to be unfamiliar to the non-Egyptian reader. These are explained in the Glossary at the end of the book. Quotations from the Qur'an are italicized and Arberry's translation has been used (Arthur J. Arberry, *The Koran Interpreted*, Oxford University Press, 1998); a list of references follows the Glossary.

While taking full responsibility for any errors, the translator acknowledges his debt to Siham Abdel Salam, Jacinthe Assaad, Madiha Doss, Maria Golia, Fawzi Mansour, A. Rushdi Nasef, Sayed Ragab, Diya Rashwan, and, above all, the author for help on various aspects of the text.

This translation is dedicated to Gasim.

The Yacoubian Building

✑ 1 ✑

The distance between Baehler Passage, where Zaki Bey el Dessouki lives, and his office in the Yacoubian Building is not more than a hundred meters, but it takes him an hour to cover it each morning as he is obliged to greet his friends on the street. Clothing- and shoe-store owners, their employees (of both sexes), waiters, cinema staff, habitués of the Brazilian Coffee Stores, even doorkeepers, shoeshine men, beggars, and traffic cops—Zaki Bey knows them all by name and exchanges greetings and news with them. Zaki Bey is one of the oldest residents of Suleiman Basha Street, to which he came in the late 1940s after his return from his studies in France and which he has never thereafter left. To the residents of the street he cuts a well-loved, folkloric figure when he appears before them in his three-piece suit (winter and summer, its bagginess hiding his tiny, emaciated body); with his carefully ironed handkerchief always dangling from his jacket pocket and always of the same color as his tie; with his celebrated cigar, which, in his glory days, was Cuban deluxe but is now of the foul-smelling, tightly packed, low-quality local kind; and with his old, wrinkled face, his thick glasses, his gleaming false teeth, and his dyed black hair, whose few locks are arranged in rows from the leftmost to the rightmost side of his head in the hope of covering the broad, naked, bald patch. In brief, Zaki Bey el Dessouki is something of a legend, which makes his presence both much looked for and completely unreal, as though he might disappear at any moment, or as though he were an

3

actor playing a part, of whom it is understood that once done he will take off his costume and put his original clothes back on. If we add to the above his jolly temperament, his unceasing stream of scabrous jokes, and his amazing ability to engage in conversation anyone he meets as though he were an old friend, we will understand the secret of the warm welcome with which everyone on the street greets him. Indeed Zaki Bey has only to appear at the top end of the street at around ten in the morning for the salutations to ring out from every side, and often a number of his disciples among the young men who work in the stores will rush up to him to ask him jokingly about certain sexual matters that remain obscure to them, in which case Zaki Bey will draw on his vast and encyclopedic knowledge of the subject to explain to the youths—in great detail, with the utmost pleasure, and in a voice audible to all—the most subtle sexual secrets. Sometimes, in fact, he will ask for a pen and paper (provided in the twinkling of an eye) so that he can draw clearly for the young men some curious coital position that he himself tried in the days of his youth.

Some important information on Zaki Bey el Dessouki should be provided. He is the youngest son of Abd el Aal Basha el Dessouki, the well-known pillar of the Wafd who was prime minister on more than one occasion and was one of the richest men before the Revolution, he and his family owning more than five thousand feddans of prime agricultural land.

Zaki Bey studied engineering in Paris. It had been expected, of course, that he would play a leading political role in Egypt using his father's influence and wealth, but suddenly the Revolution erupted and everything changed. Abd el Aal Basha was arrested and brought before the revolutionary tribunal and, though the charge of political corruption failed to stick, he remained in detention for a while and most of his possessions were confiscated and distributed among the peasants under the land reform. Under the impact of all this the Basha soon died, the father's misfortune leaving its mark also on the son. The engineering office that he opened in the Yacoubian Building quickly failed and was transformed with time into the place where Zaki Bey spends his free time each day reading the newspapers, drinking coffee, meeting friends and lovers, or sitting for hours on the balcony contemplating the passersby and traffic on Suleiman Basha.

It must be said, however, that the failure that Engineer Zaki el Dessouki has met with in his professional life should not be attributed entirely to the Revolution; it stems rather, at base, from the feebleness of his ambition and his obsession with sensual pleasure. Indeed his life, which has lasted sixty-five years so far, revolves with all its comings and goings, both happy and painful almost entirely around one word— women. He is one of those who fall completely and hopelessly into the sweet clutches of captivity of the female and for whom women are not a lust that flares up and, once satisfied, is extinguished, but an entire world of fascination that constantly renews itself in images of infinitely alluring diversity—the firm, voluptuous bosoms with swelling nipples like delicious grapes; the backsides, pliable and soft, quivering as though in anticipation of his violent assault from behind; the painted lips that drink kisses and moan with pleasure; the hair in all its manifestations (long, straight, and demure, or long and wild with disordered tresses, or medium-length, domestic and well-settled, or that short hair *à la garçon* that evokes unfamiliar, boyish kinds of sex). And the eyes . . . ah, how lovely are the looks from those eyes—honest or dissimulating and duplicitous; bold or demure; even furious, reproachful, and filled with loathing!

So much and even more did Zaki Bey love women. He had known every kind, starting with Lady Kamla, daughter of the former king's maternal uncle, with whom he learned the etiquette and rites of the royal bed chambers—the candles that burn all night, the glasses of

French wine that kindle the flames of desire and obliterate fear, the hot bath before the assignation, when the body is anointed with creams and perfumes. From Lady Kamla (she of the inexorable appetite) he learned how to start and when to desist and how to ask for the most abandoned sexual positions in extremely refined French. Zaki Bey has also slept with women of all classes — oriental dancers, foreigners, society ladies and the wives of the eminent and distinguished, university and secondary school students, even fallen women, peasant women, and housemaids. Every one had her special flavor, and he would often laughingly compare the bedding of Lady Kamla with its rules of protocol and that of that beggar woman he picked up one night when drunk in his Buick and took back to his apartment in Baehler Passage, and whom he discovered, when he went into the bathroom with her to wash her body himself, to be so poor that she made her underwear out of empty cement sacks. He can still remember, with a mixture of tenderness and distress, the woman's embarrassment as she took off her bloomers, on which was written in large letters "Portland Cement—Tura." He remembers too that she was one of the most beautiful of all the women he has known and one of the most ardent in love.

All these varied and teeming experiences have made of Zaki el Dessouki a true expert on women, and in "the science of women," as he calls it, he has strange and eccentric theories that, whether one accepts or rejects them, definitely deserve consideration. Thus he believes, for example, that the outstandingly lovely woman is usually a cold lover in bed, while women of middling beauty or even of a certain degree of ugliness are always more passionate because they are truly in need of love and will make every effort in their power to please their lovers. Zaki Bey also believes that how a woman pronounces the letter "s"—specifically—is a clue as to how ardent she will be when making love. Thus, if a woman says a word such as "Susu" or "basbusa," for example, in a tremulous, arousing way, he concludes immediately that she is gifted in bed, and that the opposite will also be true. Zaki Bey also believes that every woman on the face of the earth is surrounded by a sort of ethereal field inhabited by vibrations that though invisible and inaudible can nevertheless be vaguely felt, and that one who has trained himself to read these vibrations can divine the degree to which that woman is sexually satisfied. Thus no matter how respectable and modest the woman, Zaki Bey is able to sense her sexual hunger from the trembling of her voice or her nervous, affectedly exaggerated laugh, or even from the warmth radiated by her hand when he shakes it. As for the women who are possessed by a satanic lust that they can never quench (*"les filles de joie,"* as Zaki Bey calls them)—those mysterious women who feel that they truly exist only when in bed and making love and who place no other pleasure in life on the same footing as sex, those unhappy beings fated by virtue of their excessive thirst for pleasure to meet with a terrifying and unavoidable fate—those women, Zaki el Dessouki asserts, are all the same, even though their faces may vary. He will invite any who doubt this fact to inspect the pictures published in the newspapers of women sentenced to be executed for participating with their lovers in the murder of their husbands, saying, "We shall discover—with a little observation—that they all have the same countenance: the lips generally full, sensual, relaxed, and not pressed together; the features thick and libidinous; and the look bright and empty, like that of a hungry animal."

It was Sunday. The stores on Suleiman Basha closed their doors, and the bars and cinemas were full of customers. With its locked stores and old-fashioned, European-style buildings the street seemed dark and empty, as though it were in a sad, romantic, European film. At the start of the day, Shazli, the old doorman, moved his seat from next to the elevator to the sidewalk in front of the Yacoubian Building to watch the people going in and out on their day off.

Zaki el Dessouki got to his office a little before noon and from the first instant Abaskharon, the office servant, took in the situation. After twenty years of working for Zaki Bey, Abaskharon had learned to understand his moods at a single glance, knowing full well what it meant when his master arrived at the office excessively elegantly dressed, the scent of the expensive perfume that he kept for special occasions preceding him, and appeared tense and nervous, standing up, sitting down, walking irritably about, never settling to anything, and hiding his impatience in brusqueness and gruffness—it meant that the Bey was expecting his first meeting with a new girlfriend. As a result Abaskharon didn't get angry when the Bey started berating him for no reason, but shook his head as one who understands how things stand, quickly finished sweeping the reception room, and then grabbed his wooden crutches and pounded vigorously and rapidly off down the long tiled corridor to the large room where the Bey was sitting. In a voice that experience had taught him to make completely neutral, he said, "Do you have a meeting, Excellency? Should I get everything ready, Excellency?"

The Bey looked in his direction and contemplated him for an instant as though making up his mind as to the proper tone of voice to use in reply. He looked at Abaskharon's striped flannel gallabiya, torn in numerous places, at his crutches and his amputated leg, at his aged face and the grizzled stubble on his chin, at his cunning, narrow eyes and the familiar unctuous, scared smile that never left him, and said, "Get everything ready for a meeting, quickly."

Thus spoke the Bey in brusque tones as he went out onto the balcony. In their common dictionary, "a meeting" meant the Bey's spending time alone with a woman in the office, and "everything" referred to certain rites that Abaskharon performed for his master just before the love-making, starting with an injection of imported Tri-B vitamin supplement that he administered to him in the buttock and that hurt him so much each time that he would moan out loud and pour curses on "that ass" Abaskharon for his heavy, brutish touch. This would be followed by a cup of sugarless coffee made of beans spiced with nutmeg that the bey would imbibe slowly while dissolving beneath his tongue a small piece of opium. The rites concluded with the placing of a large plate of salad in the middle of the table next to a bottle of Black Label whisky, two empty glasses, and a metal champagne bucket filled to the brim with ice cubes.

Abaskharon quickly set about getting everything ready while Zaki Bey took a seat on the balcony overlooking Suleiman Basha, lit a cigar, and settled down to watch the passersby. His feelings swung between bounding impatience for the beautiful meeting and promptings of anxiety that his sweetheart Rabab would fail to turn up for the appointment, in which case he would have wasted the entire month of effort that he had expended in pursuit of her. He had been obsessed with her since he first saw her at the Cairo Bar in Tawfikiya Square where she worked as a hostess. She had bewitched him completely and day after day he had gone back to the bar to see her. Describing her to an aged friend, he had said, "She represents the beauty of the common people in all its vulgarity and provocativeness. She looks as though she had just stepped out of one of those paintings by Mahmoud Said." Zaki Bey then expatiated on this to make his meaning clearer to his friend, saying, "Do you remember that maid at home who used to beguile your dreams when you were an adolescent? And of whom it was your dearest wish that you might stick yourself to her soft behind, then grab her tender-skinned breasts with your hands as she washed the dishes at the kitchen sink? And that she would bend over in a way that made you stick to her even more closely and whisper in provocative refusal, before giving herself to you, 'Sir. . . . It's wrong, sir . . . ?' In Rabab I have stumbled onto just such a treasure."

However, stumbling onto a treasure does not necessarily mean possessing it and, for the sake of his beloved Rabab, Zaki Bey had been compelled to put up with numerous annoyances, like having to spend whole nights in a dirty, cramped, badly lit and poorly ventilated place like the Cairo Bar. He had been almost suffocated by the crowds and the thick cigarette smoke and had come close to being deafened by the racket of the sound system that never even for an instant stopped emitting disgusting, vulgar songs. And that was to say nothing of the foul-mouthed arguments and fistfights among the patrons of the establishment, who were a mixture of skilled laborers, bad types, and foreigners, or of the glasses of foul, stomach-burning brandy that he was forced to toss down every night and the exorbitant mistakes in the checks to which he turned a blind eye, even leaving a big tip for the house plus another even bigger one that he would thrust into the cleavage of Rabab's dress, feeling, as soon as his fingers touched her full, swaying breasts, the hot blood surging in his veins and a violence of desire that almost hurt him it was so powerful and insistent.

Zaki Bey had put up with all of this for the sake of Rabab, inviting her again and again to meet him outside the bar. She would refuse coquettishly and he would repeat his invitation, never losing hope, and then just yesterday she had agreed to visit him at the office. So overjoyed had he been that he had thrust a fifty-pound note into her dress without the slightest feeling of regret, and she had come up to him so close that he had felt her hot breath on his face and, biting her lower lip with her teeth, she had whispered in a provocative voice that demolished what equanimity he had left, "Tomorrow, I'll pay you back, sir . . . for everything you've done for me. . . ."

Zaki Bey bore the painful Tri-B injection, dissolved the opium, and started slowly drinking the first glass of whisky, followed by a second and a third, which soon released him from his tension. Good humor enveloped him and pleasant musings started gently caressing his head like soft tunes. Rabab's appointment was for one o'clock, and by the time the wall clock struck two, Zaki Bey had almost lost hope, when suddenly he heard the sound of Abaskharon's crutches striking the hallway tiles, followed immediately by his face appearing around the door as he said, his voice panting with excitement as though the news genuinely made him happy, "Madame Rabab has arrived, Excellency."

In 1934, Hagop Yacoubian, the millionaire and then doyen of the Armenian community in Egypt, decided to construct an apartment block that would bear his name. He chose for it the best site on Suleiman Basha and engaged a well-known Italian engineering firm to build it, and the firm came up with a beautiful design—ten lofty stories in the high classical European style, the balconies decorated with Greek faces carved in stone, the columns, steps, and corridors all of natural marble, and the latest model of elevator by Schindler. Construction continued for two whole years, at the end of which there emerged an architectural gem that so exceeded expectations that its owner requested of the Italian architect that he inscribe his name, Yacoubian, on the inside of the doorway in large Latin characters that were lit up at night in neon, as though to immortalize his name and emphasize his ownership of the gorgeous building.

The cream of the society of those days took up residence in the Yacoubian Building—ministers, big land-owning bashas, foreign manufacturers, and two Jewish millionaires (one of them belonging to the famous Mosseri family). The ground floor of the building was divided equally between a spacious garage with numerous doors at the back where the residents' cars (most of them luxury makes such as Rolls-Royce, Buick, and Chevrolet) were kept overnight and at the front a large store with three frontages that Yacoubian kept as a showroom for the silver products made in his factories. This showroom remained in business successfully for four decades, then little by little declined, until recently it was bought by Hagg Muhammad Azzam, who reopened it as a clothing store. On the broad roof two rooms with utilities were set aside for the doorkeeper and his family to live in, while on the other side of the roof fifty small rooms were constructed, one for each apartment in the building. Each of these rooms was no more than two meters by two meters in area and the walls and doors were all of solid iron and locked with padlocks whose keys were handed over to the owners of the apartments. These iron rooms had a variety of uses at that time, such as storing foodstuffs, overnight kenneling for dogs (if they were large or fierce), and laundering clothes, which in those days (before the spread of the electric washing machine) was undertaken by professional washerwomen who would do the wash in the room and hang it out on long lines that extended across the roof. The rooms were never used as places for the servants to sleep, perhaps because the residents of the building at that time were aristocrats and foreigners who could not conceive of the possibility of any human being sleeping in such a cramped place. Instead, they would set aside a room in their ample, luxurious apartments (which sometimes contained eight or ten rooms on two levels joined by an internal stairway) for the servants.

In 1952 the Revolution came and everything changed. The exodus of Jews and foreigners from Egypt started, and every apartment that was vacated by reason of the departure of its owners was taken over by an officer of the armed forces, who were the influential people of the time. By the 1960s, half the apartments were lived in by officers of various ranks, from first lieutenants and recently married captains all the way up to generals, who would move into the building with their large families. General El Dakrouri (at one point director of President Muhammad Naguib's office) was even able to acquire two large apartments next door to one another on the tenth floor, one of which he used as a residence for himself and his family, the other as a private office where he would meet petitioners in the afternoon.

The officers' wives began using the iron rooms in a different way: for the first time they were turned into places for the stewards, cooks, and young maids that they brought from their villages to serve their families to stay in. Some of the officers' wives were of plebeian origin and could see nothing wrong in raising small animals (rabbits, ducks, and chickens) in the iron rooms, and the West Cairo District's registers saw numerous complaints filed by the old residents to prevent the raising of such animals on the roof. Owing to the officers' pull, however, these always got shelved, until the residents complained to General El Dakrouri, who, thanks to his influence with the former, was able to put a stop to this unsanitary phenomenon.

In the seventies came the "Open Door Policy" and the well-to-do started to leave the downtown area for El Mohandiseen and Medinet Nasr, some of them selling their apartments in the Yacoubian Building, others using them as offices and clinics for their recently graduated sons or renting them furnished to Arab tourists. The result was that the connection between the iron rooms and the building's apartments was gradually severed, and the former stewards and servants ceded them for money to new, poor residents coming from the countryside or working somewhere downtown who needed a place to live that was close by and cheap.

This transfer of control was made easier by the death of the Armenian agent in charge of the building, Monsieur Grigor, who used to administer the property of the millionaire Hagop Yacoubian with the utmost honesty and accuracy, sending the proceeds in December of each year to Switzerland, where Yacoubian's heirs had migrated after the Revolution. Grigor was succeeded as agent by Maître Fikri Abd el Shaheed, the lawyer, who would do anything provided he was paid, taking, for example, one large percentage from the former occupant of the iron room and another from the new tenant for writing him a contract for the room.

The final outcome was the growth of a new community on the roof that was entirely independent of the rest of the building. Some of the newcomers rented two rooms next to one another and made a small residence out of them with all utilities (latrine and washroom), while others, the poorest, collaborated to create a shared latrine for every three or four rooms, the roof community thus coming to resemble any other popular community in Egypt. The children run around all over the roof barefoot and half naked and the women spend the day cooking, holding gossip sessions in the sun, and, frequently, quarreling, at which moments they will exchange the grossest insults as well as accusations touching on one another's honor, only to make up soon after and behave with complete goodwill toward one another as though nothing has happened. Indeed, they will plant hot, lip-smacking kisses on each other's cheeks and even weep from excess of sentiment and affection.

The men pay little attention to the women's quarrels, viewing them as just one more indication of that defectiveness of mind of which the Prophet—God bless him and grant him peace—spoke. These men of the roof pass their days in a bitter and wearisome struggle to earn a living and return at the end of the day exhausted and in a hurry to partake of their small pleasures—tasty hot food and a few pipes of tobacco (or of hashish if they have the money), which they either smoke in a water-pipe on their own or stay up to smoke while talking with the others on the roof on summer nights. The third pleasure is sex, in which the people of the roof revel and which they see nothing wrong with discussing frankly so long as it is of a sort sanctioned by religion. Here there is a contradiction. Any of the men of the roof would be ashamed, like most lower-class people, to mention his wife by name in front of the others, referring to her as "Mother of So-and-so," or "the kids," as in "the kids cooked mulukhiya today," the company understanding that he means

14

his wife. This same man, however, will feel no embarrassment at mentioning, in a gathering of other men, the most precise details of his private relations with his wife, so that the men of the roof come to know almost everything of one another's sexual activities. As for the women, and without regard for their degree of religiosity or morality, they all love sex enormously and will whisper the secrets of the bed to one another, followed, if they are on their own, by bursts of laughter that are carefree or even obscene. They do not love it simply as a way of quenching lust but because sex, and their husbands' greed for it, makes them feel that despite all the misery they suffer they are still women, beautiful and desired by their menfolk. At that certain moment when the children are asleep, having had their dinner and given praise to their Lord, and there is enough food in the house to last for a week or more, and there is a little money set aside for emergencies, and the room they all live in is clean and tidy, and the husband has come home on Thursday night in a good mood because of the effect of the hashish and asked for his wife, is it not then her duty to obey his call, after first bathing, prettying herself up, and putting on perfume? Do these brief hours of pleasure not furnish her with proof that her wretched life is somehow, despite everything, blessed with success? It would take a skilled painter to convey to us the expressions on the face of a woman on the roof of a Friday morning, when, after her husband has gone down to perform the prayer and she has washed off the traces of love-making, she emerges to hang out the washed bedding—at that moment, with her wet hair, her flushed complexion, and the serene expression in her eyes, she looks like a rose that, watered with the dew of the morning, has arrived at the peak of its perfection.

The darkness of night was receding, heralding a new morning, and a dim, small light on the roof shone from the window of the room belonging to Shazli the doorkeeper, where his teenage son Taha had spent the night sleepless with anxiety. Now he performed the dawn prayer, plus the two superrogatory prostrations, then sat on the bed in his white gallabiya reading from *The Book of Answered Prayer* and repeating in a frail whisper in the silence of the room, "O God, I ask You for whatever good this day may hold and I take refuge with You from whatever evil it may hold and from any evil I may meet within it. O God, watch over me with Your eye that never sleeps and forgive me through Your power, that I perish not; You are my hope. My Lord, Master of Majesty and Bounty, to You I direct my face, so bring Your noble face close to me and receive me with Your unalloyed forgiveness and generosity, smiling on me and content with me in Your mercy!"

Taha continued to read the prayers until the light of morning shone into the chamber and little by little life started to stir in the iron rooms—voices, cries, laughter and coughing, doors shutting and opening, and the smell of hot water, tea, coffee, charcoal, and tobacco. For the inhabitants of the roof it was just the start of another day; Taha el Shazli, however, knew that on this day his fate would be decided forever. After a few hours, he would present himself for the character interview at the Police Academy—the last hurdle in the long race of hope. Since childhood, he has dreamed of being a police officer and has devoted all his efforts to realizing that dream. He has applied himself to memorizing everything for the general secondary examination and as a result obtained a score of 98 percent (Humanities) without private tutoring (apart from a few review groups at the school, for which his father had only just been able to come up with the money). During summer vacations he joined the Abdeen Youth Center (for ten pounds a month) and put up with the exhausting body-building exercises in order to acquire the athletic physique that would allow him to pass the physical fitness tests at the Police Academy.

In order to realize this dream, Taha has courted the police officers in the district until they are all his friends, both those of the Kasr el Nil police station and of the Kotzika substation that belongs to it. From them, Taha has learned all the details relating to the admission tests for the police and found out too about the twenty thousand pounds that the well-to-do pay as a bribe to ensure their children's acceptance into the college (and how he wishes he possessed such a sum!). In order to realize this dream, Taha el Shazli has also put up with the meanness and the arrogance of the building's inhabitants.

Since he was little he had helped his father run errands for people, and when his intelligence and academic excellence manifested themselves, the inhabitants reacted in different ways. Some encouraged him to study, gave him generous gifts, and prophesied a glorious future for him. Others, however (and there were many of these), were somehow disturbed by the idea of "the high-flying doorkeeper's son" and tried to convince his father to enroll him in vocational training as soon as he finished intermediary school "so that he can learn a trade that will be of use to you and to himself," as they would say to elderly "uncle" Shazli, with a show of concern for his welfare. When Taha enrolled in general secondary school and continued to do well, they would send for him on exam days and entrust him with difficult tasks that would take a long time, tipping him generously to tempt him, while concealing a malign desire to keep him from his studies. Taha would accept these tasks because of his need for cash but would go on wearing himself out with study, often going one or two days without sleep.

When the general secondary exam results came out and he obtained a higher score than the children of many in the building, the grumblers started to talk openly. One of them would run into another in front of the elevator and ask him sarcastically if he had offered his congratulations to the doorkeeper on his son's high marks; then he would add bitingly that the doorkeeper's son would soon join the Police Academy and graduate as an officer with two stars on his epaulettes. At this point the other person would candidly reveal his annoyance, first praising Taha's character and his hard work, then going on to say in a serious tone of voice (as though he had the general principle and not the individual in mind) that jobs in the police, the judiciary, and sensitive positions in general should be given only to the children of people who were somebody because the children of doorkeepers, laundrymen, and such like, if they attained any authority, would use it to compensate for the inferiority complexes and other neuroses they had acquired during their early childhood. Then he would bring his speech to an end by cursing Abd el Nasser, who had introduced free education, or quote as authority the saying of the Prophet—God bless him and grant him peace—"Teach not the children of the lowly!"

These same residents started picking on Taha when the results appeared and finding fault with him for the most trivial of reasons, such as washing the car and forgetting to put the floormats back in place, or being a few minutes late in the performance of an errand to somewhere far away, or buying ten things for them from the market and forgetting one. They would insult him deliberately and unmistakably in order to push him into responding that he would not put up with such insults because he was an educated person, which would be their golden opportunity to announce to him the truth—that here he was a mere doorkeeper, no more and no less, and if he didn't like his job he should leave it to someone who needed it. But Taha never gave them that opportunity. He would meet their outbursts with silence, a bowed head, and a slight smile, his handsome brown face at these moments giving the impression that he did not agree with what was directed at him and that it was entirely in his power to rebut the insult but that respect for the other's greater age prevented him from so doing.

This was one of a number of fall-back positions, tantamount to defensive tactics, that Taha used under difficult circumstances in order to express what he felt while at the same time avoiding problems, positions that had initially been a matter of acting for him but which he soon performed sincerely and as though they were the truth. For example, he did not like to sit on the doorkeeper's bench so that he had to get up respectfully for every resident, and if he was sitting on the bench and he saw a resident coming, he would busy himself with something that would obviate his duty to stand up. Similarly, he was accustomed to addressing the residents with a carefully calculated modicum of respect and to treating them as an employee would his superior and not as a servant his master. As for the children of the residents who were close to him in age, he treated them as complete equals. He would call them by their first names and converse and play around with them like close friends, borrowing from them schoolbooks that he might not actually need in order to remind them that despite his position as a doorkeeper he was their colleague when it came to study.

These were the commonplaces of his day-to-day life—poverty, back-breaking hard work, the arrogance of the residents, and the five-pound note, always folded, that his father bestowed on him every Saturday and on which he practiced every stratagem to make last the whole week; the smooth, warm hand of a resident extended lazily and graciously from a car window to give him a tip (at the sight of which he had to raise his hand in a military-style salute and thank his benefactor enthusiastically and audibly); that look, impertinent and full of smugness or covertly sympathetic and tolerant, inspired by embarrassment at the "issue," which he noted in the eyes of his school friends when they visited him and discovered that he lived in the doorkeeper's quarters "up on the roof"; that hateful, embarrassing question "Are you the doorkeeper?" that strangers to the building addressed to him; and the deliberate slowing down of the residents as they entered the building so that he would hurry to relieve them of whatever they were carrying no matter how light or unimportant.

It is with annoyances such as these that the day passes, but when Taha gets into bed at the end of the evening, it is always in a state of purity and with his ablutions made, after he has first performed the evening prayer, plus superrogatory odd and even series of prostrations. Then he stares long into the darkness of the room, gradually soaring until he beholds himself in his mind's eye as a police officer strutting proudly in his beautiful uniform with the brass stars gleaming on his shoulder and the impressive government-issue pistol dangling from his belt. He imagines that he has married his sweetheart Busayna el Sayed and that they have moved to a suitable apartment in an up-market district far from the noise and dirt of the roof.

He firmly believed that God would make all his dreams come true—first of all because he made the utmost effort to honor God's commandments, observing the obligatory prayers and avoiding major sins (and God had given to the observant in a noble verse of the Qur'an the good news that *Had the people of the cities believed and been God-fearing, We would have opened upon them blessings from heaven and earth*) and second because he had the highest expectations of God's good intentions (given that the Almighty and Glorious had said, in words revealed to the Prophet, "I am according to my slaves' expectations of me: if good, then good, and if bad, then bad"). And see—God had fulfilled his promise and granted him success in the general secondary exams, and he had passed, praise God, all the tests for the Police Academy. All that remained for him to do was the character interview, which he would pass that same day, God willing.

Taha rose and prayed the two morning prostrations, plus two more in supplication for the achievement of his wish, then washed, shaved, and began to get dressed. He had bought a new gray suit, a shining white shirt, and a beautiful blue tie for the character interview, and when he glanced at himself for the last time in the mirror, he looked very smart. As he kissed his mother goodbye, she put her hand on his head muttering an incantation, then started praying for him with an ardor that made his heart pound. In the lobby of the building, he found his father sitting with his legs tucked up under him on the bench as was his habit. The old man rose slowly and looked at Taha for a moment. Then he put his hand on his shoulder and smiled, his white mustache quivering and revealing his toothless mouth, and he said proudly, "Congratulations in advance, Mr. Officer!"

It was past ten o'clock and Suleiman Basha was crowded with cars and pedestrians, and most of the stores had opened their doors. It occurred to Taha that he had a whole hour ahead of him before the exam and he decided that he would take a cab for fear of spoiling his suit on the crowded buses. He wished he could spend the remaining time with Busayna. Their agreed method was that he should pass in front of the Shanan clothing store where she worked; when she saw him she would ask permission from Mr. Talal, the owner, to leave, using the excuse that she had to fetch something or other from the store-room, and then catch up with him at their favorite place in the new garden in Tawfikiya Square.

Taha did the usual routine and sat there for about a quarter of an hour before Busayna appeared. At the sight of her, he felt his heart beating hard. He loved the way she walked, moving with small, slow steps, looking at the ground, and giving the impression that she was embarrassed or for some reason regretful, or was walking over a fragile surface with extreme care, so as not to break it with her footsteps. Noticing that she was wearing the tight-fitting red dress that revealed the details of her body and whose wide and low-cut front showed her full breasts, he experienced a surge of anger and remembered that he had quarreled with her before in an attempt to make her stop wearing it. However, he suppressed his annoyance, not wishing to spoil the occasion, and she smiled, showing her small, white, regular teeth and the two wonderful dimples on either side of her mouth and lips, which she had painted dark red. She sat down next to him on the low marble garden wall, turned toward him and looked at him, with her wide seemingly astonished honey-colored eyes and said, "What a dandy!"

He answered in an urgent whisper, "I'm going for the character interview now and I wanted to see you."

"The Lord be with you!" said Busayna with true tenderness. His heart beat hard and at that moment he wished he could clasp her to his chest.

"Are you scared?" she asked.

"I have placed myself in the hands of God, Almighty and Glorious, and whatever Our Lord may do I shall gladly accept, God willing."

He spoke fast, as though he had prepared the answer ahead of time or as though he were trying to convince himself with his own words. He was silent for a moment, then went on gently, looking into her eyes, "Pray for me."

"The Lord grant you success, Taha," she exclaimed warmly.

Then she went on, as though she thought she had gone too far in showing her feelings, "I have to go now because Mr. Talal is waiting for me."

As she withdrew, he tried to make her stay, but she put out her hand and shook his, her eyes avoiding him, and said in an ordinary, formal way, "Best of luck." Later, when he was sitting in the taxi, Taha reflected that Busayna's attitude toward him had changed and there was no point in ignoring it; that he knew her well and that one look was enough for him to penetrate her innermost thoughts. He had memorized everything about her—her face, whether radiant with happiness or sad, her uncertain smile and the way she blushed when she was embarrassed, her wildcat glances and glowering (but still beautiful) features when she was angry; he even loved to look at her when she had just woken up and the traces of sleep were still on her face, making her look like a compliant, gentle-hearted child.

He loved her and he preserved in his memory the image of her as a little girl when she would play with him on the roof and he would run after her and deliberately hang on to her so that the smell of soap from her hair would tickle his nose; of her as a student at the commercial secondary school wearing the white shirt, blue skirt, and short white school socks above black shoes as she walked hugging her bag as though to hide her ripening bosom; and the beautiful images of them wandering together at the Barrages and the Zoo, and of the day when they revealed their love to each other and agreed to marry and how after that she had clung to him and asked him questions about the details of his life, as though she were his young wife looking after him. They had agreed on everything for the future, even the number of children they would have and their names and what their first apartment would look like.

Then suddenly she had changed. She had become less interested in him and took to talking about "their project" listlessly and sarcastically. She would often quarrel with him and avoid meeting him, using a variety of excuses. This had happened right after her father died. Why had she changed? Was their love just an adolescent thing to be grown out of as they got older? Or had she fallen in love with someone else? This last thought pricked him like a thorn till he bled. He started to picture Mr. Talal the Syrian (owner of the store where she worked) taking her arm in his and wearing a wedding suit.

Taha became aware of a heavy worry weighing on his heart, then awoke from his thoughts as the taxi came to a halt in front of the Police Academy building, which at that moment appeared impressive and historic, as though it were the fortress of fate in which his destiny would be decided. His exam nerves came back to him and he started reciting the Throne Verse in a whisper as he approached the gate.

The information available about Abaskharon in his youth is extremely sparse.

We don't know what he did before the age of forty or the circumstances in which his right leg was amputated. Everything we know starts with that rainy winter's day twenty years ago when Abaskharon arrived at the Yacoubian Building in the black Chevrolet of Madame Sanaa Fanous, a widowed Copt of Upper Egyptian origin, rich, and with two children to whose upbringing she had devoted her life following the death of her husband. Despite her devotion to her children, however, she responded from time to time to the whimsical demands of her body and Zaki el Dessouki had got to know her at the Automobile Club and had been her companion for a while. Much as she enjoyed the relationship, her religious conscience gave her no rest and would often make her break into painful tears as she lay in Zaki's arms after the accomplishment of their pleasure and go and appease her guilt by taking on an abundance of good works through the church. Thus it was that no sooner did Borei, Zaki's former office servant, die than she insisted on his appointing Abaskharon (whose name was on the assistance list at the church), and suddenly there he was, standing hunched up like a mouse and staring at the ground, at his first meeting with Zaki Bey, who was so disappointed at his shabby appearance, his amputated leg, and his crutches, which marked him with the stamp of a beggar, that he said sarcastically to his friend Sanaa in French, "But, my dear, I'm running an office, not a charity!"

She continued trying to win him over with blandishments until in the end he grudgingly agreed to employ Abaskharon, with the idea that he would do what she wanted for a few days then throw him out . . . but here they were! Abaskharon had demonstrated from the first day an unusual competence: he had an uncommon capacity for uninterrupted, exhausting work and even asked the Bey daily to give him new things to add to his list of duties. He also possessed a sharp intelligence, adroitness, and shrewdness, which made him do the right thing in any given situation and with a capacity for absolute discretion, for he would see and hear nothing of what took place in front of him, be it even murder.

By dint of these great virtues, before a few months had passed Zaki Bey couldn't do without Abaskharon for so much as an hour. He even had a new bell put in the kitchen of the apartment so that he could summon him whenever he needed him, and he gave him a generous salary and allowed him to stay overnight in the office (which was something he hadn't done with anyone before). Abaskharon for his part had fathomed the Bey's nature from the first day and realized that his master was self-indulgent, a pleasure-seeker, and given to sudden whims and caprices and that his head was rarely free of the effect of narcotics. This sort of man (as per Abaskharon's wide experience of life) was quick to get angry and had a sharp temper but rarely did any harm, and the worst that one was likely to suffer from him was verbal abuse or a dressing down. Abaskharon promised himself that he would never argue with or question his master about what he asked for and that he would always take the initiative in apologizing and ingratiating himself, in order to gain his affection. Likewise he never addressed him by any term other than "Excellency," which he would insert into any sentence he uttered. Thus, if the Bey asked him, for example, "What time is it now?" Abaskharon would reply, "Five o'clock, Excellency."

To tell the truth, Abaskharon's adaptation to his work is somewhat reminiscent of a biological phenomenon. Thus, in the midst of the quiet darkness that reigns over the apartment during the daylight hours and of the ancient musty smell that emanates from the mixing of the scent of old furniture with that of the damp and of the double-strength carbolic acid that the Bey insists be used to clean the bathroom—in this "medium," when Abaskharon emerges from one of the corners of the apartment with his crutches, his ever-dirty gallabiya, his aged hang-dog face, and his ingratiating smile, he seems like a creature functioning effectively in its natural surroundings, like a fish in water, or a cockroach in the drain. Indeed whenever for some reason he leaves the Yacoubian Building and walks down the sunny street through the passersby and the noise of the cars, he looks odd and out of place, like a bat in daylight, and his integrity is restored only when he returns to the office where he has spent two decades concealed in darkness and damp.

We must not, however, be fooled into thinking of Abaskharon as no more than an obedient servant, for the truth is that there is much more to him than that, and behind his servile, weak exterior lies concealed a strong will and precise goals that he will fight courageously and obstinately to achieve. In addition to the raising and educating of his three daughters, he has taken on his shoulders the care of his younger brother Malak and his children too. This gives us the clue to understanding what he does every evening when, alone in his small room, he extracts from the pocket of his gallabiya every coin and small, sweat-soaked, folded banknote, whether obtained directly as tips or that he has succeeded in filching from the purchases for the office. (Abaskharon's brokering methods may be taken as a model of precise, skillful fraud, for he does not, like an amateur, inflate the prices of what he buys, since the prices are known, or may be known, at any moment. Instead he will, for example, filch each day from the coffee, tea, and sugar an amount too small to be noticed, then repackage the stolen provisions in new bags and resell them to Zaki Bey, presenting genuine invoices that he has obtained through a private agreement with the pious, bearded Muslim grocer on Marouf Street.)

In the evening, before retiring to his bed, Abaskharon counts his money twice with care, then pulls out the little blue indelible pencil that he always keeps behind his ear and writes down the balance of his earnings, subtracting from them the amount he is going to save (which he will place in his savings account on Sunday and never thereafter touch), then pay off mentally out of the remainder of what he has received the needs of his large family. And whether he has anything left over after that or not, Abaskharon, the believing Christian, cannot sleep until he has chanted the prayer of thanks to the Lord, his voice reverberating in the silence of the night as he whispers with genuine piety before the figure of the crucified Christ that hangs on the kitchen wall, "because, O Lord, Thou hast fed me and fed my children; thus, I praise You as Your name is glorified in Heaven. Amen."

A word, unavoidably, about Malak.

The fingers of the hand differ from one another in appearance, but all move together in coordination to carry out a given task. Similarly, on the soccer pitch, the mid-field player shoots the ball with the utmost precision to land at the feet of the striker so that he can score a goal. Abaskharon's relationship with his brother Malak was conducted with the same extraordinary harmony.

Malak learned tailoring in shirt-making workshops when he was young; thus domestic service has not left its stamp of abjection upon him, and the fact is his short stature, his cheap, dark-colored "people's suit," his huge belly, and his plump face devoid of any good looks leave a disturbing first impression. However, he hastens to take the initiative with anyone he meets by smiling his broad smile and shaking his hand warmly, talking to him like an old friend and concurring with all his opinions (so long as they do not touch his vital interests), then insistently offering him a Cleopatra cigarette from the wrinkled pack that he carefully extracts from his pocket, checking each time that it is okay, as though it were a jewel. This excessive pleasantness has another side to it, however. If necessary, Malak will switch, in an instant and with the greatest of ease, to the utterly foul language that is to be expected of someone who has received most of his upbringing on the street. Since he combines two opposites—viciousness and cowardice, the violent desire to hurt his opponents and excessive fear of the consequences—he has become accustomed in his battles to attacking with everything he has. If he finds no resistance, he will go to any lengths in his aggression, without the slightest mercy, as though he doesn't know the meaning of fear. And if he meets with serious resistance from his foe, he will back off immediately without thinking twice. To all these high-level skills of Malak's are added the sagacity and cunning of Abaskharon, so that the two of them work together in perfect coordination and are able, truth to tell, to pull off the most amazing feats.

The two brothers wanted to get a room on the roof, so they had planned and schemed for many months till, on this very day, the hour for action had arrived and no sooner had Rabab entered to see Zaki Bey than Abaskharon, standing in the doorway, bowed and said with a slight, crafty smile, "Excellency. Your permission to run a quick errand?" Before he had finished the sentence, the Bey (who was preoccupied with his girlfriend) had gestured to him to go. Abaskharon closed the door quietly, and his face, as his wooden crutches struck the tiles of the hallway, seemed to change. The servile, ingratiating smile disappeared and a serious, anxious expression appeared in its place. Abaskharon made for the small kitchen that was next to the entrance to the apartment and looked around cautiously. Then he stretched up, leaning on a crutch, until he was able carefully to remove the picture of the Virgin that hung on the wall and behind which was a niche. Sticking his hand into this, he pulled out several large bundles of banknotes, which he set about concealing carefully in his vest and pockets. Then he left the apartment, closing the door gently and firmly behind him. Reaching the entrance of the building, he turned, using his crutch, to the right and approached the doorkeeper's room, from which his brother Malak, who had been waiting for him, quickly emerged. The brothers exchanged a single look of understanding and a few minutes later were making their way down Suleiman Basha on their way to the Automobile Club to meet Fikri Abd el Shaheed, the lawyer who was the agent for the Yacoubian Building.

They had prepared themselves for this meeting and talked it over between themselves for a period of months till there was nothing left to discuss. Thus, they proceeded in silence, though Abaskharon started to mutter prayers to the Virgin and Christ the Savior to grant them success in their mission. Malak, on the other hand, was racking his brains for the most effective words with which to open the conversation with Fikri Bey. He had spent the last weeks gathering information about him and was now aware that the man would do anything for money and that he liked drink and women. He had been to meet him at his office on Kasr el Nil Street and presented him with a gift of a bottle of fine Old Parr whisky before opening the subject of the iron room at the entrance to the roof that had been left empty by the death of Atiya, the newspaper seller, who had lived and died unmarried, his room thus reverting to the owner. Malak had been dreaming of opening this room as a shirt shop ever since he had turned thirty and found himself still a journeyman, moving from store to store as circumstances required. When he broached the topic, Fikri Bey asked for time to think and after much pressure from Malak and his brother had agreed to give it to them in return for the sum of six thousand pounds and not a penny less, and had given them an appointment at the Automobile Club, where he was accustomed to take lunch every Sunday. When the brothers reached the club, Abaskharon felt overwhelmed at the grandness of the place and stared at the real marble that covered the walls and the floor and the luxurious red carpet that extended up to the elevator. Malak seemed to sense this and pressed his arm in encouragement, then advanced and warmly shook hands with the doorman of the club, asking him for Fikri Abd el Shaheed. In preparation for this day, Malak had got to know the workers at the Automobile Club over the past two weeks and gained their friendship with kind, flattering words and a few white gallabiyas that he had presented them as gifts. The waiters and workers hastened therefore to welcome the brothers and led them to the restaurant on the second floor where Fikri Bey was taking lunch with a fat white lady friend of his. Naturally, it wouldn't do for the brothers to interrupt the Bey, so they sent someone to him to inform him of their presence and waited for him in a side room.

Only a few minutes passed before Fikri Abd el Shaheed appeared, with his corpulent body, his large bald patch, and his face ruddy and white as a foreigner's; it became immediately obvious from the redness of his eyes and the slight slur in his speech that he had drunk a lot. After the greetings and compliments Abaskharon launched into a long interlude in praise of the Bey, his kind-heartedness, and his similarity in all his doings to Christ. He went on to tell (his brother Malak listening attentively and with affected admiration) how the Bey would exempt many of his clients from the costs of cases if he was sure that they had been wronged and were poor and unable to pay.

"Do you know, Malak, what Fikri Bey says to a poor client if he tries to pay?" Having posed the question, Abaskharon quickly answered it himself. "He says, 'Go and prostrate yourself in thanks to the Lord Jesus, for He has paid me the fees for your case in full!'" Malak sucked his lips, folded his hands over his protruding stomach, looked at the ground as though completely overcome, and said, "There you see a true Christian!"

Fikri Bey, however, though drunk, was attentive to the way the conversation was going and did not much like its drift; so to bring matters to a head he said in a no-nonsense tone, "Did you bring the money as agreed?"

"Of course, Your Honor," cried Abaskharon, as he handed him two pieces of paper. "Here's the contract as agreed with Your Honor, and God bless you."

Then he thrust his hand into his vest to pull out the money. He had brought the agreed-upon six thousand, but had distributed the notes about his person in order to leave himself room for maneuver. He started by pulling out four thousand pounds and held out his hand with these in it to the Bey, who cried out angrily, "What's that? Where's the rest?" At this, the brothers burst out with one voice, as though singing an aria, into a joint plea—Abaskharon in his hoarse, phlegmy, panting tones and Malak in his sharp, high-pitched, loud ones, their words overlapping until they became incomprehensible, though taken as a whole they were intended to awaken the Bey's sympathy by speaking of their poverty and noting that they had, by the Living Christ, gone into debt to get the money and that in all honesty they were unable to pay more than that. Fikri Bey didn't relent for a second. Indeed he got angrier and saying, "This is how children behave! This is no use to me!" he turned around to go back into the restaurant. Abaskharon, however, who had been expecting this move, threw himself so forcefully toward the Bey that he stumbled and was about to fall but with a lightning movement pulled another bundle of notes, worth a thousand pounds, out of the pocket of his gallabiya and thrust it with the other bundles into the pocket of the Bey, who displayed no serious resistance and allowed this to happen. At this Abaskharon was obliged to launch into another interlude of pleading during which he attempted to kiss the Bey's hand more than once and finally brought his ardent importunities to a close with a special move that he kept in reserve for emergencies, suddenly bending his torso backward and pulling his worn, dirty gallabiya upward with both hands so that his truncated leg, attached to the depressingly dark-colored prosthesis, was displayed. In a hoarse, disjointed, voice designed to evoke pity he shouted, "I'm a cripple, sir, and my leg's gone! A cripple with a parcel of children to look after, and Malak has four children and their mother to support! If you love the Lord Christ, sir, don't turn me away brokenhearted!"

This was more than Fikri Bey could withstand and a little while later the three of them were sitting and signing the contract—Fikri Bey, who was furious at what he afterward called, as he recounted what had happened to his lady friend, "moral blackmail," Malak, who was thinking about the first steps he would take in his new room on the roof and Abaskharon, who kept in place on his face his final, affecting expression (a sad, broken look, as though he had been vanquished and subjected to unbearable burdens); inside, however, he was happy both because the rental contract had been signed and because he had managed with his skill to save a one-thousand-pound bundle, whose delicious warmth he could feel in the right-hand pocket of his gallabiya.

Downtown remained, for at least a hundred years, the commercial and social center of Cairo, where were situated the biggest banks, the foreign companies, the stores, the clinics and the offices of famous doctors and lawyers, the cinemas, and the luxury restaurants. Egypt's former élite had built the downtown area to be Cairo's European quarter, to the degree that you would find streets that looked the same as those to be found in any of the capitals of Europe, with the same style of architecture and the same venerable historic veneer. Until the beginning of the 1960s, Downtown retained its pure European stamp and old-timers doubtless can still remember that elegance. It was considered quite inappropriate for natives to wander around in Downtown in their gallabiyas and impossible for them to be allowed in this same traditional dress into restaurants such as Groppi's, À l'Américaine, and the Odéon, or even the Metro, Saint James, and Radio cinemas, and other places that required their patrons to wear, for men, suits, and, for the ladies, evening dresses. The stores all shut their doors on Sundays, and on the Catholic Christian holidays, such as Christmas and New Year's, Downtown was decorated all over, as though it were in a foreign capital. The glass frontages scintillated with holiday greetings in

French and English, Christmas trees, and figures representing Father Christmas, and the restaurants and bars overflowed with foreigners and aristocrats who celebrated with drinking, singing, and dancing.

Downtown had always been full of small bars where people could take a few glasses and tasty dishes of *hors d'œuvres* in their free time and on weekends at a reasonable price. In the thirties and forties, some bars offered in addition to the drinks small entertainments by a Greek or Italian musician or a troupe of foreign Jewish women dancers. Up to the end of the 1960s, there were on Suleiman Basha alone almost ten small bars. Then came the 1970s, and the downtown area started gradually to lose its importance, the heart of Cairo moving to where the new élite lived, in El Mohandiseen and Medinet Nasr. An inexorable wave of religiosity swept Egyptian society and it became no longer socially acceptable to drink alcohol. Successive Egyptian governments bowed to the religious pressure (and perhaps attempted to outbid politically the opposition Islamist current) by restricting the sale of alcohol to the major hotels and restaurants and stopped issuing licenses for new bars; if the owner of a bar (usually a foreigner) died, the government would cancel the bar's license and require the heirs to change the nature of their business. On top of all this there were constant police raids on bars, during which the officers would frisk the patrons, inspect their identity cards, and sometimes accompany them to the police station for interrogation.

Thus it was that as the 1980s dawned, there remained in the whole of Downtown only a few, scattered, small bars, whose owners had been able to hang on in the face of the rising tide of religion and government persecution. This they had been able to do by one of two methods— concealment or bribery. There was not one bar downtown that advertised its presence. Indeed, the very word "Bar" on the signs was changed to "Restaurant" or "Coffee Shop," and the owners of bars and wine stores deliberately painted the windows of their establishments a dark color so that what went on inside could not be seen, or would place in their display windows paper napkins or any other items that would not betray their actual business. It was no longer permitted for a customer to drink on the sidewalk in front of the bar or even in front of an open window that looked on to the street, and stringent precautions had to be taken following the burning of a number of liquor stores at the hands of youths belonging to the Islamist movement.

At the same time, it was required of the few remaining bar owners that they pay large regular bribes to the plainclothes police officers to whose districts they belonged and to governorate officials in order for these to allow them to continue. Sometimes the sale of cheap locally produced alcohol would not realize enough income for them to pay the fine, so that the bar owners found themselves obliged to find "other ways" of adding to their income. Some of them turned to facilitating prostitution by using fallen women to serve the alcohol, as was the case with the Cairo Bar in El Tawfikiya, and the Mido and the Pussycat on Emad el Din Street. Others turned to manufacturing alcohol in primitive laboratories instead of buying it, so as to increase profits, as at the Halegian Bar on Antikkhana Street and the Jamaica on Sherif Street. These disgusting industrially produced drinks led to a number of unfortunate accidents, the most celebrated of which befell a young artist who lost his sight after drinking bad brandy at the Halegian Bar. The public prosecutor's office ordered the bar closed, but its owner was able to reopen later, using the usual methods.

Consequently, the small remaining downtown bars were no longer cheap, clean places for recreation as they had been before. Instead, they had turned into badly lit, poorly ventilated dens frequented mostly by hooligans and criminal types, though there were a few exceptions to this rule, such as Maxim's in the passage between Kasr el Nil and Suleiman Basha streets, and the Chez Nous, located beneath the Yacoubian Building.

The Chez Nous is a few steps below street level, and thanks to the thick curtains the lighting is dim and shadowy even during the day. The large bar is to the left and the tables are benches of natural wood painted a dark color. The old lanterns of Viennese design, the works of art sculpted from wood or bronze and hung on the wall, the Latin-script writing on the paper tablecloths, and the huge beer glasses—all these things give the bar the appearance of an English "pub." In summer, as soon as you penetrate the Chez Nous, leaving behind you Suleiman Basha with its noise, heat, and crowds, and seat yourself to drink an ice-cold beer in the midst of the quiet, the powerful air conditioning, and the low, relaxing lighting, you feel as though you had gone into hiding from daily life in some way. This feeling of privacy is the great distinguishing feature of Chez Nous, which made its name basically as a meeting place for homosexuals (and which has made its way into more than one Western tourist guide under this rubric).

The owner of the bar is called Aziz. He is nicknamed "the Englishman" (because, with his white complexion, yellow hair, and blue eyes, he resembles one) and he is a victim of that same condition. They say he took up with the old Greek who used to own the bar and that the latter fell in love with him and made him a present of the establishment before his death. They whisper too that he organizes outrageous parties at which he introduces homosexuals to Arab tourists and that homosexual prostitution brings him in huge profits with which he pays the bribes that have made his place into a safe haven from the annoying attentions of the security forces. He is blessed with a strong presence and *savoir-faire,* and under his supervision and care homosexuals meet at Chez Nous and form friendships there, released from the social pressures that prevent them from advertising their tendencies.

Places where homosexuals meet are like hashish cafés and gambling dens in that their patrons belong to all social levels and are of varying ages. You find among them skilled workers and professionals, young people and old, all united by their homosexuality. By the same token, homosexuals, like burglars, pickpockets, and all other groups outside the laws and norms of society, have created for themselves a special language that enables them to understand one another when among strangers. Thus, they call a passive homosexual a "kudyana" and give him a girl's name by which he is known among them, such as Souad, Angie, Fatma, and so on. They call an active homosexual a "barghal," and if he is ignorant and simple, they call him a "rough barghal." They call male-to-male sex a "hook-up." They make themselves known to one another and hold secret conversations by means of hand movements. Thus, if one of them takes the other's hand and strokes his wrist with his finger while shaking it, that means that he desires him, and if a man brings two fingers together and moves them while talking to someone, this means that he is inviting his interlocutor to have sex, and if he points to his heart with one finger, it means that his lover has sole possession of his heart, and so on.

Just as Aziz the Englishman looks out for the comfort and good cheer of the Chez Nous patrons, so by the same token he permits them no indecent behavior. As the night and the patrons' indulgence in drink progress, their voices grow louder, rise in pitch, and interrupt one another, for the desire to talk takes possession of them, as happens in all bars. The drunkards at Chez Nous, however, fall prey to a combination of lust and intoxication, exchanging endearments and dirty jokes, and one of them will sometimes stretch out his fingers to caress his friend's body—at which point, Aziz the Englishman intervenes at once, using every means to re-impose order, starting with a polite whisper and ending with a threat to throw the delinquent customer out of the bar. Often the Englishman gets so excited that his face turns red while he berates the homosexual whose lust has been aroused, saying, "Listen. As long as you're at my place, behave yourself. If you fancy your friend that much, get up and go off with him, but don't you lay a hand on him in this bar!"

The Englishman's sternness here does not stem from any concern for morality of course but from calculations of profit and loss, since plain-clothes officers often visit the bar. True, they satisfy themselves with a quick glance from a distance and don't disturb the patrons at all (thanks to the large bribes they receive), but if they were to witness any scandalous act there, they would make a huge fuss, since that would be their opportunity to blackmail the Englishman into paying even more.

A little before midnight, the door of the bar opened and Hatim Rasheed appeared with a dark-complexioned young man in his twenties wearing inexpensive clothes, his hair cropped like a soldier's. The people in the bar were drunk, shouting and singing loudly. All the same, as soon as Hatim entered, their racket diminished and they took to observing him with curiosity and a certain awe. They knew that he was a kudyana, but a forbidding natural reserve prevented them from acting familiarly with him and even the most impudent and obscene of the customers could do no other than treat him with respect.

There were a number of reasons for this. Hatim Rasheed is a well-known journalist and editor-in-chief of the newspaper *Le Caire*, which comes out in Cairo in French. He is an aristocrat of ancient lineage whose mother was French and whose father was Dr. Hassan Rasheed, the famous jurist and dean of the College of Law in the 1950s. In addition, Hatim Rasheed is a conservative homosexual, if that is the right expression: he does not sacrifice his dignity, put powder on his face, or stoop to using provocative ways as do many kudyanas. In appearance and behavior he always chooses a skillful compromise between elegance and femininity. Tonight, for instance, he is wearing a dark wine-red suit and has knotted around his slender neck a yellow scarf, most of which he has tucked under his pink, natural-silk shirt, the two ends of the latter's broad collar flopping over the front of his jacket. With his smart clothes, svelte figure, and fine French features, he would look like a scintillating movie star were it not for the wrinkles that his riotous life has left on his face and that sad, mysterious, gloomy look that often haunts the faces of homosexuals.

Aziz the Englishman went toward him to welcome him and Hatim shook his hand affectionately, gesturing gracefully toward his young friend and saying, "My friend Abd Rabbuh, who's doing his military service in Central Security."

"Pleased to meet you," said Aziz, smiling and looking the strong, muscular young man over. Then he led his two guests to a quiet table at the end of the bar and took their orders—gin and tonic for Hatim, an imported beer for Abd Rabbuh, and some hot *hors d'œuvres*. Gradually, the customers lost interest in them and resumed their talk and raucous laughter.

The two friends appeared to be engrossed in a long and wearisome argument, Hatim speaking in a low voice and looking at his friend as though trying to convince him of something, Abd Rabbuh listening unmoved and then replying vehemently. Hatim would remain silent for a moment, his head bowed, then resume the attempt. The conversation went on this way for almost half an hour, during which the two companions drank two bottles of beer and three glasses of gin, and at the end of which Hatim leaned his back once more against the back of the seat and directed a penetrating glance at Abduh.

"That's your last word?"

Abduh replied in a loud voice, the alcohol having gone quickly to his head, "Yes!"

"Abduh, come with me tonight and we'll work things out in the morning."

"No."

"Please, Abduh."

"No."

"Very well. Can we work things out quietly? None of that quick temper of yours!" whispered Hatim winningly, touching with his fingers his friend's huge hand as it lay on the table. This insistence seemed to exasperate Abduh who let out his breath in annoyance and said, "I told you I can't stay with you tonight. I was late three times last week because of you. The officer will refer me for disciplining."

"Don't worry! I've found someone who can put in a good word for you with the officer."

"Ouff!" screamed Abduh with annoyance, pushing the beer glass with his hand so that it fell over with a ringing crash. Then he got up, directed an angry look at Hatim, and rushed to the exit. Hatim pulled some notes out of his wallet, threw them on the table, and hurried after his friend. For a few moments, silence reigned in the bar. Then the drunken comments rang out:

"A barghal with attitude, me boys!"

"Pity the one who loves and can't get no satisfaction!"

"What to do, Honey, now you done used up all my money?"

The men laughed uproariously and burst enthusiastically and with resonant voices into a round of indecent songs, so that Aziz the Englishman was obliged to intervene to restore order.

Like most Egyptians from the countryside, Muhammad el Sayed, cook's assistant at the Automobile Club, had suffered from bilharzia, which he contracted early on in life and which had led to inflammation and failure of the liver by the time he reached fifty. Busayna, his eldest daughter, remembers well the day in Ramadan when, after the family had eaten its breakfast meal in their small apartment with its two rooms and a latrine on the roof of the Yacoubian Building and her father had gone to perform the evening prayer, they suddenly heard the sound of something heavy falling to the ground. Busayna remembers too her mother's agonized scream, "Go help your father!" They all ran to him—Busayna, Sawsan, Fatin, and little Mustafa. Their father was lying on the bed in his white gallabiya, his body completely still and his face a dull blue. Once they had called the ambulance and the raw young doctor had made a quick examination and announced the sad news, the girls let out piercing screams and their mother started slapping hard at her face, keeping it up till she fell to the floor.

At the time Busayna was studying for a commercial diploma and had dreams for the future that it would never have occurred to her might not come true: she was going to graduate and marry her sweetheart Taha el Shazli after he graduated from the Police Academy, and they would live in a nice spacious apartment a long way from the Yacoubian roof, and they would have just one boy and one girl so that they could raise them properly. They had everything worked out, but her father had died suddenly and with the passing of the mourning period the family found itself destitute. The pension was meager and did not cover the costs of schooling, food, clothes, and rent. Her mother soon changed. She always wore black, her body withered and dried out, and her face took on that stern, masculine, prickly look that poor widows have. Little by little she grew bad-tempered and took to quarreling all the time with the girls; even little Mustafa wasn't spared her beatings and abuse. After each scene she would abandon herself to a long bout of crying. She stopped talking about the departed with the great affection she had shown in the early days and instead starting talking about him in a bitter and disappointed way, as though he had let her down and deliberately left her in this mess. She started disappearing two or three days a week, leaving in the morning and returning at the end of the day exhausted, silent, and distracted, carrying bags of cooked food all mixed up together (rice and vegetables and little bits of meat or chicken) which she would heat and give them to eat.

The day Busayna passed her exams and got her diploma her mother waited until night had fallen and the rest of the family was asleep and took her out onto the roof. It was a hot summer night and men were smoking goza and chatting the evening away while a few women were sitting in the open air to escape the heat of their cramped iron rooms. The mother greeted them and pulled Busayna by her hand to a distant part of the roof, where they stood next to the wall. Busayna can still recall the sight of the cars and the lights of Suleiman Basha as they appeared that night from the roof, along with her mother's frowning face, her stern, penetrating looks, and her harsh, strange voice as she spoke to her of the burden the departed had left her with to endure on her own, and informed her that she was working in the house of some good-hearted people in Zamalek but had kept it a secret so that it wouldn't affect Busayna's or her sisters' marriage prospects (when people found out that their mother was working as a maid). The mother asked Busayna to look for a job for herself, starting the next day. Busayna did not reply but looked at her mother for a little, overwhelmed by tenderness. Then she bent down toward her and hugged her. It occurred to her as she kissed her that her face had gotten dry and coarse and that a new, strange smell came off her body—the smell of sweat mixed with dust that maids give off.

The next day Busayna put everything she had in her into finding a job and in one year she went through lots—secretary in a lawyer's office, assistant to a women's hairdresser, trainee nurse at a dentist's. Every job she left for the same reason and after going through the same rigmarole—the warm welcome from the boss accompanied by enormous, burning interest, followed by the little kindnesses and the presents and small gifts of money, with the hints that there was more where that came from, all to be met from her side with a refusal well coated in politeness (so that she wouldn't lose the job). However, the boss would keep at it till the business reached its logical conclusion, that final scene that she hated and feared and that always came about when the older man would insist on kissing her by force in the empty office, or press up against her, or start opening his fly to confront her with some "facts on the ground." Then she would push him away and threaten to scream and make a scene, at which point he would switch and show his vengeful face by throwing her out, after mocking her by calling her "Khadra el Shareefa." Or sometimes he would pretend that he was just testing her morals and assure her that he loved her like his own daughter, in which case he would wait for the right time (after any danger of scandal had passed) and throw her out on any other excuse.

During that year Busayna learned a lot. She discovered, for example, that her beautiful and provocative body, her wide, dark-brown eyes and full lips, her voluptuous breasts and tremulous, rounded backside with its soft buttocks, all had an important role to play in her dealings with people. It became clear to her that all men, however respectable in appearance and however elevated their position in society, were utter weaklings in front of a beautiful woman. This drove her to try out some wicked but entertaining tests. Thus, if she met a respectable old man whom she thought it would be fun to test, she would put on a girlish voice and bend over and stick out her voluptuous breasts, then immediately enjoy the sight of the sober-sided gentleman going soft and trembly, his eyes clouding over with desire. The way men panted after her gave her a gloating pleasure similar to that of revenge. It also became clear to her during that year that her mother had changed completely, for whenever Busayna left a job because of the men's importunities, her mother would greet the news with a silence akin to exasperation and on one occasion, after it had happened several times, she told Busayna as she got up to leave the room, "Your brother and sisters need every penny you earn. A clever girl can look after herself and keep her job." This sentence saddened and puzzled Busayna, who asked herself, "How can I look after myself when faced with a boss who opens his fly?"

She remained in the same state of puzzlement for many long weeks, until Fifi, the daughter of Sabir the laundryman, who was a neighbor of theirs on the roof, appeared. She had heard that Busayna was looking for work and had come to tell her about a job as a salesgirl at the Shanan clothing store. When Busayna told her about her problem with earlier bosses, Fifi let out a great sigh, struck her on her chest, and shouted in her face in disbelief, "Don't be a fool, girl!" Fifi explained to her that more than ninety percent of bosses did that with the girls who worked for them and that any girl who refused was thrown out and a hundred other girls who didn't object could be found to take her place. When Busayna started to object, Fifi asked her sarcastically, "So Your Ladyship has an MBA from the American University? Why, the beggars in the street have commercial diplomas the same as you!"

Fifi explained to her that going along with the boss "up to a point" was just being smart and that the world was one thing and what she saw in Egyptian movies was another. She explained to her that she knew lots of girls who had worked for years at the Shanan store and given Mr. Talal, the owner of the store, what he wanted "up to a point" and were now happily married with kids, homes, and husbands who loved them lots. "But why go so far afield?" Fifi asked, citing herself as an example. She had worked in the store for two years and her salary was a hundred pounds, but she earned at least three times that much by "being smart," not to mention the presents. And all the same, she had been able to look after herself, she was a virgin, and she'd scratch out the eyes of anyone who said anything against her reputation. There were a hundred men who wanted to marry her, especially now that she was earning and putting her money into saving co-ops and setting money aside to pay for her trousseau.

The next day Busayna went with Fifi to Mr. Talal at the store. He turned out to be over forty, fair-complexioned, blue-eyed, balding, and stout. He was snub-nosed and had a huge black mustache that hung down on either side of his mouth. Mr. Talal was not at all handsome, and Busayna found out that he was the only son, among a bunch of girls, of Hagg Shanan, a Syrian, who had come from Syria during the Union and settled in Egypt and opened this store. Once he started getting on, he had handed his business over to his only son. She learned too that he was married and that his wife was Egyptian and pretty and had borne him two sons, though despite all that his predations on women never stopped. Talal shook Busayna's hand (giving it a squeeze) and never raised his eyes from her chest and body while he spoke. After a few minutes, she started her new job.

In just a few weeks, Fifi had taught her all she had to do: how she had to take care of her appearance, paint her fingernails and her toenails, open the neck of her dress a little, and take her dresses in a bit at the waist to show off her backside. It was her job to open the store in the morning and mop it out along with her colleagues, then set her clothes straight and stand at the door (a way of attracting customers familiar to all the clothing stores). When she had a customer, she had to talk to him nicely, comply with his requests, and persuade him to buy as much as possible (she got a half of one percent of the value of all sales). Naturally, she had to put up with the customers' flirting, however obnoxious.

That was the job. As for "the other thing," Mr. Talal started in on it the third day after she came. It was the time of the afternoon prayer and the store was empty of customers. Talal asked her to go with him to the storeroom so that he could explain to her the different items they had in stock. Busayna followed him without a word, noting the shadow of an ironic smile on the faces of Fifi and the other girls.

The storeroom consisted of a large apartment on the ground floor in the building next to the À l'Américaine café on Suleiman Basha. Talal entered and locked the door from the inside. She looked about her. The place was damp and badly lit and ventilated and was stacked to the ceiling with boxes. She knew what was coming and had readied herself on the way to the storeroom, repeating to herself in her head her mother's words, "Your brother and sisters need every penny you earn. A clever girl can look after herself and keep her job." When Mr. Talal came close to her, she was struck by strong and conflicting feelings—determination to make the best of the opportunity and the fear which despite everything still wracked her and made her fight for breath and feel as though she was about to be sick. There was also a sneaking, covert curiosity that urged her to find out what Mr. Talal would do to her. Would he woo her and tell her, "I love you," for example, or try to kiss her right away? She found out quickly enough because Talal pounced on her from behind, flung his arms around her hard enough to hurt her and started rubbing up against her and playing with her body without uttering a single word. He was violent and in a hurry to get his pleasure and the whole business was over in about two minutes. Her dress was soiled and he whispered to her, panting, "The bathroom's at the end of the corridor on the right."

As she washed her dress in the water, she thought to herself that the whole thing was easier than she'd imagined, like some man rubbing up against her in the bus (something that happened a lot) and she remembered what Fifi had told her to do after the encounter. She went back to Talal and said to him in a voice she made as smooth and seductive as she could, "I need twenty pounds from you, sir." Talal looked at her for a moment, then quickly thrust his hand into his pocket as though he had been expecting the request and said in an ordinary voice as he took out a folded banknote, "Nah. Ten's enough. Come back to the store after me as soon as your dress is dry." Then he went out, closing the door behind him.

Ten pounds a time, and Mr. Talal would ask for her twice, sometimes three times a week, and Fifi had taught her how from time to time to show her liking for a dress in the shop and keep on at Talal until he made her a present of it. She started making money and wearing nice clothes and her mother was pleased with her and was comforted by the money that she took from her and tucked into the front of her dress, uttering warm blessings for her after doing so. Listening to these, Busayna was overwhelmed with a mysterious, malign desire to start giving her mother clear hints about her relationship with Talal, but her mother would ignore any such messages. Busayna would then go to such lengths with her hints that the mother's refusal to acknowledge them became obvious and extremely fragile, at which point Busayna would feel some relief, as though she had snatched away her mother's mask of false innocence and confirmed her complicity in the crime.

As time passed her rendezvous with Talal in the storeroom had an impact on her that she would never have imagined. She found herself no longer able to perform the morning prayer (the only one of the required prayers that she had performed) because inwardly she was ashamed to face "Our Lord," because she felt herself unclean, however much she performed the ablutions. She started having nightmares and would start up from her sleep terrified. She would go for days depressed and melancholy and one day when she went with her mother to visit the tomb of El Hussein, no sooner had she entered the sanctuary and found herself surrounded by the incense and lights and felt that deeply-rooted hidden presence that fills the heart than she burst into a long, unexpected bout of weeping.

On the other hand, since retreat was not an option and she could not stand her feelings of sin, she started to resist the latter fiercely. She took to thinking of her mother's face as she told her that she was working as a servant in people's houses. She would repeat to herself what Fifi had said about the world and how it worked and often she would contemplate the shop's rich, chic, women customers and ask herself with spiteful passion, "I wonder how many times that woman surrendered her body to get to where she is now?"

This violent resistance to her feelings of guilt left a legacy of bitterness and cruelty. She stopped trusting people or making excuses for them. She would often think (and then seek forgiveness) that God had wanted her to fall. If He had wanted otherwise, He would have created her a rich woman or delayed her father's death a few years (and what could have been easier for Him?). Little by little, her resentment extended to include her sweetheart Taha himself. A strange feeling that she was stronger than he was by far would creep over her—a feeling that she was mature and understood the world, while he was just a dreamy, naïve boy. She started to get annoyed at his optimism about the future and speak sharply to him, mocking him by saying, "You think you're Abd el Halim Hafez? The poor, hard-working boy whose dreams will come true if he struggles?"

At first, Taha didn't understand the reason for this bitterness. Then her sarcasm at his expense started to provoke him and they would quarrel, and when he asked her once to stop working for Talal because he had a bad reputation, she looked at him challengingly and said, "At your service, sir. Give me the two hundred and fifty pounds that I earn from Talal and you'll have the right to stop me showing my face to anyone but you." He stared at her for a moment as though he did not understand and then his anger erupted and he shoved her on the shoulder. She screamed insults at him and threw at him an outfit in silver he'd bought for her. In the depths of her heart, she craved to rip her relationship with him to pieces so that she might be freed of that painful feeling of sin that tortured her as soon as she set eyes on him, yet it was not in her power to leave him completely. She loved him and they had a long history full of beautiful moments. The instant she saw him sad or anxious, she would forget everything and envelop him in genuine, overflowing tenderness as though she was his mother.

However bad the quarrels between them got, she would make up with him and go back to him, and their affair was not without rare and wonderful times. Very soon, however, the gloom would return.

Busayna spent the whole day blaming herself for her cruelty to him that morning when he had been in need of a word of encouragement from her as he set off for a test that she knew he had been waiting for for many years. How cruel that had been of her! What would it have hurt her to encourage him with a word and a smile? If only she had spent a little time with him! After work she found herself anxious to meet him, so she went to Tawfikiya Square and sat waiting for him on the wall of the flowerbed where they usually met each evening. Night had fallen and the square was crowded with passersby and vendors; sitting on her own she was subjected to a lot of harassment but she kept waiting for him for almost half an hour. When he didn't come, she thought he must be angry with her because she had put him off that morning, so she got up and climbed the stairs to his room on the roof. The door was open and Taha's mother was sitting there alone, anxiety showing on her aged face. The mother hugged her and kissed her, then sat her down next to her on the bench and said, "I'm very scared, Busayna. Taha left for the exam in the morning and still hasn't come back. Pray God he's all right!"

Were it not for his advanced age and the years of hardship that have left their traces on his countenance, Hagg Muhammad Azzam would look like a movie star or a crowned head, with his towering height and imperturbable gravitas, his elegance and his wealth, his face rosy with overflowing good health and his complexion all polished and shiny thanks to the skill of the experts at La Gaité Beauty Center in El Mohandiseen where he goes once a week. He owns more than a hundred suits of the most luxurious kind and wears a different one every day, with a showy necktie and elegant imported shoes.

Each day, in the middle of the morning, Hagg Azzam's red Mercedes rolls down Suleiman Basha from the direction of the À l'Américaine with him seated in the back absorbed in telling the small amber prayer beads that never leave his hand. His day starts with an inspection of his properties—two large clothing stores, one of them opposite the À l'Américaine, the other on the ground floor of the Yacoubian Building where his office is situated; two automobile show-rooms; and a number of spare parts shops in Marouf Street, not to mention a great deal of real estate in the downtown area and many other buildings that are under construction, soon to rise in the form of towering skyscrapers bearing the name Azzam Contractors. The car proceeds to stop in front of each establishment and the employees gather round it to offer the Hagg warm greetings, which he returns with a wave of his hand so restrained and insignificant that you might not notice it. The head employee or the most senior among them immediately approaches the car window, bends toward the Hagg, and briefs him on the work situation or seeks his advice on some matter. Hagg Azzam listens carefully with his head lowered, his thick eye-brows knotted, his lips pursed, then trains his narrow, gray foxy eyes (always slightly red from the effects of hashish) on the distance, as though he were watching something on the horizon. Finally he speaks, his voice deep, its intonation decisive, the words few and far between. He cannot abide chatter or disputatiousness.

Some attribute his love of silence to his application (with his strictly observant piety) of the noble hadith that says, "If one of you speaks let him be brief, or let him stay silent"—though at the same time, with his vast wealth and extraordinary influence, he does not in fact need to talk much because his word is generally final and has to be obeyed. To this should be added his wide experience of life that enables him to grasp things at a glance, for the aging millionaire, who is past sixty, started out thirty years ago as a mere migrant worker who left Sohag governorate for Cairo looking for work, and the older people on Suleiman Basha remember him sitting on the ground in the passage behind the À l'Américaine in a gallabiya, vest, and turban with a small wooden box in front of him—for that is where he started, shining shoes. He worked for a time as an office servant in the Babik office supplies store, then disappeared for more than twenty years, suddenly to reappear having made a lot of money. Hagg Azzam says that he was working in the Gulf, but the people in the street do not believe that and whisper that he was sentenced and imprisoned for dealing in drugs, which some insist he continues to do to this day, citing as evidence his exorbitant wealth, which is out of all proportion to the volume of the sales in his stores and the profits of his companies, indicating that his commercial activities are a mere front for money laundering.

Whatever the accuracy of these rumors, Hagg Azzam has become the unrivaled Big Man of Suleiman Basha and people seek him out to get their business done and settle their differences, while his influence has been consolidated recently by his joining the Patriotic Party and by his youngest son Hamdi subsequently joining the judiciary as a public prosecutor. Hagg Azzam has an overwhelming urge to buy property and shops in the downtown district specifically, as though to stress his new situation in the area that once witnessed him as a poor down-and-out.

It was about two years ago that Hagg Azzam woke to perform the dawn prayer, as was his custom, and found his nightwear wet. He was disturbed and it occurred to him that he might be sick, but when he went into the bathroom to wash, he ascertained that the cause of the wetness was a sexual urge and he remembered the distorted image of a naked, distant woman that he had seen in his dreams. This strange phenomenon in an old man like himself astonished him. He forgot about it during the busy day but it happened again several times thereafter, so that he had to bathe daily before the dawn prayer to cleanse himself of the defilement. Nor did things end there, for he caught himself several times stealing glances at the bodies of the women working for him in the store, and some of them, instinctively sensing his lust, started to walk with a deliberately provocative gait and talk coquettishly in front of him to seduce him, so that several times he was forced to scold them.

These sudden importunate sexual urges disturbed Hagg Azzam greatly, firstly because they were inappropriate to his age and secondly because he had kept to the straight and narrow all his life and believed that his uprightness and avoidance of anything that might make God angry was the main reason for all the success he had achieved—for he never drank alcohol. (As for the hashish that he smoked, many religious experts had assured him that it was merely "reprehensible" and neither created uncleanness nor was absolutely prohibited. In addition it neither took away the mental faculties nor drove man to commit indecencies or crimes as did alcohol; on the contrary, hashish calmed a man's nerves, brought him greater equipoise, and sharpened his mind.) Likewise, the Hagg had never committed fornication in his entire life, immunizing himself, like most Sa'idis, by marrying early; also over the course of his long life he had witnessed wealthy men surrender to their lusts and lose vast fortunes.

The Hagg confided his problem to certain older friends of his and they assured him that what was happening was an ephemeral phenomenon that would soon disappear forever. "It's just an excess of good health," said his friend Hagg Kamil the cement trader, laughing. But the urges continued as the days passed and intensified until they became a heavy burden on his nerves and, even worse, were the cause of a number of tiffs with Hagga Salha, his wife, who was a few years younger than he but was caught unprepared by this sudden blossoming of youthfulness and then got upset because she was unable to satisfy him. More than once she rebuked him and told him that their children were grown men and that as two older spouses they ought to adorn themselves with an appropriate sedateness.

Nothing was left to Hagg Azzam but to take the matter to Sheikh El Samman, the celebrated man of religion and president of the Islamic Charitable Association, whom Azzam considers his spiritual leader and guide in all matters pertaining to this world and the next, to the degree that he will not reach a firm decision on any subject that concerns him in his work or his life without having recourse to him. He puts at his disposal thousands of pounds, to be spent, with his knowledge, on charitable works, not to mention the valuable gifts that he gives him every time a good business deal has gone through as a result of his prayers and blessings.

After the Friday prayer and the weekly class in religion that Sheikh El Samman delivers at the Salam Mosque in Medinet Nasr, Hagg Azzam requested a private interview with the sheikh and talked to him about his problem. The sheikh listened attentively, was silent for a while, then said with a vehemence that was not far from anger, "Glory be, Hagg! Why, my brother, make things difficult for yourself when God has made them easy for you? Why open the door for Satan, so that you can fall into error? You have to protect yourself, as God commanded. God has made marriage to more than one wife lawful for you so long as you behave with justice. Put your trust in God and make haste to do what is right before you fall into what is wrong!"

"I'm an old man. I'm afraid of what people might say if I married."

"If I didn't know your righteousness and God-fearingness, I would think badly of you. Which is worthier of your fear, man? What people say, or the anger of the Merciful, Glorious, and Magnificent? Would you make forbidden what God has made lawful? You are potent, your health is excellent, and you find in yourself a desire for women. Marry and treat both your wives equally. God loves you to make lawful use of what He has permitted."

Hagg Azzam hesitated for a long while (or made a show of doing so), but Sheikh El Samman kept on at him until he convinced him. He even (and for this he was to be thanked) undertook to convince his three sons, Fawzi, Qadri, and Hamdi (the public prosecutor). The last two received the news of their father's wish to get married with astonishment but accepted it anyway. Fawzi, the elder son and his father's right hand at work, seemed not to approve, though he did not make his reason for objecting explicit. In the end, he said grudgingly, "If the Hagg has to marry, then it's up to us to make sure he chooses well, so he doesn't fall into the hands of some bitch who will make his life hell."

The principle was established, then, and it remained to mount a search for a suitable wife. Hagg Azzam commissioned his most trusted friends to look for a nice girl and during the next few months saw many candidates but with his broad experience refused any in whose conduct he found anything to object to. This one was outstandingly lovely but had her face uncovered, was pert, and he could not entrust her with his honor; that one was young and spoiled and would exhaust him with her demands; and the one after was greedy and loved money. Thus, the Hagg refused all candidates until he met Souad Gaber, a salesclerk in the Hannaux department store in Alexandria. She was divorced and had one son, and as soon as the Hagg saw her she beguiled his heart— a light-skinned woman, full-bodied, beautiful, who covered her hair, which was black and smooth and flowing, the tresses peeking out from beneath her headscarf. The eyes were black, wide, and bewitching, the lips plump and sensual, and she was clean, and her attention to the min-utiae of her body was outstanding as is usually the case with the women of Alexandria. Her finger- and toenails were clipped and the tips were cleaned, though they were not painted (so that the varnish would not form an impediment to the water she used for her ritual ablutions). Her hands were soft, tender-skinned, and rubbed with cream. Even her heels were extremely clean, smooth, firm, and free of any cracking, and were suffused with a delicate redness as a result of being polished with pumice.

Souad left a delicate, fascinating impression on the Hagg's heart. What pleased him specially was the meekness that poverty and a hard life had left her with. He considered that her history was in no way blameworthy: she had married a house painter, who had left her a son and then abandoned her and gone off to Iraq, where nothing more was heard from him; the court had granted her a divorce so that her situation should not lead to social problems.

The Hagg sent people secretly to ask about her at her work and home, and everyone praised her for her morals. Then he performed the prayer for guidance in choice and Souad Gaber appeared to him in a dream in all her beauty (but decently dressed and not naked and vulgar like the women of whom he usually dreamed). As a result, Hagg Azzam put his trust in God and visited Souad's family in Sidi Bishr, sat down with Rayyis Hamidu, her elder brother (who worked as a waiter in a café in El Manshiya), and agreed with him on everything. Hagg Azzam, who was, as usual when conducting a business transaction, clear and frank and not disposed to bargain, married Souad Gaber on the following conditions:

1   That Souad come and live with him in Cairo and leave her small son Tamir with her mother in Alexandria, it being understood that she could go and visit him "when convenient."

2   That he should buy her jewelry to a value of ten thousand pounds as an engagement present and that he should pay a bride price of twenty thousand pounds, it being understood that the amount to be paid in the case of an eventual divorce should not exceed five thousand pounds.

3   That the marriage should remain a secret and that it be clearly understood that in the case of Hagga Salha, his wife, finding out about

his new marriage, he would be compelled to divorce Souad forthwith.

    4   That, while the marriage was to be conducted according to the norms set by God and His Prophet, he had no desire whatsoever for offspring.

Hagg Azzam stressed this last condition, making it extremely clear to Rayyis Hamidu that neither his age nor his circumstances permitted him to be father to a child at this time and that if Souad got pregnant, the agreement would be considered abrogated forthwith.

"What's wrong?"

The two of them were on the bed: Souad in her blue nightgown that revealed her full, trembling breasts, her thighs, and her amazingly white arms, Hagg Azzam stretched out beside her on his back wearing his white gallabiya. This was their hour—every day after the Hagg had performed the afternoon prayer in his office and gone up to her in the luxury apartment that he had bought her on the seventh floor of the building to take his lunch, after which he would sleep with her till before the last prayer and then leave her until the following day. This was the only regime that allowed him to see her without disturbing his family life.

Today, however, he was, unlike his usual self, exhausted and anxious. He was thinking about something that had kept him distracted all day long but now he was tired of thinking and had a headache and nausea from the several hand-rolled cigarettes he had smoked after eating and he wished Souad would leave him to sleep for a little. She, however, stretched out her hands, took his head between their soft palms with their sweetly perfumed scent, looked at him for a while with her wide, black eyes, and whispered, "What's wrong, my dear?"

The Hagg smiled and mumbled, "Lots of problems at work."

"Praise God you've got your health. That's the most important thing."

"Praise God."

"I swear to Almighty God, the world isn't worth a second's worry!"

"You're right."

"Tell me what's bothering you, Hagg."

"As though you don't have enough problems of your own!"

"Go on with you! Are my problems more important than yours?"

The Hagg smiled and looked at her gratefully. Then he moved closer, planted a kiss on her cheek, pulled his head back a little, and said in a serious voice, "God willing, I intend to put myself forward for the People's Assembly."

"The People's Assembly?"

"Yes."

She was taken aback for a moment because it was so unexpected, but she soon pulled herself together and wreathed her face in a happy smile, saying gaily, "What a wonderful day, Hagg! Should I whoop for joy or what?"

"Let's just hope that things go well and I get elected."

"God willing."

"You know, Souad, if I get into the Assembly . . . I can do business worth millions."

"Of course you'll get in. Could they find anyone better than you?"

Then she puckered up her lips as though talking down to a child and said to him (using the words one would to a little girl), "But I'm scared, sweetie, that when you appear on television and everyone sees you looking so cute, they'll go steal you away from me!"

The Hagg burst into laughter and she moved up close so he could feel the warmth of her excited body. Then she reached over with her hand in an unhurried, practiced, long-lasting caress that finally yielded its fruits, and let out a ribald laugh when she saw that in his enthusiasm and haste, he had got his head stuck in the neck of his gallabiya.

It was just like when you watch a film—you get engrossed in it and you react to it, but in the end the lights go back on, you return to reality, you leave the cinema, and the cold air of the street, crowded with cars and passersby, strikes you on the face; everything returns to its normal size and you think of everything that happened as just a movie, just a lot of acting.

That's how Taha el Shazli recalls the events of the day of the character interview: the long corridor of luxurious red carpet, the huge spacious room with its lofty ceiling, the large desk raised enough above floor level to make it seem like the dais in a courtroom, the low leather seat on which he sat, the three generals with their huge flabby bodies, white suits, shiny brass buttons, signs of rank, and glittering decorations on their chests and shoulders, and the presiding general, who welcomed him with a precisely measured, disciplined smile and then nodded to the committee member on his right. The latter propped his arms on the desk, stuck his bald head forward, and started asking him questions, the other two watching him closely as though weighing every word he spoke and observing every expression that appeared on his face. The questions were what he'd expected, his officer friends having assured him that the character interview questions were always the same and well known, the whole test being no more than a formality carried out for appearance's sake, either to exclude radical elements (based on the National Security Service reports) or to confirm the acceptance of those blessed with influential friends. Taha had memorized the expected questions and their model answers and proceeded steadily and confidently to give his answers before the committee. He said that he had obtained high enough marks to qualify for one of the good colleges but preferred the Police Academy so that he could serve his country from his position as a police officer. He stressed that the job of the police was not simply to maintain order, as many thought, but social and humanitarian (giving examples of what he meant). Next he spoke about preventive security, in

57

terms of definition and methods, approval appearing clearly on the examiners' faces and the presiding general even nodding his head twice in confirmation of Taha's answer. The former then spoke for the first time and asked Taha what he would do if he went to arrest a criminal and found him to be one of his childhood friends. Taha was expecting the question and had prepared the reply, but he made a show of thinking a bit to increase the impact of his answer on the examiners. Then he said, "Sir, duty knows nothing of friends or relatives. A policeman is like a soldier in battle—he must carry out his duty irrespective of all other considerations, for the sake of God and his country."

The presiding general smiled and nodded with frank admiration and the silence that comes before the end reigned. Taha expected that the order to dismiss would be given, but the presiding general suddenly looked hard at the papers as though he had just discovered something. He raised the sheet of paper a little to make sure of what he had read, then asked Taha, avoiding his eyes, "Your father—what's his profession, Taha?"

"Civil servant, sir."

(This is what he had written on the application form, after paying the Community Liaison Officer a bribe of a hundred pounds to sign off on it.) The general searched through the papers again and said, "Civil servant or property guard?"

Taha said nothing for a moment. Then he said in a low voice, "My father is a property guard, sir."

The presiding general smiled and looked embarrassed. Then he bent over the papers, carefully wrote something on them, raised his head with the same smile, and said, "Thanks, son. Dismissed."

His mother sighed and quoted the Qur'anic verse, *"It may happen that you will hate a thing which is better for you."*

Busayna cried out vehemently, "What's so special about being a police

58

officer? Police officers are as common as dirt. How happy I would have been to see your officer's uniform, when you were earning pennies!"

Taha had spent the day roaming the streets till he was exhausted and then come home to the roof and sat with his head bowed on the bench, the suit that he had put on that morning stripped of its glamour, baggy now and looking cheap and wretched. His mother tried to cheer him up.

"Son, you're making things too complicated. There are lots of other good colleges apart from the police."

Taha remained bowed and silent. It seemed it was beyond his mother's words to deal with the matter and she disappeared into the kitchen, leaving him with Busayna, who moved over to sit next to him on the bench. She drew close to him and whispered, "Please don't upset yourself, Taha."

Her voice set him off and he cried out bitterly, "I'm upset because of all my wasted effort. If they'd set a particular profession for the father from the start, I would have known. They should have said 'No children of doorkeepers.' And what they did is against the law, too. I asked a lawyer and he told me that if I brought a case against them, I'd win."

"We don't want a court case or anything of that sort. Know what I think? With the grades you've got, you should enter the best college in the university, graduate with top marks, go off to an Arab country and earn some money, then come back here and live like a king."

Taha looked at her for a while, then hung his head again. She went on, "Look, Taha. I know I'm a year younger than you, but I've worked and work has taught me a few things. This country doesn't belong to us, Taha. It belongs to the people who have money. If you'd had twenty thousand pounds and used them to bribe someone, do you think any one would have asked about your father's job? Make money, Taha, and you'll get everything, but if you stay poor they'll walk all over you."

"I can't let them get away with it. I must make a complaint."

Busayna laughed bitterly. "Complain about who and to who? Do as I say and no more useless ideas. Work hard, get your degree, and don't come back here till you're rich. And if you never come back, better still."

"So you think I should go to one of the Arab countries?"

"Certainly."

"Will you come with me?"

The question took her by surprise and she mumbled, avoiding his eyes, "God willing." But he said sadly, "You've changed toward me, Busayna. I know it."

Busayna could see another quarrel coming, so she said with a sigh, "You're tired out now. Go get some sleep and we'll talk tomorrow."

She left but he didn't sleep. He stayed awake for a long while thinking, recalling a hundred times the face of the presiding general as he asked him slowly, as though reveling in his humiliation, "Your father's a property guard, son?" "Property guard?"—an unfamiliar expression, one that he'd given no thought to and that he'd never expected. An expression that was his whole life. He had lived it for long years, suffered its oppression, resisted it with all his might, and tried to rid himself of it. He had struggled so that he might escape through the opening provided by the Police Academy into a respectable, decent life, but that expression—"property guard"—was waiting for him at the end of the exhausting race, to ruin everything at the final moment. Why hadn't they told him at the beginning? Why had the general left it to the end and shown how pleased he was with his answers to the questions, then directed his final thrust at him, as much as to say to him, "Get out of my sight, you son of a doorkeeper! You want to get into the police, you son of a doorkeeper? The son of the doorkeeper wants to be an officer? That's a good one, I swear!"

Taha started to pace the room for he had made up his mind that he had to do something. He told himself that he could not remain silent while they humiliated him in this way. Slowly, he started to imagine fantastic scenes of revenge: he saw himself, for example, delivering the generals on the committee a speech about equal opportunity, rights, and the justice that God and his Prophet—God bless him and grant him peace—had bidden us to. He went on rebuking them until they melted in shame for what they had done and apologized to him and announced his acceptance into the academy. In the final scene, he saw himself grasping the presiding general's collar and shouting in his face, "What business is it of yours what my father's job is, you cheating bribe-taker!" Then he directed at it a number of violent blows, in response to which the general fell to the ground, drowning in his own blood. It was his habit to imagine scenes like these whenever he found himself in difficult situations that he could not control. This time, however, the scenes of revenge, for all their power, could not assuage his thirst. Feelings of humiliation continued to bear down on him, until an idea occurred to him that he could not get out of his head. Sitting down at the small desk and taking out a piece of paper and a pen, he wrote in large letters at the top of the page, "In the Name of God, the Merciful, the Compassionate. Complaint presented to His Excellency the President of the Republic." He stopped for a moment and tipped his head back, feeling some comfort at the grandiloquence of the words and their solemnity. Then he applied himself diligently to writing.

I have left this space empty because I couldn't think what to write in it.

Words are all right to describe ordinary sorrows or joys, but the pen is incapable of describing great moments of happiness, such as those lived by Zaki el Dessouki with his sweetheart Rabab and, despite the unfortunate incident, Zaki Bey will always remember the lovely Rabab with her magical, golden-brown face, her wide, black eyes, and her full, crimson lips when she had undone her hair so that it hung down her back and sat in front of him drinking whisky and caressing him with her provocative voice, and how she excused herself to go to the bathroom and came back wearing a short nightdress, opened to reveal her charms; and he will remember that playful smile of hers as she asked him, "Where shall we sleep?" and the irresistible pleasure that her soft, warm body bestowed on him. Zaki Bey remembers every detail of that superb lovemaking and then suddenly the picture in his head becomes distorted and is violently disturbed, and finally cuts out altogether, leaving behind it a dark emptiness and a painful feeling of headache and nausea. The last thing he remembers is a low sound like the hissing of a snake, followed by a penetrating smell that stung the membranes of his nose, at which moment Rabab started examining him with a strange look as though watching for something. After that, Zaki Bey remembers nothing. . . .

He awoke with difficulty, the hammers of an appalling headache banging on his head, and found Abaskharon standing next to him, showing signs of apprehension and whispering insistently, "Your Excellency is unwell. Shall I call a doctor?"

Zaki shook his heavy head with difficulty, making an extraordinary effort at the same time to gather his scattered thoughts. He thought he must have been asleep for a long while and wanted to know the time, so he looked at his gold wristwatch, but it wasn't there. Nor was his wallet on the table next to him where he'd left it. At this, he knew for sure he'd been robbed and little by little started to make an inventory of what was missing: in addition to the gold watch and the five hundred pounds that were in his wallet, Zaki Bey lost a set of gold Cross pens (unused, in their case) and a pair of Persol sunglasses. The worst blow, however, was the theft of the diamond signet ring belonging to his elder sister Dawlat el Dessouki.

"I've been robbed, Abaskharon! Rabab robbed me!"

Zaki Bey kept repeating this as he sat almost naked on the edge of the couch that shortly before had been a cradle of love. At that moment, in his underwear and with his frail body and empty, collapsed mouth (he had removed his false teeth so as to be able to kiss the Beloved), he looked very much like some wretched comic actor, resting between scenes. Overwhelmed by misery he put his head in his hands while Abaskharon, agitated by this momentous event and excited as a locked-up dog, started to strike the ground with his crutch and pace the room in every direction. Then he bent over his master and gasped out, "Excellency, should we report the bitch to the police?"

Zaki thought a little, then shook his head and remained silent. Abaskharon came closer and whispered, "Excellency, did she give you something to drink or spray something in Your Excellency's face?"

Zaki el Dessouki had needed that question in order to be able to articulate his anger and he flared up, raining insults on the unfortunate Abaskharon. In the end, however, he accepted his help in getting up and dressing, for he had decided to leave.

It was past midnight and the stores on Suleiman Basha had closed their doors. Zaki Bey walked with dragging steps, staggering from the effects of the headache and fatigue, an enormous fury slowly building up inside him. He thought of the efforts and the money that he had spent on Rabab and the valuable things she had stolen from him. How could all this have happened to him? Zaki Bey the distinguished, the woman charmer and lover of noblewomen, tricked and robbed by a low prostitute! Perhaps she was with her lover at this minute, giving him the Persol glasses and the gold Cross pens (unused) and laughing with him at the gullible old man who had "fallen for it."

His ire was increased by the fact that he could not inform the police for fear of the scandal, echoes of which would inevitably reach his sister Dawlat. Likewise he could not go after Rabab or make a complaint against her at the Cairo Bar where she worked since he knew for sure that the owner of the bar and everyone who worked there were hardened criminals with previous convictions and that the robbery might even have been carried out for them. In any case there was no possibility they would support him against Rabab, and it was even on the cards that they would beat him up, as he had actually seen them do with disorderly customers.

There was nothing for it therefore but to forget the whole incident, and how difficult and painful that was—not to mention the anxiety weighing on his heart over the theft of his sister's ring. He started blaming himself: when he had got the ring back from Papasian the jeweler's after it was mended, why had he kept it in the office instead of hurrying to return it to Dawlat? What was he to do now? He could not afford to buy a new ring and even if he could, Dawlat knew her jewelry as she did her own children. He feared his confrontation with Dawlat more than anything else—so much so that when he arrived in front of their apartment in Baehler Passage, he stood hesitating at the entrance and it occurred to him to go and spend the night at one of his friends' houses, and this he almost did. But it was late and his exhaustion was driving him to go upstairs, so he went.

"And just where has His Lordship been?"

These were Dawlat's opening words to him as he stepped into the apartment. She was waiting for him in the reception room, on the seat facing the front door. She had wrapped her chestnut-dyed hair on her "*boucles*" and covered her lined face with thick layers of powder, while a lighted cigarette in a small gold holder dangled from the corner of her mouth. She had on a blue house robe that covered her thin body and had stuffed her feet into her "*pantoufles*," which were shaped like white rabbits. She sat knitting, her hands moving in a quick, mechanical way, never stopping or slackening their pace, as though they were divorced from the rest of her body. Habit had taught her the skill of smoking, knitting, and talking simultaneously.

"Good evening."

Zaki said the words quickly and tried to move on directly to his room, but Dawlat launched her attack immediately, screaming in his face, "What do you think you are? Living in an hotel? Three hours I've been waiting for you, to and fro between the door and the window. I was just going to call the police. I thought something must have happened to you. It's too bad of you! I'm sick. Do you want to kill me? Have mercy on me, Lord! Lord, take me and let me rest!"

This was a kind of brief overture to a quarrel in four movements that might stretch out till the morning and Zaki, quickly crossing the hall, said, "I'm sorry, Dawlat. I'm extremely tired. I'm going to sleep and in the morning I'll tell you what happened, God willing."

Dawlat, however, was alert to his attempt at flight and, throwing the knitting needles from her hands, rushed at him screaming at the top of her voice, "Tired from what, you poor thing? From the women you spend all your time sniffing after like a dog? Wise up, mister! You could die any day. When you meet Our Lord, what are you going to tell Him then, *mister*?"

With the last cry, Dawlat gave Zaki a hard shove in the back. He staggered a little but rallied his forces and slipped inside his room, where despite Dawlat's fierce resistance he managed to lock his door, stuffing the key into his pocket. Dawlat continued to shout and rattle the doorknob to make him open up, but Zaki felt that he'd made it to safety and told himself that it wouldn't be long before she got tired and went away. Then he lay down fully clothed on the bed. He was tired and sad and he started to review the events of the day, muttering in French, "*Quelle journée horrible!*" Then he thought of Dawlat and asked himself how his beloved sister could have been transformed into this vicious, hateful old woman.

She is only three years older than he, and he still remembers her as a beautiful delicate girl wearing the yellow and navy school uniform of the Mère de Dieu and learning selections of La Fontaine's animal verses by heart. In the evenings she would play the piano in the reception room of their old house in Zamalek (which the Basha had sold following the Revolution). She played so well that Mme. Chedid the music teacher approached the Basha about the possibility of her applying for the international amateurs' competition in Paris, but the Basha refused and Dawlat soon married Airforce Captain Hassan Shawkat and had a boy and a girl (Hani and Dina). Then the Revolution came and Shawkat was pensioned off because of his close relations with the royal family and soon after died a sudden death while still less than forty-five years of age.

Dawlat remarried twice after him but had no more children—two failed marriages that left her bitter, nervy, and a cigarette smoker. Then her daughter grew up, married, and emigrated to Canada. When her son graduated from the School of Medicine, Dawlat waged a fierce battle to stop him emigrating. She wept and screamed and implored all her relatives to convince him to remain with her, but the young doctor, like most of his generation, was sick to despair of the situation in Egypt. He was determined to emigrate and offered to take his mother with him but she refused and was left on her own.

She rented out her flat in Garden City furnished and moved in to live with Zaki downtown, and from the first day the two old people had not stopped feuding and battling as though they were sworn enemies. Zaki had got used to his independence and freedom and it had become difficult for him to accept anyone else sharing his life—to accept that he would have to stick to appointed times for sleeping and eating and that he would have to tell Dawlat ahead of time if he intended to stay out late. Her presence prevented him from inviting girlfriends home, and her barefaced interference in his most private affairs and her constant attempts to dominate him made her even harder to put up with.

From her side, Dawlat endured loneliness and unhappiness and it grieved her that she should end her life without accomplishments or achievements after failing in marriage and seeing her children leave her in her old age. It provoked her greatly that Zaki seemed in no way like a failing old man waiting for death, but still wore scent and played the fop and chased women. No sooner did she catch sight of him smiling and humming in front of the mirror as he primped his clothes or notice that he was happy and in high spirits than she would feel a resentment that wouldn't subside until she'd picked a quarrel with him and flayed him with her tongue. She attacked his childish ways and whims not from a standpoint based on any moral objections but simply because his clinging to life in this way didn't match her own despair, her fury at him being akin to that felt by mourners at the man who guffaws in the middle of a funeral.

In addition, there lay between the two old people all the irritability, impatience, and obstinacy that go with old age, plus that certain tension that develops when two individuals live in too close proximity to one another—from one using the bathroom for a long time when the other wants it, from one seeing the sullen face the other wears when he wakes from sleeping, from one wanting silence while the other insists on talking, from the mere presence of another person who never leaves you day and night, who stares at you, who interrupts you, who picks on everything you say, and the grating of whose molars when he chews sets you on edge, and the ringing noise of whose spoon striking the dishes disturbs your quiet every time he sits down to eat with you.

Zaki Bey el Dessouki stayed stretched out on the bed going over these events and gradually drowsiness started to overcome him. However, his bad day wasn't over yet, for it was not long before he heard, as he lay between sleeping and waking, the grating of the spare key, which Dawlat had known where to find. She opened the door, approached him, and, eyes wide with resentment and voice gasping with emotion, said, "Where's the ring, Zaki?"

Thus Your Excellency Mr. President will see that your son Taha Muhammad el Shazli has suffered injustice and the violation of his rights at the hands of the presiding general of the interviewing committee at the Police Academy. The Prophet—God bless him and give him peace—has said, in a sound hadith, "Verily, your people who were before you would leave alone a nobleman if he stole, and would invoke the punishment against a poor man if he stole. By God, even if Fatima, daughter of Muhammad, stole, I would cut off her hand." The Prophet of God has spoken truly.

Mr. President, I went to great trouble and made great efforts in order to obtain a score of 98 (Humanities), and I was able, through God's bounty, to pass all the tests for admission to the Police Academy. Is it then just, Mr. President, that I should be denied admission to the police force for no better reason than that my father is a decent but poor man who works as a property guard? Is not the guarding of property a decent occupation, and is not every decent occupation to be respected, Mr. President? I ask you, Mr. President, to look into this complaint with the eye of a loving father who will never agree that injustice be done to one of his sons. My future, Mr. President, awaits a decision from Your Excellency and I am confident that, the Almighty willing, I shall meet with fair treatment at your noble hands.

May God preserve you as an asset for Islam and the Muslims,
Your sincere son, Taha Muhammad el Shazli
Identity Card No.19578, Kasr El Nil
Address: The Yacoubian Building, 34 Talaat Harb Street, Cairo

꿈:

Like a victorious wartime general who enters in triumph a city he has
conquered after bitter fighting, Malak Khilla appeared on the roof of
the building to take possession of his new room in a happy and vainglo-
rious mood. He was wearing his blue people's suit that he kept for special occasions and had hung around his neck a long tape measure that
was for him—like an officer's pips or a doctor's stethoscope—the distinguishing mark of his professional status as a master shirtmaker. That
morning he brought with him a number of workmen to get the room
ready—a smith, an electrician, a plumber, and some young male assistants to help them.

Master craftsman Malak muttered a prayer of thanks to the Virgin
and Christ the Savior, then stretched out his hand to open the door to
the room for the first time. The air inside was musty because it had
been closed for a whole year following the death of Atiya the newspaper seller (some of whose effects Malak found and had one of the boys
collect in a large cardboard box).

Now Malak stands in the middle of the room after opening the window and letting sunlight flood the place and issues detailed instructions to the workmen as to what they have to do. From time to time,
one of the residents of the roof stops and watches what's going on out
of curiosity. Some watch for a short while, then move on. Others offer
Malak their congratulations on taking possession of the new room and
shake his hand, wishing him well in his enterprise.

Not all the residents of the roof, however, are so well mannered.
After less than half an hour, word has spread on the roof and soon two
individuals appear who do not seem to be the least bit eager to welcome the new arrival—Mr. Hamid Hawwas and Ali the Driver.

The first is a civil servant in the National Sanitation Authority whose
boss got angry with him and transferred him from his hometown of El

Mansoura to Cairo, so he rented a room on the roof where he lives alone, expending all his energy for more than a year now to get his arbitrary transfer cancelled and return home. Mr. Hamid Hawwas is a major writer of official complaints, and finds a genuine and all-encompassing pleasure in selecting the subject of the complaint and formulating it eloquently, then writing it out in a neat, easy-to-read hand and subsequently following it through to the end at whatever cost this may impose upon him, for he considers himself to be responsible to some degree for the proper performance of all public utilities in any area in which he may be residing, or even passing through. He always finds the time to make a daily round of the District Administration, the Governorate, and the Utilities Police, during which he pertinaciously and single-mindedly follows up on the complaints he has made against street vendors who may stand in locations far distant from his place of residence but whom, as violators of the law, he nevertheless believes it to be his duty to pursue with one complaint after another, never tiring and never despairing, until the Utilities Police finally move and arrest them and confiscate their goods—at which point Mr. Hamid watches from a distance, feeling the ease of conscience of one who has gone that extra mile to do his duty in full.

As for Ali the Driver, he's an alcoholic, over fifty, never married, who works as a driver at the Holding Company for Pharmaceuticals, going straight from work every day to the Orabi Bar in El Tawfikiya, where he eats and sits sipping a drink until midnight. Loneliness and the cheap alcohol to which he is addicted have had their effect on him, making him gross, violent, and ever in search of a quarrel on which to expend his aggression.

Mr. Hamid Hawwas approached Malak and greeted him, then opened the conversation in an extremely refined way by saying, "About this room, my friend. Do you have a contract from the owner of the building giving you the right to use it as a commercial establishment?"

"Of course I have a contract," answered Malak excitedly, and he pulled out of his small leather purse a copy of the contract that he had signed with Fikri Abd el Shaheed. Hamid took the piece of paper, put on his glasses, and examined it carefully. Then he handed it back to Malak, saying quietly, "The contract is invalid in this form."

"Invalid?" repeated Malak, apprehensively.

"Of course invalid. According to the law the roof is a common resource for the residents and a common resource may not be rented out for commercial purposes."

Malak didn't understand and stared angrily at Mr. Hamid, who went on to say, "The Court of Cassation has issued more than one ruling on the issue and the matter is closed. The contract is invalid and you have no right to the use of the room."

"Yes, but all of you are living on the roof, so why not me?"

"We are employing our rooms for residential purposes, and that is legal. You, however, are exploiting your room for commercial ends, and that is illegal and we cannot allow it."

"Okay. Go complain to the owner of the place since he's the one who gave me the contract."

"Certainly not. The law itself forbids you to make use of the room, and we, as injured residents, are obliged to prevent you."

"What does that mean?"

"*It means you'd better get a move on and scram or else!*"

These last words were spoken by Ali the Driver in his husky voice as he looked challengingly at Malak. Laying his hand on Malak's shoulder in a clearly threatening way, he went on, "Listen, sonny boy. This roof is for respectable folk. You can't just turn up here in your own sweet time and open a shop, with workers and customers looking at the ladies going in and out. Got it?"

Malak, who now felt the danger of the situation, responded quickly, "My dear sir, all my workers are educated people, praise God!

They're the most polite and discreet people in the world. And the people living on the roof and their ladies have my utmost respect."

"Listen. Forget the chitchat. Pick up your stuff and get going!"

"Dear me! What's going on? Are you going to behave like ruffians or what?"

"That's it, momma's boy, we're going to behave like ruffians."

As Ali the Driver said this, he pulled Malak toward him by his collar and gave him a slap to announce that battle was about to commence. He conducted his quarrels with ease and proficiency as though he were carrying out simple, routine procedures or practicing a sport of which he was fond. He started with a well-placed head butt at Malak, followed by two punches to the stomach and a third, powerful and audible, that struck his nose. A thread of blood flowed down Malak's face and he tried to resist by aiming a useless, symbolic punch at his opponent, but it missed. Then as violent blows fell on him, he started screaming in protest and chaos reigned, while the workmen, not wanting problems, quietly fled and people gathered from every direction to watch. Abaskharon appeared suddenly on the roof and started screaming and wailing for help and the fight continued until Ali the Driver succeeded in expelling Malak from the room.

Mr. Hamid Hawwas had slipped away at the beginning and called the Emergency Response Police from the telephone in the cigarette stand on the opposite side of the street and it wasn't long before a young police officer and a number of policemen and goons took everyone involved into custody—Malak, his assistants, Abaskharon, and Ali the Driver.

Approaching the officer, Hamid Hawwas greeted him politely and said, "You've studied law, of course, sir. Now our friend here"—pointing to Malak—"wants to open a commercial establishment on the roof, while the roof is a common resource that may not be exploited commercially. As you know full well, sir, this is a crime, known in legal terminology as 'extortion of possession,' and is punishable by imprisonment for a period of up to three years."

"Are you a lawyer?" the officer asked Mr. Hamid, who responded confidently, "No, sir. I, sir, am Hamid Hawwas, deputy director of auditing in the National Sanitation Authority, El Mansoura Branch. Equally, I am one of the residents whose rights to the common resource of the roof have been usurped. How could the owner, my dear sir, go and rent the roof for a commercial purpose? This is a flagrant attack on the common resources of the residents. If he gets away with this, he could rent out the elevator, or the entrance to the building! Has the country gone to the dogs or what?"

Mr. Hamid Hawwas posed the last question with a theatrical flourish, looking hard at the assembled residents, who, stirred by his words, muttered in protest. Confusion appeared on the young officer's face, and after thinking for a little he said disgustedly, "Okay, come on. Everyone to the station!"

Dr. Hassan Rasheed was a leading figure in the law in Egypt and the Arab world. Like Taha Hussein, Ali Badawi, Zaki Naguib Mahmoud, and others, he was one of the great intellectuals of the 1940s who completed their higher studies in the West and returned to their country to apply what they had learned there—lock, stock, and barrel—within Egyptian academia. For people like them, "progress" and "the West" were virtually synonymous, with all that that entailed by way of positive and negative behavior. They all had the same reverence for the great Western values—democracy, freedom, justice, hard work, and equality. At the same time, they had the same ignorance of the nation's heritage and contempt for its customs and traditions, which they considered shackles pulling us toward Backwardness from which it was our duty to free ourselves so that the Renaissance could be achieved.

During his studies in Paris, Dr. Rasheed met a French woman, Jeanette, and fell in love with her. Then he brought her with him to Egypt and married her and they had their only son, Hatim. The family lived a life that was European in both form and essence. Hatim could not remember ever seeing his father pray or fast. The pipe never left his mouth, there was always French wine at his table, the most recent records from Paris resounded through the house, and French was the main language of conversation at home. In the Western manner, everything about the family's life took place according to a set time and schedule, Dr. Rasheed even setting aside special times during each week for meeting friends and relatives and writing his personal correspondence.

The fact is that in addition to his exceptional mental capacities he possessed an astonishing appetite for uninterrupted work and was able in two decades to bring about a real blossoming of Egyptian civil law studies. With time his star rose till he assumed the deanship of the Faculty of Law at Cairo University. Then the International Law Society in Paris chose him as one of the hundred most prominent lawyers in the world.

Since Dr. Rasheed was always absorbed in his research and lecturing and because his wife Jeanette's job as a translator at the French embassy occupied all her time, their son Hatim spent his childhood sad and lonely, to the point that in contrast to all other children he even liked school days and hated the long summer vacations, which he spent on his own with no friends to play with. And along with the painful loneliness, there were the feelings of alienation and mental confusion from which the children of mixed marriages suffer.

Little Hatim spent a lot of time with the servants, and his parents (being always busy) would often send him with one of them to the Gezira Club or the cinema. Among the many servants in the house, little Hatim was particularly fond of the steward Idris, with his flowing white caftan, broad red cummerbund and tall fez, and his tall, strong, slim body, his handsome brown face, his intelligent, bright eyes, and his beaming smile from which his gleaming, white, regular teeth shone out. It was Idris's habit to sit with Hatim in his large room overlooking Suleiman Basha, playing with his toys with him, telling him stories about animals, singing beautiful Nubian songs to him and translating for him what they meant. Idris's voice would tremble and the tears would glisten in his eyes when he spoke to him of his mother and his brothers and sisters and his village that they had taken him away from when he was young to go work in people's houses. Hatim loved Idris and their relationship grew till they were spending many hours together every day, and when Idris started kissing Hatim on his face and neck and whispering, "You're beautiful. I love you," Hatim felt no revulsion or fear. On the contrary, the burning sensation that his friend's breath left on his body excited him. They continued to exchange kisses until one day Idris asked him to take off his clothes. Hatim was nine at the time and felt embarrassed and confused, but in the end he gave in to the insistence of his friend. The latter was so aroused by the sight of his smooth, white body that during the encounter he sobbed with pleasure and whispered incomprehensible Nubian words. Idris, despite his lust and vigor, entered Hatim's body gently and carefully and asked him to tell him if he felt the slightest pain. This approach was so successful that when Hatim now thinks back to that first time with Idris, the same strange, piercing sensation that he knew that day for the first time comes back to him but he cannot remember feeling any distress at all.

When Idris was finished, he turned Hatim to face him and kissed him ardently on the lips, then looked into his eyes and said, "I did that because I love you. If you love me, don't tell anyone what happened. If you tell them, they'll beat you and throw me out and your father may put me in prison or kill me and you'll never see me again."

Hatim's relationship with Idris lasted years, until Dr. Rasheed suddenly died of a brain hemorrhage caused by overwork and his widow was obliged to get rid of many of the servants because of the expense. Idris left the house and nothing more was heard of him. His absence affected Hatim so much psychologically that that year he got a poor score in the general secondary exam. Thereafter he plunged into his tumultuous homosexual life and two years later his mother passed away.

This released him from the last constraint on his pleasures. He had inherited a solid income which along with his reasonable salary from the newspaper underwrote an opulent lifestyle. He redid the large apartment in the Yacoubian Building to liberate it from its traditional style, turning it into something closer to a Bohemian artist's studio than the home of an established family. It was now in his power to invite lovers to share his bed for days and sometimes months at a time. Hatim had relationships with many men and left them for a variety of reasons, but his covert, sinful desire remained forever linked to Idris the steward and, as a man searches among women for the image of his first love, with whom he first became acquainted with pleasure, so Hatim sought among all other men for Idris—the rough-hewn, primitive male whom civilization had not refined, and with all the hardness, crudity, and vigor that such a man represented. He never ceased thinking about Idris and often would relive, with a delicious, burning tenderness, his feeling as he lay facedown on the floor of his room (like a little rabbit surrendering itself to its fate) following with his eyes the Persian designs drawn on the carpet as Idris's hot, bursting body clung to his, wringing it and melting it. The strange thing was that their sexual encounters, many as they were, always ended up on the floor and they never got into the bed, a fact probably attributable to Idris's feelings of insignificance as a servant and his psychological inability to use his master's bed even when having sexual intercourse with him.

It had happened one night a few months ago that drunkenness got the better of Hatim and an implacable urge to have sex had swept over him. He left his apartment and wandered the downtown area. It was ten o'clock (the hour when the police privates change guard, one known to every Downtown homosexual as the hour at which they rush to meet their lovers among them) and Hatim was looking over the simple conscripts as they prepared to quit their shift when he saw Abd Rabbuh (who looked a lot like Idris). He got him into the car, gave him money, and kept fondling him until he succeeded in seducing him.

Later Abd Rabbuh made many violent attempts to put an end to his relationship with Hatim, who was well aware from his long experience in homosexual love that the active homosexual who is just starting out, such as Abd Rabbuh, is usually possessed by a terrible sense of sin that soon develops into bitterness and black hatred for the passive homosexual who seduces him. He was also aware that the homosexual experience when repeated and the savoring of its sensual pleasures turn bit by bit into genuine desire on the part of the active partner, however much he may hate it and shy away from it at the beginning. As a result, Hatim and Abduh's relationship swung from attempts at separation to reunions.

Yesterday Abduh had left Chez Nous to escape from Hatim, but Hatim had caught up with him and insisted until he went with him to the apartment, where they had drunk a whole bottle of strong French wine together before making love—and now here was Hatim the next morning lying stretched out in the bathtub, surrendering himself to the jets of hot water spurting from the showerhead which felt to his body like armies of delicious ants, while he recalled, smiling, his passionate night with Abduh, whose body, its lust inflamed by the wine, had been wrung by numerous, successive spasms. Hatim stood up to dry himself in front of the mirror and clean his private parts with care, applying scented cream, then wrapped himself in a rose cashmere dressing gown, left the bathroom for the bedroom, and settled down to watch Abduh as he slept—his dark brown face, his thick lips, his snub Negroid nose, and the heavy eyebrows that gave his face its stern cast. He bent over him and kissed him and Abduh awoke and opened his eyes slowly.

"Good morning! *Bonjour!*" whispered Hatim gently, smiling at Abduh, who sat up a little and leaned against the back of the bed, revealing his broad, dark chest covered with a forest of thick hair. Hatim pursued him with kisses, but Abduh pushed his face away with his hand, then looked downward and said bitterly as though breaking into a lament, "Hatim Bey, I'm in a real mess. Any day now the officer will refer me for punishment."

"Abduh! Do we have to start talking about the officer again? I told you not to worry. I've found someone who can put in a good word for you with him, a very important general in the Ministry."

"By the time you talk to him, I'll have been flung in prison. My wife and little boy back in the village live off what I earn, Excellency. I wish I could get out of the army right away—if I go to prison, my family will be done for."

Hatim gazed at him tenderly and smiled. Then he got up slowly, went over to his small purse, took out a hundred-pound note, and thrust it toward him, saying, "Here. Send this to your wife and son, and if they ask for anything from me, I'll take care of it for you. Tomorrow I'll meet my relative the general and we'll put in a word for you with the officer. Just please, for my sake, don't upset yourself, Abduh."

Abduh looked down and whispered words of thanks. Hatim moved up to him until their bodies were completely joined and said to himself in French as he approached Abduh's thick lips, "*Quelle belle journée!*"

To: Taha Muhammad el Shazli, Citizen
Yacoubian Building
34, Talaat Harb Street
Cairo

Greetings:

With reference to your complaint presented to the Presidency of the Republic concerning your rejection by the acceptance examination at the Police Academy: We have to inform you that the matter has been reviewed with the director of the Police Academy and it is evident to us that the complaint is unfounded. We wish you success.

Please accept the assurance of our highest respect, General Hassan Bazaraa

Director, Public Complaints Administration

Presidency of the Republic

The neighbors were used to hearing the sounds of Zaki el Dessouki and his sister Dawlat quarreling. It happened a lot and no longer aroused their surprise or curiosity. This time, however, the quarrel was different—more like a terrible explosion. Screams, ugly insults, and the loud sounds of hand-to-hand fighting reached the residents, who opened their doors and came out to reconnoiter. Some murmured nervously, preparing to intervene. Dawlat shouted in an angry voice, "You lost my diamond ring, you shit?"

"Talk decently, Dawlat!"

"I wouldn't be surprised if you didn't give it to one of your prostitute friends!"

"I'm telling you, talk decently!"

"I am still decent, in spite of you! It's you that's the laughingstock everyone despises! Get out of my house, you son of a bitch, you junkie!"

"This is *my* apartment," shouted Zaki Bey in an exhausted voice.

"Not so, sweetheart. It's the house of my father, the respected basha, which you have defiled with your filth!"

Sounds of slaps and a battle followed, the door of the apartment opened, and Dawlat pushed Zaki outside, shouting, "Get out! I don't ever want to see your miserable face again!"

Zaki Bey came out and, catching sight of the throng of neighbors, turned around and said, "As you wish, Dawlat. I'm going."

Dawlat slammed the door and the sound of the bolt was heard as she locked it. The neighbors went up to Zaki Bey and said that what had happened just now was quite inappropriate and that whatever differences there might be, it was shameful for respectable people such as Zaki Bey and his sister to fight like that. Zaki Bey nodded, smiling sadly as he withdrew, and before entering the elevator told the neighbors in a conciliatory, apologetic tone, "Sorry to have disturbed you, everyone. It's just a misunderstanding. God willing, everything will get sorted out."

The numerous, oft-repeated stories about the politician Kamal el Fouli assert that he grew up in an extremely poor family from Shibin el Kom, in the governorate of El Minoufiya. Despite his poverty he was extremely intelligent and ambitious, obtaining a general secondary certificate in 1955 with one of the top placements in the nation, and he plunged into politics the moment he joined the Faculty of Law. Kamal el Fouli became a member of each of the regime's political structures in succession—the Liberation Organization and the National Union, followed by the Socialist Union and the Vanguard Organization, then the Center Platform, the Egypt Party, and, finally, the Patriotic Party. Throughout these shifts, he was always the most enthusiastic and loudest voice in support of the principles of the governing party. During Nasser's era he gave lectures and wrote works on the necessity for and historical inevitability of the socialist transformation. And when the state switched to capitalism, he became one of the greatest supporters of privatization and the free economy, mounting from beneath the parliament dome a fierce and celebrated campaign against the public sector and totalitarian ideas in general. He was one of the few Egyptian politicians who had managed to keep a seat in parliament for more than thirty consecutive years.

While it's true that Egyptian elections are always fixed in favor of the ruling party, it is also true that Kamal el Fouli is endowed with a real talent for politics that would necessarily have enabled him to assume the highest positions of state even in a democratic society. This same authentic talent, however, like so many talents in Egypt, has been diverted, distorted, and adulterated by lying, hypocrisy, and intrigue till the name of Kamal el Fouli has come to represent in the minds of Egyptians the very essence of corruption and hypocrisy.

He has risen through the party hierarchy to become secretary of the Patriotic Party and the primary arbiter of elections for the whole of Egypt, for he nominates or rejects whomever he wishes to or from the party's list and personally supervises the fixing of elections from Alexandria to Aswan. He takes large bribes from the candidates to guarantee that the elections are fixed in their favor while at the same time covering up his corruption with all sorts of tricks, such as swapping favors and financial privileges that divert millions to leading politicians.

El Fouli also keeps secret security reports and documents proving the malfeasances of officials so that he can use them to blackmail or if need be destroy them. At political meetings, whether in the People's Assembly or the Patriotic Party, everyone shuts up when Kamal el Fouli speaks. Indeed a single stern look from him is enough to strike terror into the heart of any official. There are numerous celebrated incidents related about him in this context in which he made mincemeat of leading officials in public because they said something that he didn't like, an example being the ruthless campaign that he led a few years ago (on behalf of leading officials) against Dr. El Ghamrawi, governor of the Bank of Egypt, which led in the end to the latter's resignation. A more recent example occurred last year and affected the minister of religious endowments, who enjoyed a certain popularity that made him imagine that he was powerful and influential. Under the influence of this mistaken impression, the minister got up at a meeting of the Political Bureau of the Patriotic Party and made a violent attack on political corruption, demanding that party posts be cleansed of deviant elements and profiteers. Kamal el Fouli made a sign to the minister to bring his speech to a close, but the minister continued, ignoring him. At this point El Fouli interrupted him mockingly and, turning dramatically to those present, said, "Well, well! Whatever's got into you, my dear minister? Given that Your Excellency is so concerned about fighting corruption, you might want to begin with yourself, sport. You borrowed ten million pounds from the Development Bank and for the last five years you've refused to pay the installments. By the way, the officials at the Bank intend to bring a case and make an example of you"—at which, the minister turned pale and sat down in silence amid the wisecracks and laughter of those present.

Hagg Azzam was well aware of all this and so as soon as he decided to put himself forward as a candidate in the elections for the People's Assembly he sought an appointment with Kamal el Fouli, who kept him waiting for a few weeks, then finally gave him one at the office of his son, the lawyer Yasser el Fouli, on Shihab Street in El Mohandiseen. After Friday prayers, Hagg Azzam and his son Fawzi went to the appointment. The office was empty except for security staff, Kamal el Fouli, and his son. Azzam and El Fouli embraced and exchanged prayers, compliments, and jokes, and one might have been forgiven for thinking the two were old friends who loved, understood, and respected each other.

After a long conversation ranging over a number of topics by way of preparation, Azzam broached the subject. He spoke of how he loved the people and of his desire to serve them, quoting more than one of the Prophet's noble hadiths concerning the rewards waiting for those who strive to meet the needs of the Muslims, Kamal el Fouli nodding in agreement. Finally Azzam came to the critical point. He said, "This is why I have sought God's guidance, placed my trust in Him, and decided, God willing, to put myself forward as a candidate in the coming elections for my constituency, Kasr el Nil. I hope that the Patriotic Party will agree to nominate me and I'm yours to command, Kamal Bey, for anything you may need."

El Fouli made a show of thinking deeply, even though he had been expecting Azzam to say this.

El Fouli made contradictory impressions on people who saw him. There were his intelligence, quick-wittedness, and overwhelming presence on the one side and on the other his corpulent body, his sagging belly, his always slightly loosened neck tie, the hideous, mismatched colors of his clothes, his crudely dyed hair, his coarse, fat face, his lying, vicious, impertinent looks, and his plebeian manner of speaking, when he would stretch his arms out in front of him, waggling his fingers and shaking his shoulders and belly as he talked, like a woman of the lower classes. All the preceding gave him a somewhat comic appearance, as though he were putting on a turn for the amusement of the bystanders. It also left one with an unpleasant feeling of vulgarity.

El Fouli asked his helpers for pen and paper. Then he started to draw and for a few moments was so absorbed in his task that Hagg Azzam thought that something was wrong. El Fouli soon finished, however, and turned the piece of paper toward Azzam, who was astonished to see that the drawing represented a large rabbit. He said nothing for a moment, then asked him in an amicable way, "I don't understand what you mean, Your Excellency."

El Fouli answered quickly, "You want to guarantee your success in the elections, and you're asking what's needed. I've drawn you a picture of what's needed."

"A whole 'rabbit'? A million pounds, Kamal Bey? That's a huge amount!"

Azzam had been expecting the amount but preferred to bargain, just in case. El Fouli said, "Listen, Hagg, as God is my witness . . ."

(Here all present repeated, "There is no god but God.")

". . . in constituencies smaller than Kasr el Nil I take a million and a half, two million, and my son Yasser is standing here in front of you and he can tell you. But I love you, I swear to God, Hagg, and I really want you with us in the Assembly. Plus, I don't take all that for myself. I'm just the postman—I take from you and deliver to others, and a nod's as good as a wink."

Hagg Azzam put on a show of uneasiness for a moment, then asked, "You mean, if I pay that sum, Kamal Bey, I'll be sure of winning the elections, God willing?"

"Shame on you, Hagg! You're talking to Kamal el Fouli! Thirty years' experience in parliament! There's not a candidate in Egypt can win without our say-so, God willing!"

"I hear there are some big fish intending to nominate themselves for Kasr el Nil."

"Don't worry about it. If we come to an understanding, God willing, you'll win in Kasr el Nil even if the devil himself stands against you. Just leave it to me, Hagg."

El Fouli then laughed and leaning back and rubbing his big belly said complacently, "People are naïve when they get the idea that we fix elections. Nothing of the kind. It just comes down to the fact that we've studied the Egyptian people well. Our Lord created the Egyptians to accept government authority. No Egyptian can go against his government. Some peoples are excitable and rebellious by nature, but the Egyptian keeps his head down his whole life long so he can eat. It says so in the history books. The Egyptians are the easiest people in the world to rule. The moment you take power, they submit to you and grovel to you and you can do what you want with them. Any party in Egypt, when it makes elections and is in power, is bound to win, because the Egyptian is bound to support the government. It's just the way God made him."

Azzam pretended to be confused and unconvinced by El Fouli's words. Then he asked him about the payment details and the other said simply, "Listen up, Hagg. If it's in cash, I'll take it. If it's a check, make it out to 'Yasser el Fouli, Lawyer' and make a contract with him for any case, as though you were hiring him for it. You understand, of course, that these are mere formalities."

Hagg Azzam was silent for a moment. Then he took out his checkbook and said as he undid his gold pen, "Fine. Let's do it. I'll write a check for half. Then when I win, God willing, I'll pay the rest."

"No way, sugar! Shame on you—you'll get me upset if you go on like that. Keep that kind of stuff for school kids. The way I do things is pay first, take later. Pay the whole amount and I'll congratulate you on getting into the Assembly and read the Fatiha with you right now!"

It had been Azzam's last ploy, and when it failed, he surrendered. He wrote out the check for a million pounds, examined it carefully as was his custom, and then handed it to El Fouli, who took it and gave it to his son. Then El Fouli grinned all over his face and said gaily, "Congratulations, Hagg! Come on, let's read the Fatiha. May the Lord be generous to us and grant us success! You'll find the contract ready with Yasser."

The four of them—El Fouli, Azzam, and their two sons—closed their eyes, held their hands before their breasts in supplication, and set to reciting the Fatiha under their breath.

Hagg Azzam paid the money to El Fouli and imagined the elections had been decided in his favor, but that was not the case. There was fierce competition in the Kasr el Nil constituency among a number of businessmen, each of whom wanted to win the Workers' seat in the People's Assembly. Hagg Azzam's strongest competitor was Hagg Abu Himeida, owner of the famous Approval and Light clothing store chain. Just as the two poles repel one another in nature, so the sharp dislike between the two Haggs derived in essence from their many points of similiarity. Thus Abu Himeida, like Azzam, had originally been a simple laborer in Port Said. Then in less than twenty years his wealth increased vastly till he became one of Egypt's millionaires.

People had heard about Abu Himeida for the first time some years before when he opened a chain of large shops in Cairo and Alexandria. He had flooded the newspapers and television with advertisements undertaking to give any woman a number of new, "modest" dresses and colored headscarves if the same woman would take the decision to observe religiously sanctioned dress and agreed to hand in her old, revealing clothes to the store management as a sign of her seriousness. At the time people were amazed at this strange offer and their astonishment grew when the Approval and Light stores did in fact receive the old clothes of dozens of women, to whom it handed over new and expensive Islamic garments as free replacements. The project's noble objectives did not prevent the infiltration of certain women who already wore "modest dress" but who wanted to take advantage of the free clothes. These would pretend that they had not worn modest dress before and present the store with revealing garments that did not belong to them so that they could receive new ones in return. The Approval and Light stores caught on to this ruse and published announcements everywhere warning these tricksters of the punishment they faced in law, as the contract that the woman signed in the store included a penalty clause if she lied.

Despite these setbacks, the project achieved enormous success and helped thousands of Muslim women to adopt modest dress. Paid advertisements in the form of journalistic reports about the project appeared in the press where Hagg Abu Himeida went on record as saying that he'd sworn to set aside a large sum of money to be spent on charitable works in the hope of winning the favor of God, Almighty and Glorious, and that following consultation with qualified men of religion he'd discovered that the best method by which he might serve the call was to help Muslim women to observe modesty, as a first step toward a total commitment to God's true path. When he was asked how much the distribution for free of thousands of new modest garments had cost him, Abu Himeida refused to say how much he had spent, asserting that he anticipated that God, Almighty and Glorious, would compensate him for the money; and there can be no doubt that the "modest dress" project catapulted Abu Himeida's name into the world of celebrity and turned him into one of Egyptian society's leading figures. Despite this, rumors constantly circulated that Abu Himeida was one of Egypt's biggest heroin dealers, that the Islamic project was a money-laundering front, and that the bribes he paid to top officials protected him from arrest.

Abu Himeida had expended enormous effort to get the Patriotic Party nomination for the Kasr el Nil constituency, and when the party nominated Hagg Azzam, he was furious and made strenuous representations to important people, but in vain. El Fouli's word was supreme. In fact, a high official who was a strong friend of Abu Himeida's listened to him complaining against El Fouli, then smiled and said, "Listen, Abu Himeida. You know that I love you and look out for your interests. Under no circumstances escalate your differences with El Fouli. If you don't get into the People's Assembly this time, there'll be other times, God willing. But you don't ever lose El Fouli because he has backers and contacts beyond anything you can think of. Plus, he's cunning, and if he gets mad, he'll cause you problems you can't even imagine."

Abu Himeida wouldn't, however, back down. On the contrary, he put himself forward officially as an independent, flooding the Kasr el Nil constituency with hundreds of election posters bearing his name, his portrait, and his election symbol (the chair). He also erected large election marquees every night in the downtown area where his supporters would gather and he would make speeches to them attacking Hagg Azzam and hinting at the illicit sources of his wealth and his dedication to the pleasures of the senses (an allusion to his new wife). Azzam got angry at this smear campaign, went to El Fouli, and told him frankly, "What's the benefit of being the party's candidate, if it doesn't protect me from being insulted every night in public?"

El Fouli shook his head and promised that everything would be all right, then the next day put out a statement that was prominently displayed on the front pages of all the newspapers, in which he said, "The Patriotic Party has one candidate in every constituency and it is the duty of all party members to stand with all their strength behind the party's candidate. By the same token any member of the party who puts himself up against the party's candidate will be tried by the party and stripped of his membership once the elections are over."

The statement clearly applied to Abu Himeida, who, however, was unfazed by the threat and continued his violent campaign against Azzam, the marquees being set up now every day while hundreds of gifts were distributed to constituents. The two sides competed at collecting followers and supporters by any means possible, and violent fights broke out daily, leading to many injuries. In view of the great influence that both the opponents enjoyed, the security forces always adopted a neutral stance. Thus, the police would usually arrive at the site of the fight after it had broken up, or make symbolic arrests of some of those involved, who no sooner reached the police station than they were released without interrogation.

For some reason, the Faculty of Economics and Political Sciences of Cairo University is associated in people's minds with affluence and chic. Its students, if asked which faculty they are in, are accustomed to reply, "Economics and Political Science" in a complacent, confident, and nonchalant way (as though saying, "Yes indeed. We are, as you can see, the tops."). No one knows the reasons behind this mystique that surrounds the faculty. It may be because it was created separately, many years after the other faculties, that it acquired a special cachet, or because the government established it specifically—or so they say—so that the daughter of the Leader, Gamal Abd el Nasser, could go to it, or because the political sciences put those who study them in close daily contact with world events, which lends a certain stamp to their way of thinking and behaving, or finally perhaps because this faculty was for a long time the royal gateway to a job in the Ministry of Foreign Affairs and the children of the great would join it as a sure first step to a diplomatic career.

Despite all of this, no such ideas were in Taha el Shazli's mind when he stuck the Faculty of Economics sticker onto his placement application as his first choice. His hope for a place in the Police Academy was gone forever, and he wanted to exploit his high marks to the maximum; that was all there was to it.

On the first day of studies, when he passed beneath the university clock and listened to its celebrated chimes, he was seized by that certain sense of awe and majesty, and when he entered the lecture hall filled with the reverberating buzz given off by the chatter and mingled laughter of hundreds of students as they began getting to know one another and swap merry small talk, Taha felt that he was something extremely small in the midst of a terrible congregation that resembled nothing so much as a mythical animal with a thousand heads whose eyes were all looking at, and examining, him. He found himself climbing up to sit far away at the highest point in the lecture hall, as though hiding himself in a safe place from which he could see everyone without their seeing him.

He was wearing blue jeans and a white T-shirt and had continued to believe as he left the house that he looked smart. But when he saw his student colleagues, he discovered that his clothes were not at all what was called for and that the jeans in particular were nothing but a cheap, second-rate imitation of the original. He made up his mind to persuade his father to buy even just one outfit from El Mohandiseen or Zamalek instead of the Approval and Light store from which he bought his cheap clothes.

Taha decided that he would not get to know anyone because getting to know people meant exchanging personal details and he might be standing in the midst of a group of his colleagues (including girls, maybe) and one of them would ask him what his father did. What would he say then? Next he was overcome by a strange feeling that one of the students sitting in the hall was the son of one of the residents of the Yacoubian Building and Taha might have bought him a pack of cigarettes once or washed his car, and he started to think what would happen if the unknown resident's son found that the son of the doorkeeper was a colleague of his in the same faculty.

He kept thinking like this as the lectures went by one after the other until the call to the noon prayer rang out and a number of the students rose to pray. Taha followed these to the Faculty's mosque and noticed with relief that like him they were poor, most of them being apparently of rural origin. This encouraged him to ask one of them when the prayer was over, "Are you first year?"

He replied with a friendly smile, "God willing."

"What's your name?"

"Khalid Abd el Rahim, from Asyut. What's yours?"

"Taha el Shazli, from here in Cairo."

This was the first acquaintance Taha made and in fact from the first moment, just as oil separates from water and forms a distinct layer on top, so the rich students separated themselves from the poor and made up numerous closed coteries formed of graduates from foreign language schools and those with their own cars, foreign clothes, and imported cigarettes. It was to these that the most beautiful and best-dressed girls gravitated. The poor students, on the other hand, clung to one another like terrified mice, whispering to one another in an embarrassed way.

In less than a month, Taha had become friends with the whole mosque group. Khalid Abd el Rahim, however, with his short stature, his body that was as dry and thin as a piece of sugarcane, his deep brown complexion, and his glasses with the black frames that lent his face a serious, self-possessed cast, so that, in his modest, classic clothes he looked much like a recently graduated teacher in a state school, remained the one for whom he felt the greatest affection. Taha's affection for him may have been due to the fact that he was as poor as or even poorer than he was (as witnessed by the darns in his socks, which always showed during prayer). He was also fond of him because he was deeply religious and when praying would stand and invoke God's presence in the full meaning of the words, placing his folded hands over his heart and bowing his head in total submission so that anyone who saw him at that moment might have imagined that if a fire broke out or shots were fired next to him, these would not distract him from his prayer for an instant. How Taha wished he could attain the same faith and love for Islam as Khalid! Their friendship grew stronger and they spoke to each other frankly and confided in each other, sharing the same distaste at the daily displays of frivolity they saw on the part of some of their affluent male colleagues and at their abandonment of the True Religion, as well as at the shamelessness of some of their female colleagues, who would come to the university dressed as though for a dance party.

Khalid introduced his friend Taha to others from the university dormitories—all country boys, good-hearted, pious, and poor—and Taha started to visit them every Thursday evening to pray the final evening prayer and stay up with them chatting and discussing. Indeed, he benefited greatly from these discussions, for he learned for the first time that Egyptian society was at the same stage that had prevailed before Islam and it was not an Islamic society because the ruler stood in the way of the application of God's Law, while God's prohibitions were openly flouted and the law of the state permitted alcohol, fornication, and usury. He learned too the meaning of communism, which was against religion, and of the crimes committed by the Abd el Nasser regime against the Muslim Brothers, and he read with them books by Abu el Aala el Mawdudi, Sayed Kutb, Yusef el Karadawi, and Abu Hamid el Ghazali. After several weeks, the day came when following an enjoyable evening with his friends from the dorms, they stood up to bid him farewell as usual and at the door Khalid Abd el Rahim said to him suddenly, "Where do you do your Friday prayer, Taha?"

"At a small mosque near the house."

Khalid and his brethren exchanged a look and Khalid then said gaily, "Listen, Taha. I've decided to use you to get myself some reward in Heaven. Wait for me tomorrow at ten in Tahrir Square in front of the Ali Baba café. We'll pray together at the Anas ibn Malik Mosque and I'll introduce you to Sheikh Shakir, God willing."

Two hours before the Friday call to prayer, the mosque of Anas ibn Malik filled to capacity with worshippers. They were all Islamist students, some wearing Western clothes but most in Pakistani dress—a white or blue gallabiya that reached to just below the knees with trousers of the same color beneath it and on their heads a white turban whose tail dangled at the back of the neck. These were all devotees and followers of Sheikh Muhammad Shakir and they came to the mosque early on Fridays to reserve their places before the crowd came and pass the time making acquaintances, reciting the Qur'an, and engaging in religious discussions. Their numbers grew until the place became too small to hold them all and the mosque officials brought out dozens of mats and spread them in the square opposite the mosque. This too filled to capacity with worshippers so that the traffic was brought to a standstill; even the enclosed balcony of the mosque, which was reserved for female students, despite being hidden from sight was the source of a loud murmuring that indicated that it was filled to overflowing as well.

Someone turned on the mosque's loudspeaker and it emitted a loud squeal; then the sound cleared and one of the students started to chant the Qur'an in a sweet, submissive voice, the students listening to him with rapt attention. The atmosphere was fabulous, authentic, and pure, the ascetic, homespun, primitive scene bringing to mind the first days of Islam. Suddenly, shouts of "There is no god but God" and "God is most great" rang out and the students, rising, crowded one another to shake the hand of Sheikh Shakir, who had finally arrived. He was about fifty and stocky, with a sparse beard dyed with henna, a face not without certain good looks, and wide, impressive, honey-colored eyes. He was dressed in the Islamist fashion like the students, with a black shawl over his robes. He knew most of the students crowding around him, and shook their hands and embraced them, asking them how they were. It took a long time for him to mount the pulpit and take from his pocket a siwak, with which he purified and sweetened his teeth. Then he said, "In the name of God, the Merciful, the Compassionate," and the cries of "God is most great" redoubled in strength until the walls of the mosque shook. The sheikh made a gesture with his hand and immediately complete silence reigned.

Starting his sermon with praise and thanks to God, he continued, "Beloved sons and daughters, I want every one of you to ask himself this question: 'How many years does a man live on this earth?' The answer is that the average lifespan, at the best estimate, does not exceed seventy years. This, when we come to think about it, is a very short time indeed. Moreover, a man may be afflicted at any moment with a disease or by an accident and die. If you ask among your acquaintances and friends, you will find more than one who has died suddenly while young, and it would never have occurred to any of those who died young that they would die. Pursuing this line of thinking, we find that Man has two choices before him, no more. He may focus all his efforts on his life in this fleeting, brief world that may come to an unexpected end at any moment, in which case he is like the man who wants to build himself a luxurious, elegant house but makes it of sand, on the seashore, so that the house is exposed to the possibility that at any moment a wave may come and knock it down; this is the choice that is doomed to failure. As for the second choice, that to which our Lord, Almighty and Glorious, calls us, it requires that the Muslim live in this world from the perspective that it is a brief and passing stage in the life of the immortal soul. One who lives their life in this way will gain both this world and the next and be always happy, content in mind and conscience, and courageous, fearing none but our Lord, Almighty and Glorious. The true believer has no fear of death because he does not consider it the end of existence, as the materialists believe it to be. Death for the believer is the transition of the soul from the ephemeral body to everlasting life. It was this sincere faith that allowed a few thousand of the first Muslims to be victorious over the armies of the great empires of that time, such as Persia and Byzantium. Those simple Muslims were successful in raising the banner of Islam in every part of the world through the strength of their faith, their true love for death in God's cause, and their deep contempt for the evanescent pleasures of this world. God has made it incumbent upon us to struggle to raise high His word. Gihad is a pillar of Islam, exactly like prayer and fasting. Indeed, gihad is the most important of those pillars but the corrupt rulers dedicated to the pursuit of money and the pleasures of the flesh who have ruled the Islamic world in times of decadence have attempted, with the help of their hypocritical men of religion, to exclude gihad from the pillars of Islam, knowing that if the people cleaved fast to gihad, it would in the end be turned against them and cost them their thrones. In this way, by eliminating gihad, Islam was robbed of its real meaning and our great religion was transformed into a collection of meaningless rituals that the Muslims performed like athletic exercises, mere physical movements without spiritual significance. When the Muslims abandoned gihad, they became slaves to this world, clinging to it, shy of death, cowards. Thus their enemies prevailed over them and God condemned them to defeat, backwardness, and poverty, because they had broken their trust with Him, the Almighty and Glorious.

"Beloved sons and daughters, our rulers claim that they are applying the Law of Islam and assert at the same time that they are governing us by democracy. God knows they are liars in both. Islamic law is ignored in our unhappy country and we are governed according to French secular law, which permits drunkenness, fornication, and perversion so long as it is by mutual consent. The state itself in fact benefits from gambling and the sale of alcohol, then spews out its ill-gotten gains in the form of salaries for the Muslims, who as a result are cursed with the curse of what is forbidden and God expunges His blessings from their life. The supposedly democratic state is based on the rigging of elections and the detention and torture of innocent people so that the ruling clique can remain on their thrones forever. They lie and lie and lie, and they want us to believe their revolting lies. We say to them, loud and clear, 'We do not want our Islamic Nation to be either socialist or democratic. We want it Islamic-Islamic, and we will struggle and give up our lives and all we hold dear till Egypt is Islamic once more.' Islam and democracy are opposites and can never meet. How can water meet with fire, or light with darkness? Democracy means people ruling themselves by themselves. Islam knows only God's rule. They want to submit God's Law to the People's Assembly so that the honorable representatives may decide whether God's Law is worthy of application or not! *A monstrous word it is, issuing from their mouths; they say nothing but a lie.* The Law of the Truth, Glorious and Sublime, is not to be discussed or scrutinized; it is to be obeyed and implemented immediately, by force, unhappy as that may make some people. Come, my children, let us prepare our hearts to receive God's presence, and while we are in this blessed congregation of ours, let us contract with Him, Great and Glorious, to be faithful to Him in our religion, struggle for His cause with every atom of our beings, give our lives gladly until it is God's word that is supreme. . . ."

Shouts and cries of "God is most great!" arose, shaking the place to its foundations, and the sheikh stopped speaking and bowed his head for a short while till silence had returned. Then he resumed, "My children, the task before Muslim youth today is to reclaim the concept of gihad and bring it back to the minds and hearts of the Muslims. It is precisely this that terrifies America and Israel and with them our traitorous rulers. They tremble in fear at the great Islamic Awakening that gains greater momentum and whose power becomes more exigent in our country day by day. A handful of warriors from Hizbollah and Hamas were able to defeat Almighty America and Invincible Israel, while Abd el Nasser's huge armies were routed because they fought for this world and forgot their religion."

The sheikh's enthusiasm now reached its climax, and he shouted, "Gihad! Gihad! Gihad! Children of Abu Bakr and Umar, Khalid, and Saad! The hopes of Islam today are pinned on you as once they were on your mighty forefathers! Struggle then for God's cause and divorce yourselves once and for all from this world as did the Imam Ali ibn Abi Talib, may God be pleased with him! God looks to you to implement His covenant with you, so stand firm and retreat not, lest you be among those who lose all! Millions of Muslims humiliated and subjected to dishonor by the Zionist occupation appeal to you to restore for them their ruined self-respect. Youth of Islam, the Zionists get drunk and commit fornication with whores in the forecourt of your el Aqsa Mosque! What then will you do?"

The students' excitement intensified and one of their number arose from the front row, turned toward the congregation, and shouted in a voice breaking with excess of emotion, "Islamic! Islamic! Not socialist and not democratic!" and the cry was taken up by hundreds of throats behind him and all the students started chanting the paean to gihad with one powerful, thunderous voice while joyful ululations rang out from the area reserved for the female students. The voice of Sheikh Shakir rose again, his excitement mounting to a new peak, "By God, I see that this place is pure and blessed, the angels surrounding it! By God, I see that the Islamic state lies in your hands and that it has been reborn mighty and proud! Our time-serving, traitorous rulers, servants of the Crusader West, will meet their just fates at your pure hands, cleansed for prayer, if God so wills!"

Then the prayer commenced and with the hundreds of students congregated behind him he recited in a sweet, affecting voice from the chapter of the House of Imran,

In the name of God, the Merciful, the Compassionate . . .
who said of their brothers (and they themselves held back),
"Had they obeyed us, they would not have been slain,"

Say: "Then avert death from yourselves, if you speak truly."
Count not those who were slain in God's way as dead,
but rather living with their Lord, by Him provided,
rejoicing in the bounty that God has given them,
and joyful in those who remain behind and have not joined them,
because no fear shall be upon them, neither shall they sorrow,
joyful in blessing and in bounty from God,
and that God leaves not to waste the wage of the believers.
And who answered God and the Messenger
after the wound had smitten them—to all those of them
who did good and feared God, shall be a mighty wage;
those to whom the people said,
"The people have gathered against you, therefore fear them";
but it increased them in faith, and they said,
"God is sufficient for us; an excellent Guardian is he."
So they returned with blessing and bounty from God, untouched by evil;
they followed the good pleasure of God; and God is of bounty abounding.
God has spoken truly.

Following the prayer, the students pushed forward to shake the sheikh's hand. Then they spread themselves out over the courtyard of the mosque in groups of four, introducing themselves to one another, chanting from and helping one another with their study of the Qur'an. Behind the pulpit Sheikh Shakir made his way through a small, low door to his office, which was filled to capacity with students who wanted to meet with him for various reasons. Those present pushed forward toward him and embraced him and some of them made to kiss his hand, which, however, he would pull firmly away. He sat and listened with interest to each student's issue, then a whispered conversation would take place between them after which the student would leave.

By the end, only a few students were left in the room, among them Khalid Abd el Rahim and Taha el Shazli. The students who remained were those who were particularly close to the sheikh, and at a signal from the latter, one of them rose and bolted the door. The conversation was opened by a huge student with a long beard, who said to the sheikh in a loud, excited voice, "Master, I'm not looking for a quarrel with the security forces. They are the ones who attacked us. They seized our colleagues from their homes and put them in detention even though they'd done nothing. All I'm asking for is some kind of protest. A sit-in or a demonstration for the release of our brothers in detention."

Khalid whispered to Taha, pointing to the huge student, "Brother Tahir, the Emir of the Gamaa for the whole of the University of Cairo. He's a final-year medical student."

The sheikh listened to the young man, thought for a little, and said quietly, a smile never leaving his lips, "There's nothing to be gained by provoking the security forces against us at this time. The regime has got itself involved in the coalition with the Americans and the Zionists in the name of liberating Kuwait. In a few days an unjust, infidel war will commence in which Egyptian Muslims will kill their Iraqi brothers under America's leadership. When this happens, the people will turn against the government in Egypt, with the Islamic movement at their head, God willing. I think you understand now, my boy. National Security is goading us in the hope that we'll respond and provide them with a pretext to direct a comprehensive blow at the Islamists. Didn't you notice how in today's sermon I contented myself with a general discourse and didn't mention the coming war openly? If I'd attacked Egypt's membership in the coalition, they would close the mosque tomorrow, while I need the mosque to rally the young people when the war starts. No, my boy, it wouldn't be wise to put ourselves at their mercy now. Leave them be until they kill our Muslim brothers in Iraq and you'll see what we shall do on that day, God willing."

"Who says that they'll leave us alone until the war starts? What makes you so sure? Today they detained dozens of cadres of the Islamic movement and tomorrow they'll detain the rest, if we don't resist them," replied the young man vehemently.

Silence reigned and the atmosphere grew tense. The sheikh shot the young man a reproving look and said in the same calm voice, "I pray God that one day you may rid yourself of this excitable nature of yours, my boy. The strong Muslim is he who controls himself when angry, as the Beloved Prophet—God's blessings and peace upon him—has taught us. I know that it is your love for your brethren and your zeal in defense of religion that drive you to this anger, and I assure you, my boy, and I swear to you by Him who is Sublime and All-Powerful, that we shall strike this infidel regime in battle, but at the right time, God willing."

The sheikh fell silent for a moment, then looked at the young man for a while and added in a tone that brooked no reply, "This is my last word. I will do my best, God willing, to bring about the release of those detained; we have friends, praise God, everywhere. But I will not agree to a sit-in or demonstration at this stage."

The young man hung his head, giving the impression that he had conceded only grudgingly, and it was not long before he asked permission to leave. He shook hands with those present, and when he came to the sheikh, he bent over him and kissed his brow twice, as though to erase any trace of the tiff. The sheikh responded with a kindly smile and patted him on the shoulder affectionately. After this, the students departed one after another until only Taha and Khalid were left. Khalid approached the sheikh and said, "Master. This is Brother Taha el Shazli, my colleague at the Faculty of Economics that I told you about."

The sheikh turned to Taha welcomingly and said, "Welcome, welcome. How are you, my boy? I've heard a lot about you from your friend Khalid."

At the police station, the battle heated up.

Hamid Hawwas accused Malak Khilla in an official report of usurping occupancy of the room and demanded that the matter be referred to court, while for his part Malak affixed to the report a copy of the rental contract for the room and insisted on making a second report in which he accused Hamid Hawwas and Ali the Driver of physically assaulting him and requested that his injuries be officially noted. As a result, they sent him with a policeman to the Ahmad Mahir Hospital, from which he returned with a medical report. This too was affixed to the report, Ali the Driver denying absolutely that he had assaulted Malak and accusing him of faking his injuries.

So much for the legal cut and thrust. As for the psychological war, each plunged in after his own fashion. Hamid Hawwas, for instance, never for a second stopped presenting legal arguments relating to the common resource of the residents of the roof, citing among other things various Court of Cassation rulings, while Abaskharon pleaded with the officer (after pulling up his gallabiya as was his custom in times of disaster to show off his amputated leg) with loud repeated wailing cries of, "Mercy, Your Honor, mercy! We just want to make a living, and they throw us out and beat us up!"

Malak's own performance in police stations was unique. He had worked out long ago that police officers evaluated a citizen on the basis of three factors—his appearance, his occupation, and the way he spoke; according to this assessment, a citizen in a police station would either be treated with respect or despised and beaten. Given that Malak's modest people's suit could not be expected to leave any special impression on the officers and, equally, that his occupation of shirtmaker would not guarantee him sufficient respect, all that remained was how he spoke. As a result, Malak had become accustomed when for any reason he entered a police station to adopt the manner of a businessman preoccupied with urgent and serious affairs who was extremely perturbed at being detained in this fashion and would speak to the officers in a language approaching the classical tongue that would make them hesitate before underestimating him. He would say any old thing and then shout in the officers' faces to stress the point, "You, sir, are apprised of this and I am apprised of this! The honorable station chief is apprised of this! The esteemed District Chief of Police is likewise apprised of this!"

The use of the classical plus the mention of the district chief of police (as though he were an intimate acquaintance whom he intended to contact) were effective ways of making the officers grudgingly draw back from treating Malak with contempt.

So there they all were—Abaskharon and Malak and Hamid Hawwas standing in front of the officer and yelling without let-up, while behind them the drunkard Ali the Driver, like an old hand on the bass who knows how to make his contribution to the music, kept repeating in his deep, husky voice, over and over again, the same words: "Sir, there are women and families on the roof! We can't have apprentices violating the sanctity of our families, sir!"

The officer had become completely fed up with them and, were it not for his fear of the consequences, would have told the goons to hitch them all to the bastinado and beat them. In the end, however, he endorsed the report for referral to the public prosecutor and the contestants stayed in the detention room till the following morning, when the public prosecutor issued an order permitting Malak to have the use of the room "and the injured parties to have recourse to the courts." Thus, Malak returned victorious to the roof, men of goodwill subsequently intervening and reconciling him with his opponents Ali the Driver and Hamid Hawwas (who made a show of accepting the reconciliation but never stopped writing—and conscientiously pursuing—complaints against him).

The prosecutor's order was, however, a springboard for Malak, who in one week transformed the appearance of the room. He closed the door that opened onto the roof and opened a large door onto the main stairwell, where he hung a large plastic sign on which he wrote in Arabic and English *Malak Shirts*. Inside he placed a large cutting table and some chairs for waiting customers and on the wall he hung a picture of the Virgin Mary along with a copy of an article in English from the *New York Times* with the headline "Malak Khilla, Superb Egyptian Tailor," in which the American journalist spoke for a whole page about the skill of Master Craftsman Malak Khilla; in the middle was a large picture of Malak with the tape measure around his neck completely absorbed in cutting a piece of cloth and apparently unaware that he was being photographed.

If anyone asks him about the article, Malak tells them that a foreigner (who later turned out to be the Cairo correspondent of the *New York Times*) came one day to have some shirts made and that Malak had been astonished to find him returning the following day with foreign photographers and they had written this piece about him because they were so amazed at his tailoring skill. Malak tells this story in an ordinary way, then steals a look at his listeners. If he finds them fidgety and dubious, he moves on to talk of something else as though he'd said nothing. If they appear to believe him, however, Malak will continue, emphasizing that the foreigner had insisted vehemently that he should go with him to America to work there as a shirtmaker at any salary he cared to name but that he, of course, had refused the offer because he hated the idea of living away from Egypt. Malak brings his set piece to an end by saying complacently and confidently, "Everyone knows that all those foreign countries are sniffing around for clever shirtmakers."

The truth of the matter is that Basyouni, the photographer in Ataba Square, can run anyone up a newspaper piece talking of his skill for any newspaper on demand—ten pounds for Arabic and twenty for foreign. It takes Basyouni no more than the name of the newspaper and a picture of the client plus a ready-made article that he has in which the writer speaks of his great surprise at coming across in the streets of Cairo the workshop of the brilliant tailor so and so, or the establishment of the great kebab cook so and so. All of these Basyouni puts together in a certain way in the photocopier so as to make the copy come out looking as though it has been taken from the newspaper.

But what does Malak do in his new place? He makes shirts, of course; but tailoring doesn't account for more than a small part of his daily activities because, in short, he works at anything that might yield a profit, from trading in currency and smuggled liquor to brokering real estate, land, and furnished apartments, to arranging the marriage of elderly Arabs to young peasant girls whom he brings in from certain villages in Giza and Fayoum, to sending workers to the Gulf against two months' wages.

This multifaceted enterprise has made him avid for any information he can get about people and for knowledge of their most minute secrets, since anyone is a potential candidate to have dealings with him at any moment, and a little bit of information may help him at any given instant and have a decisive impact on those dealings, allowing him to sew things up the way he wants. Every day from mid-morning to ten at night, every type of humanity makes its way to Malak's workplace— poor customers and rich, elderly Arabs, brokers, maids and girls for the furnished apartments, and small traders and commission agents; and in the midst of all these Malak comes and goes, talking and shouting, laughing and wheedling, losing his temper and quarreling, swearing a hundred false oaths and making deals, like a well-known and illustrious actor performing with relish his role in a play he has rehearsed so long he has perfected it.

Malak used to see Busayna el Sayed twice a day, on her way to and from work. She had stirred his interest from the beginning because she was beautiful and her body arousing. At the same time another feeling that was difficult to put into words made him certain that the serious expression that she wore on her face was fragile and false and that she was not as virtuous as she tried to appear. When he had collected some information about her and knew everything that was going on, he started greeting her and asking her about the health of her mother the Hagga and whether the Shanan clothing store in which she worked was in need of a consignment of shirts (for which she would of course get her commission), and gradually he started talking to her about a variety of subjects—the weather, the neighbors, marriage. Busayna herself was both ill at ease with Malak and at the same time unable to keep him at a distance since she passed him every day and he was their neighbor and spoke to her politely, thus denying her the opportunity of rounding on him. All the same, she submitted to conversing with him at base because something searching and probing in his behavior toward her made her submit. No matter what topic he might be speaking to her about, the tone of his voice and his looks would get to her, as though he were saying, "Don't come on so self-righteous. I've found out every-thing." This unspoken message became so clear and strong that she started asking herself whether Talal could have revealed the secret of their relationship.

Malak got more and more familiar with her until one day he sudden-ly directed a slow, appraising look at her full bosom and luscious body and then asked brazenly, "How much does Talal Shanan pay you a month?"

Suddenly she felt furious and decided that this time she would put him in his place very firmly, but in the end she found herself answering, avoiding his eyes, "Two hundred and fifty pounds."

Her voice came out with a strange-sounding rattle as though someone else were speaking and Malak laughed, came close to her, and said, advancing his attack, "You're a stupid girl. That's pennies. Listen, I can get you work for six hundred pounds a month. Don't say anything now. Take your time to think about it—a day, two days, then come and see me."

2

At Maxim's, Zaki el Dessouki feels at home.

No sooner has he crossed Suleiman Basha Square to the small passage opposite the Automobile Club, pushed open the small wooden door with the glass panes, and passed through the entranceway, than he feels as though a magic time machine has carried him back to the beautiful years of the 1950s. Everything at Maxim's—from the brightly painted white walls hung with original works by great artists, the quiet lighting emanating from elegant wall lamps, the tables covered with gleaming white cloths on which plates, folded napkins, spoons, knives, and glasses of various sizes are set out in the French manner, and the way into the bathroom that is concealed from sight by a large blue folding screen to the small, chic bar at the far end to the left of which stands an ancient piano on which Christine, the restaurant's owner, plays for her friends—bears the stamp of the elegant past in the same way as do old Rolls-Royces, ladies' long white gloves, hats decorated with feathers, gramophones with horns and gold needles, and old black-and-white photos in wooden frames that we hang in the sitting room and forget about and which, when from time to time we do look at them, make us feel tender and melancholy.

The owner of Maxim's, Madame Christine Nicholas, is of Greek origin, born and raised in Egypt. She draws, plays the piano and violin excellently, and sings exquisitely. She has married a number of times and lived a gay and boisterous life. Her relationship with Zaki began in the 1950s with a passionate love that burned itself out and left behind a deep, unbudgeable friendship. Zaki will be preoccupied and go without seeing her for many months, but as soon as he feels oppressed or things are not going well for him, he goes to her and always finds her waiting for him. She listens attentively, gives him sincere advice, and commiserates like a mother.

Today, no sooner did she see him entering through the door of the bar than she let out a cry of joy and embraced him and kissed him on both cheeks. Then she took his hands, leaned back, and examined him for a short while with her blue eyes, saying, "You look worried, my friend."

Zaki smiled sadly and almost said something but remained silent. Christine shook her head as though she understood, then invited him to sit at his favorite table next to the piano and ordered a bottle of rosé and cold *hors d'œuvres*. Just as dried flowers retain something of their old fragrance, Christine still bore traces of her former beauty. Her body was neat and svelte, her hair dyed and swept back, and tasteful makeup gave her lined face a dignified, refined cast. When she laughed, her face would fluctuate between the tenderness and tolerance of a kindly grandmother and that old coquetry that would sometimes return in a momentary flash, then disappear. Christine tasted the wine as the traditions of the table require, then made a sign to the ancient Nubian waiter and he poured out two full glasses. As he sipped the wine, Zaki told her what had happened. She listened attentively, then said dismissively, pronouncing the French words in her own specially smooth and musical way, "Zaki, you're exaggerating. It's just an ordinary quarrel."

"Dawlat threw me out."

"Just an impulsive act born of too much anger. In a day or two, go and apologize to her. Dawlat has a short temper, but she's good-hearted. And don't forget, you did lose her valuable ring and any woman in the world will throw you out if you lose her jewelry."

Christine said this light-heartedly, but Zaki remained gloomy and said sorrowfully, "Dawlat has been planning for a long time to throw me out of the apartment and the loss of the ring has given her the excuse. I offered to buy her a new ring, but she refused."

"I don't understand."

"Dawlat wants to get her hands on the apartment for herself."

"Why?"

"My dear friend. I'm not religious, as you know, and there are things I never give any thought to, such as the estate and the division of bequests."

Christine looked at him questioningly and he went on to explain, pouring himself another glass, "I have never married and I have no children. When I die, my possessions will go to Dawlat and her children. She wants to secure everything for her children right now. Yesterday, during the quarrel, she said to me, 'I will never let you squander our rights.' Imagine! Just like that, in the clearest way possible! She considers everything I own to be her children's by right, as though I were just the steward of my wealth. She wants to inherit from me before I die. Do you understand now?"

"No, Zaki."

Christine, who seemed to have become a little inebriated, shouted the last words, and when Zaki tried to speak, she interrupted him heatedly, "Dawlat could never think that way!"

"After all these years, you're still naïve. Why are you amazed at evil? You think like a child. You think that the good people should be smiling and jolly and the bad ones have ugly faces with thick, matted eyebrows. Life's a lot more complicated than that. There's evil in the best of people and in those closest to us."

"My dear philosopher, you exaggerate. Listen. Let's bet a large bottle of Black Label. I'll call Dawlat tonight and make peace between you. Then I'll make you buy the bottle and don't you dare go back on your word!"

Zaki left Maxim's and wandered aimlessly around Downtown. Then he returned to his office, where Abaskharon (who was aware of what had happened) met him with an appropriately sad expression on his face and prepared his drink and snacks quickly and fervently, as though offering condolences. Zaki took his drink out onto the balcony, still at that point harboring some hope of making up with Dawlat. He felt that in the end she was his sister and she couldn't do him harm. Half an hour passed and then the telephone rang. He heard Christine's voice, sounding embarrassed, say, "Zaki. I called Dawlat. I'm sorry. She seems to have really gone mad and is set on expelling you from the apartment. She said she's changed the lock and she'll be sending you your clothes tomorrow. I can't believe what's happened. Can you imagine, she talked about legal measures she's going to take against you?"

"What legal measures?"

"She didn't explain, but you'd better be careful, Zaki. Expect anything from her."

The following day Abaskharon appeared with a lad from the street carrying a large suitcase in which Dawlat had sent all Zaki's clothes. This was followed by a series of summonses from the police station, as Dawlat had made a number of reports with the intention of proving her legal right to possession of the apartment and had got an undertaking of non-harassment from Zaki. Friends tried to act as go-betweens to arrange a reconciliation between the two, but Dawlat refused. Zaki called her several times on the telephone, but she hung up in his face and eventually he consulted a lawyer, who told him that his position while not bad was not especially good, since the apartment was rented in his father's name and it was Dawlat's right to live in it. He also stressed to him that the law moved slowly and that the proper thing to do in such situations was to use force. He ought—it was most unfortunate—to hire some thugs, throw Dawlat out of the apartment, prevent her from going back in, and let her go to court; this was the only way to settle such disputes.

Zaki agreed to the lawyer's idea and suggested that the door be broken and the lock changed on Sunday morning, when Dawlat normally went to the bank. He affirmed to the lawyer that neither the doorkeeper nor any of the neighbors would prevent him from carrying out the plan. He spoke enthusiastically and seriously but in his heart knew very well that he would never do any of it. He would never hire thugs, he would never throw Dawlat out, and he would never take her to court. He couldn't do it.

Is he afraid of her? Maybe. He never confronts her. He always backs down in front of her and he's not a fighter by nature; from the time he was little, he has hated conflicts and problems and avoided them at any cost. And in addition, he'll never throw her out because she's his sister. Even in the event that he should recover the apartment from her and throw her out onto the street, he wouldn't be happy. His struggle with her saddens him because he cannot bring himself to think of her as a vicious and wicked person, whatever she might do. He cannot forget the way she once was, which he loved. How delicate and shy she used to be, and how she's changed! He's sad because his relationship with his only sister has deteriorated to this point and he thinks of what she has done and asks himself where she acquired this cruelty. How could she have brought herself to throw him out in front of the neighbors? And how was she able to sit in front of the officer at the police station and make out a report against her brother? Doesn't she even once consider that he's her brother and that he's never done anything to her bad enough to deserve such a reward? And again, is a little property worth the loss of one's family? True, the land that he'd recovered from the land reform has increased several times over in value, but all of it will go back to Dawlat and her children on his death in any case, so why all the problems and disrespect?

Zaki felt the melancholy spreading little by little and throwing its black shadow over his life and he spent whole nights unable to sleep, during which he would stay up on the balcony till morning, drinking and smoking, and going over in his mind the events of the past, sometimes thinking that he had been unlucky from the time he was born. Even the timing of his birth had been inauspicious, and if he'd been born fifty years earlier, his whole life would have been different. If the Revolution had failed, if King Farouk had made haste to arrest the Free Officers—who were known to him by name—the Revolution would never have taken place and Zaki would have lived the life he was supposed to—Zaki Bey, son of Abd el Aal Basha el Dessouki. He would have made minister for sure, perhaps prime minister—a great life, truly befitting him, instead of a life of aimlessness and humiliation. A prostitute drugs him and robs him and his sister throws him out and exposes him to scandal in front of the neighbors and he ends up sleeping in his office with Abaskharon. Is it bad luck or a failing in his character that always drives him to make the wrong decision? Why did he stay in Egypt after the Revolution? He could have gone to France and started a new life, as many children of the big families had done. There he would certainly have attained a position of note as friends had done who were less than he in all respects. But he had stayed in Egypt and started to acclimatize himself to the deteriorating situation little by little until he had sunk to these depths. And then . . . why hadn't he married? When he was a young man, many rich and beautiful women had wanted him, but he'd kept refusing marriage until the chance was gone. If he had gotten married, he would now have grown-up children to take care of him and grandchildren to play with and love. If he'd had even just one child, Dawlat would not have done all that to him, and if he'd married, he wouldn't feel that killing, agonizing loneliness, that pitch-black sense of mortality that sweeps over him whenever he hears of the death of one of his friends. The unanswerable question that comes to him every night as he takes refuge in his bed is, "When will death come, and how?" He thinks now of a friend of his who prophesied his own death. He was sitting with him on the balcony of the office and directed a strange look at him, out of the blue, as though he had noticed something on the horizon. Then he said quietly, "My death is close, Zaki. I can smell it."

The strange thing was that his friend did indeed die a few days later even though he wasn't sick. This incident makes him wonder (when depressed or downcast), does death have a special smell that a person exudes at the end of his life, so that he becomes aware of his approaching end? And how will the end be? Will death be like a long sleep from which one never wakes up? Or is there a resurrection, a reward, and a punishment, as the religious believe? Will God torture him after his death? He isn't religious and he doesn't, it's true, pray or fast. But he has never hurt anyone in his life, he hasn't cheated, he hasn't stolen, he hasn't deprived others of their rights, and he's never been slow to help the poor. Apart from alcohol and women, he doesn't believe that he's committed crimes in the true sense of the word.

These dispiriting thoughts took possession of Zaki for many long days after he had spent about three weeks living in the office—three weeks of worry and care, which ended one morning with a pleasant surprise that drove away his sorrow just as a long night dissolves in one magical moment. Zaki will always remember the happy sight, rehearsing in his mind hundreds of times, accompanied by cheerful music, how he was sitting on the balcony sipping his morning coffee, smoking, and watching the crowded street when Abaskharon appeared swinging on his crutch with, on his face, instead of its usual ingratiating cast, a mysterious, cunning smile.

"What do you want?" Zaki Bey accosted him with distaste in a warning growl. But something exceptional and quite certain gave Abaskharon an unaccustomed confidence and he came up to his master and bent down and whispered, "Excellency, my brother Malak and I have something to talk about."

"What kind of thing?"

"Something about you, Excellency, as it were."

"Speak out, you donkey! I'm in no mood for your nonsense. What is it?"

At this Abaskharon leaned over him and whispered, "We have a seccaterry for Your Excellency. A very nice young girl. Excuse the boldness, but Your Excellency in these bad circumstances is in need of a seccaterry to take care of Your Excellency."

Zaki started paying attention and directed a deep, penetrating look at Abaskharon as though he had received a special coded message or heard a sentence in a secret language that he understood. He answered quickly, "And why not? Am I to see her?"

In response to the desire to torture his master a little, Abaskharon at first said nothing. Then he said slowly, "Your Excellency would like to see her?"

The Bey nodded his head quickly and pretended to look at the street to hide his excitement. In the manner of a conjurer revealing his surprise at the end of the trick, Abaskharon turned around, moved away banging the floor with his crutch, and disappeared for ten minutes. Then he came back with her.

This is the moment Zaki will never forget—when he saw her for the first time. She was wearing a white dress covered with large green flowers that clung to her body and revealed its details, her plump, soft arms emerging from the short sleeves. Abaskharon led her forward by the hand and said, "Miss Busayna el Sayed. Her late father was a good man and he lived with us here on the roof. God have mercy on him, he was more than a brother to me and Malak."

Busayna advanced with her small, swinging, undulating steps. Then she smiled, her face lighting up in a way that stole Zaki's heart, and said, "Good morning, Excellency."

Those who knew Taha el Shazli in the past might have difficulty in rec-
ognizing him now. He has changed totally, as though he had swapped
his former self for another, new one. It isn't just a matter of the Islamic
dress that he has adopted in place of his Western clothes, nor of his
beard, which he has let grow and which gives him a dignified and
impressive appearance greater than his real age, nor of the small space
for prayer that he has set up next to the elevator in the lobby of the
building, where he takes turns in giving the call to prayer with another
bearded brother who is an engineering student and lives on the fifth
floor. All these are changes in appearance. Inside, however, he has been
possessed by a new, powerful, bounding spirit. He has taken to walking,
sitting, and speaking to people in the building in a new way. Gone forever are the old cringing timidity and meekness before the residents.
Now he faces them with self-confidence. He no longer cares a hoot for
what they think, and he won't put up with the least reproach or slight
from them. He's no longer interested in those small banknotes that
they used to give him and which he used to save in order to buy his new
things, in the first place because of his firm faith that God will provide
for him and secondly because Sheikh Shakir has got him involved in
the sale of religious books—small errands that he undertakes in his
spare time and which bring him in a reasonable amount.

He is now training himself to love or hate people "in God." He has
learned from the sheikh that men are too despicable and lowly to be
loved or hated for their this-worldly characteristics. On the contrary,
our feelings toward them should be determined by the degree to which
they observe God's Law. This has changed the way he looks at many
things. He used to like a number of the residents because they were
good to him and gave generously. Now he has started to hate them "in
God" because they don't pray and some of them drink alcohol. He has

come to love his brethren in the Gamaa Islamiya so much that he would sacrifice his life for them. All his old, worldly standards have crumbled like an ancient fragile building and their place has been taken by a true, Islamic evaluation of people and things. The power of faith has filled his heart and made him into a new being, liberated from fear and evil. He no longer fears death or holds any created being in awe, no matter what its strength or influence. He no longer fears anything whatsoever in his life except that he disobey God and merit His anger.

The credit for this is due to God, Great and Glorious, and next to God, to Sheikh Shakir who has provided him whenever they meet with increased faith in God and knowledge of Islam. Taha has come to love him and cling to him and has become one of those who are so close to him that after a while the sheikh granted him permission to visit him at his home at any time, an intimate status the sheikh grants to only his most trusted associates.

Only one thing remains of the old dispensation in Taha's soul—his love for Busayna. He has tried hard to subject his feelings for her to his new way of thinking, and failed. He has striven to convince her of the need to follow God's Law. He took her the book *Dress Modestly Lest Ye Be Judged* and pressured her to read it and kept on at her until he got her to accompany him to the Anas ibn Malik mosque, where she listened with him to Sheikh Shakir's sermon. To his astonishment and disappointment, however, she was not impressed. Indeed she told him frankly that it was boring, which led to a quarrel. They have started quarreling a lot when they meet, with her always provoking him so that he gets angry and goes away each time determined to make a final break with her, seeing in his mind's eye the calm, beaming smile that Sheikh Shakir gives him whenever he speaks to him of Busayna, and of his words, "My boy, you will never guide to righteousness those whom you love, but God will guide to righteousness those whom He wills." The sheikh's words reverberate in his thoughts and he promises himself never to see her again, then he goes back on his word after a few days, distressed and yearning for her. But every time he comes back to make up with her after a quarrel, her coldness toward him increases.

Today, though, he did not go to the university, specifically so that he could see her. He waited for her at the entrance to the building as she came out in the morning and accosted her, saying, "Good morning, Busayna. I want a word with you, please."

"I'm busy."

Such was her uncivil answer as she ignored him and proceeded for a few steps. He, however, could not control himself and pulled her by the hand, though she resisted for a moment before yielding and whispering in panic, "Let go of my hand! No scenes!" The two then walked silently and warily among the people in the street till they got to their favorite place in Tawfikiya Square. As soon as they sat down, she burst out angrily, "What do you want from me? Do you have to make problems every day?"

Strangely, his own anger disappeared rapidly, as though it had never been, and he waited for a moment. Then he said in a voice that he tried hard to make calm, as though he wanted to conciliate her, "I beg you, Busayna, don't be angry with me!"

"I'm asking you, what do you want from me?"

"I want to confirm something I heard."

"Confirmed."

"Meaning what?"

"Meaning everything you've heard is true."

She was challenging him and pushing the conversation to the edge.

"You've left Talal's store?"

"I left the job at Talal's and I'm working for Zaki el Dessouki. Is that bad, or a sin, Your Reverence?"

In a weak voice he said, "Zaki el Dessouki has a bad reputation."

"Sure, he's got a bad reputation and he likes women, but he pays me

117

six hundred pounds a month. And seeing that I have a family to support and seeing that your good self can't pay me the cost of schools,
food, and drink, it's none of your business!"

"Busayna, fear God! You're a good person. Take care you don't make
Our Lord angry! Do what's right and leave it to God to provide!"

"I agree, it's up to God to provide. Unfortunately, we just aren't
finding enough to eat."

"I can find you a respectable job."

"Find yourself a job, sweetheart! I'm perfectly happy with mine."

"That's how you want it?"

"Yes, that's how I want it. Anything else?"

She asked him this sarcastically, then irritation swept over her
again, so she got up and stood in front of him and said, arranging her
hair in readiness to depart, "Listen, Taha. I'm telling you—bottom line,
it's over between us. Each one goes his own way. And there's no call for
us to meet again, if you don't mind."

Then she smiled ambiguously and said as she moved away, "You've
even grown your beard and become observant, and I wear short skirts
and go about uncovered. We don't look right together."

Sheikh Shakir's apartment is cramped and humble. The house consists
of two stories built of red brick in a narrow alley in Dar el Salam. In the
two bedrooms and a parlor live Sheikh Shakir, his two wives, and his
seven sons and daughters, who are at different stages of their schooling. The sheikh and his student visitors have agreed on a signal by
which he can recognize them—three knocks with spaces in between.

This was the knock that Taha el Shazli used, and he heard the voice
of the sheikh saying from inside, "Coming!" Then he heard a sound
which told him that the women had gone into the farther room and the
slow, heavy footsteps of the sheikh and the sound of him clearing his

throat were audible. After a short while the sheikh opened the door, saying "In the name of God, the Merciful, the Compassionate" as he did so.

"Taha! Welcome, my boy."

"Sorry to disturb you but I want to talk to you a little."

"Come in, please. You didn't go to the university today?"

Taha sat on the sofa next to the window and recounted what had happened with Busayna. He told everything and described his feelings to the sheikh, who listened carefully, playing with his prayer beads. The talk was interrupted for a few minutes when the sheikh got up to bring the tea tray, after which he continued to listen until Taha had finished talking. He thought for a while, and then said, "My boy, the True Religion does not forbid love so long as it is legitimate and does not lead to disobedience to God's Law. Indeed, the noblest of God's creations, the Chosen One—blessings and peace be upon him—loved the Lady Aisha and spoke of this in sound reports whose validity is generally accepted. The difficulty lies in choosing the woman deserving of your emotions. What should the specifications of this woman be? The Prophet—God bless him and give him peace—said, 'A woman may be taken in marriage for her beauty, her wealth, or her religion. Take you the religious woman, and, God willing, wealth will follow' (God's Prophet has spoken truly). A proper Islamic upbringing would have prevented you from falling into a difficulty such as that from which you are now suffering. You and all the children of your generation did not receive an Islamic upbringing because you grew up in the secular state and received a secular education. Thus you grew accustomed to thinking in a way that excludes religion. Now you have returned to Islam with your hearts, but your minds will take a while before they rid themselves of secularism and are purified for Islam. Learn, as I have said to you so many times, how to love in God and hate in God, for otherwise your Islam will never be complete. The distress from which you are now suffering is a natural and inevitable result of your distance from God, even though this be in only one aspect of your life. If you had asked yourself at the beginning of your relationship with this friend of yours how observant she was, if you had made her adherence to Islam a condition for your having a relationship with her, you would not find yourself where you are now."

The sheikh poured out two glasses of tea and offered one to Taha. Then he placed the pot on the metal tray, whose color had been transformed by age, and said, slowly sipping his tea, "God knows how much I love you, my boy, and I hate you to come to your sheikh in sorrow only for him to give you a lecture instead of consoling you. But, by God, my sincere advice to you is this: forget this young woman, Taha, because she's gone astray. You are an observant young man, a believer, and a girl who is a Muslim like you would be better for you. Force yourself to forget and seek help in prayer and the recitation of the Qur'an. It will be difficult at the beginning but will get easier for you later, God willing. Then again, have you forgotten your religion, Taha? What's become of gihad, Taha? What's become of your duty to Islam and the Muslims? Yesterday the filthy war began, with our rulers allowing themselves to be forced into fighting Muslims and under the command of unbelievers. It is the duty of all young Muslims in Egypt to rise up against this unbelieving government. Are you willing, Taha, to hang back in aiding the Muslims, who are being killed in their thousands every day, and occupy yourself with an erring young woman who has deserted you in favor of abomination? God, Mighty and Glorious, will not ask you on the Day of Resurrection about Busayna, but He will hold you to account for what you did to support the Muslims. What will you say to God on the day of the Great Gathering?"

Taha hung his head and appeared moved. Then he said in grief and shame, "I have promised God more than once that I'd forget her, but unfortunately I start thinking of her again."

"Satan will not give your soul up easily and you will not achieve true devotion in one go. The gihad of the soul, Taha, is the Greater Gihad, as the Messenger of God—God bless him and give him peace—called it."

"What should I do, Master?"

"You must pray and recite the Qur'an. Apply yourself constantly to them, my boy, until God brings you relief and promise me, my boy, that you will not see this young woman again, whatever the circumstances."

Taha looked at the sheikh and said nothing.

"This is an undertaking between you and me, Taha, and I'm confident that you'll keep it, God willing."

The sheikh then rose, opened the drawer of the old desk, took out some pictures from foreign newspapers and threw them in Taha's lap, saying, "Look at these pictures. Examine them well. These are your Muslim brethren in Iraq whose bodies have been torn apart by the Coalition's bombs. Look at how the bodies have been rent apart, including those of women and children. This is what they do to Muslims and their children, and our traitorous rulers participate with the unbelievers in their crimes."

Then the sheikh picked out a photo and held it in front of Taha's eyes and said, "Look at the face of this Iraqi child, ripped open by American bombs. Is not this innocent child as much your responsibility as your sister and your mother? What are you doing to aid her? Is there still a place in your heart for sorrow over your erring friend?"

The photo of the disfigured child was extremely upsetting and Taha said bitterly, "The children of Muslims are slaughtered in this hideous way, while Egyptian television is crawling with scholars from el Azhar affirming that the Egyptian government's position is sound in Islamic Law and claiming that Islam supports the alliance with America to strike Iraq."

For the first time the sheikh showed excitement and his voice rose. "Those scholars are hypocrites and evildoers. They are the pet jurists of the sultans and their sin in God's eyes is great. Islam absolutely forbids us to participate with unbelievers in the killing of Muslims, whatever the reasons. Any schoolchild doing their first class in the Law knows the authorities for this."

Taha nodded in agreement with the words of the sheikh, who suddenly said, as though he had just thought of something, "Listen. Tomorrow, God willing, our brothers are organizing a big demonstration at the university. I hope you won't stay away."

He was silent for a moment, then went on, "I shan't be able to lead the demonstration myself, but your brother Tahir will be your commander tomorrow, God willing. The assembly point is in front of the auditorium after the noon prayer."

Taha nodded, then stood up and asked permission to leave, but the sheikh asked him to wait and disappeared inside for a little. He returned smiling and said, handing him a small book, "This is the Islamic Action Charter. I'd like you to read it, then we can discuss it later. This book, Taha, will make you forget, God willing, all the bad thoughts that haunt you."

The animals were slaughtered on the Friday morning—three huge bullocks that had spent the night next to the elevator in the lobby of the Yacoubian Building. At the call to the dawn prayer, five butchers fell on them, trussed them, and slit their throats; then they spent hours flaying them, cutting them up, and loading the meat into bags, ready for distribution. No sooner had the noon prayer come to an end than the crowds in Suleiman Basha swelled with troops of people making their way to the Azzam stores. They were extremely poor: beggars, privates in the police force, barefoot boys, and women garbed in black carrying or dragging behind them their small children. All came to take their share of the sacrificial meat that Hagg Azzam was giving away to mark the occasion of his victory in the elections. In front of the main entrance to the store stood Fawzi, Hagg Azzam's eldest son, in a white gallabiya, taking the bags of meat and throwing them to the people, who had formed a surging crowd and were shoving one another to get at the meat. Fights broke out and injuries occurred, and the store's employees were obliged to make a cordon and beat the surging people back with their shoes to keep them away from the glass display windows before they broke under the weight of their bodies. Inside, Hagg Azzam sat at the front wearing a smart blue suit with a white shirt and a crumpled red tie, his face beaming with joy.

The results of the elections had been announced officially on Thursday evening, Hagg Azzam winning the People's Assembly Workers' seat for Kasr el Nil and scoring a sweeping victory over his opponent Abu Himeida, who obtained only a very few votes (El Fouli had decided that his defeat should be overwhelming and ringing, as an example to anyone else who might disobey his instructions in the future). Hagg Azzam felt a genuine, deep gratitude to God, Almighty and Glorious, who had supplied him, of His bounty and His support, a clear victory. He performed more than twenty prostrations in thankful prayer the moment he heard the news and issued his instructions for the slaughter of the bullocks. He also secretly distributed more than twenty thousand pounds to poor families whose needs he himself took care of and gave a further twenty thousand to Sheikh el Samman to be spent on charitable purposes under his supervision, not to mention the twenty golden guineas he donated to Sheikh el Samman on this occasion.

A different feeling toyed with Hagg Azzam's heart when he thought of Souad: how should he celebrate his fabulous win with her that night? He reviewed the details of her soft, warm body in his mind's eye and felt that he truly loved her. He said to himself that the Messenger of God—God bless him and give him peace—was right when he described women as bringers of good fortune. There were indeed some blessed women whom a man had only to take as a partner for him to be inundated with good fortune, and Souad was one of them. She had brought victory and blessing and here he now was, triumphant and about to enter the People's Assembly. Verily, there was nothing more wonderful than divine providence! He was now the People's Assembly member for the residents of the constituency of Kasr el Nil, who at one time had held out their shoes to him for him to clean, and looked down on him from above, and generously given him their pennies. Now he was the Honorable Member, enjoying legal immunity, which prevented anyone from taking action against him without the Assembly's permission. From now on his picture would appear in the press and on television and he would meet every day with the ministers and shake their hands, equal to equal. He was no longer merely a rich businessman, he was a statesman and he would have to deal with everyone on that basis. Starting from now, he would begin the great work that would catapult him to the level of the giants. The next step would take him to the summit; he would be one of the five or six movers and shakers in the whole country provided the deals he was planning in order to move him from the millionaire to the billionaire bracket went through. He might in fact become the richest man in Egypt and become a minister. Yes indeed! Why not? When God is willing, nothing is impossible; hadn't he dreamed of becoming a member of the People's Assembly? Money makes short work of problems and brings the distant goal within reach. One day he might achieve a ministry, just as he had the Assembly.

He remained sunk in his ponderings until the call to the afternoon prayer rang out and he led the store's employees in prayer as usual, even though (and he asked God's forgiveness for this) his mind did wander more than once as he was praying to Souad's body. As soon as he had finished the prayer and said his beads, he hurriedly left, entered the Yacoubian Building, and rode the elevator to the seventh floor. What deliciously insistent, burning desire he felt as he turned the key in the door and found before him Souad, exactly as he had imagined her, waiting for him in the red robe that showed off her stunning charms, and that smell of perfume that stole into his nose and tickled his senses! She came toward him with a vampish gait and passion took possession of him as he listened to her footsteps and the rustling of the robe on the floor. Then she took him in her arms and whispered, her lips brushing his ear, "Congratulations, my darling! A thousand congratulations!"

At rare and exceptional moments Souad Gaber appears as she really is. A look suddenly flashes from her eyes like a spark and her face recovers its original appearance, exactly as an actor returns to his own character on finishing a role, takes off his costume, and wipes the makeup off his face. On such occasions, a serious, slowly awakening look suggestive of a certain degree of hardness and determination appears on Souad's face and reveals her true nature. This may happen at any time—while she's eating with the Hagg or chatting with him of an evening; even while she's with him in bed, she may be twisting and turning in his arms as she does her best to rouse his feeble virility and that spark will flash in her eyes confirming that her mind never stops working, even in the heat of passion.

Often she astonishes even herself with her newfound capacity to take on fake roles. She was never a liar before. All her life long she has been used to saying whatever's on her mind—so where did all this acting come from? She plays with skill the role of the jealous, compassionate, yearning, loving wife and like a professional actor has learned to control her emotions perfectly: she cries, laughs, and gets angry whenever she decides to do so. Right now, in bed with Hagg Azzam, she is playing out a scene—that of the woman who, taken unawares by her husband's virility, surrenders to him so that he may do with her body whatever his extraordinary strength may demand, her eyes closed, panting, and sighing—while in reality she feels nothing except rubbing, just the rubbing of two naked bodies, cold and annoying. With that sharp, lurking, unblinking awareness of hers, she contemplates Hagg Azzam's exhausted body, whose brief last hurrah came to an end and whose feebleness manifested itself after one month of marriage, and averts her eyes from the whiteness of his old, wrinkled skin, the few, scattered hairs of his chest, and his small, dark nipples. She feels nauseated whenever she touches his body, as though she were putting her hand on a lizard or a revolting, slimy frog and each time she thinks of the slim, hard body of Masoud, her first husband, with whom she knew love for the first time.

Those were beautiful days. She smiles when she thinks how much she loved him and how she longed to see him, her body burning with his touches and the feel of his hot breath on her neck and breast. She would make love with him hotly and melt, swooning in pleasure and, when she recovered herself, feel shame. She'd turn her face well away from him and spend a while avoiding looking at his face, while he'd roar with laughter and say in his strong, deep voice, "My oh my! What's the matter with you, girl, that you're so shy? Did we do something naughty? It's God's Law, you silly girl!"

How lovely that time had been and how far away it seemed now! She had loved her husband and all that she'd wanted from the world was for them to live together and raise a boy. She swore she didn't want money and she didn't have any demands. She was happy in her small apartment in El Asafra South next to the railway tracks doing the washing and cooking, preparing Tamir's feeds, and mopping the floor. Then she would take a shower, put on makeup, and wait for Masoud at the end of the day. She thought her home was as spacious, clean, and well-lit as a palace, and when he informed her that he had got a work contract in Iraq, she had rejected the idea, flaring up and fighting and banning him from her bed for several days in order to dissuade him from traveling. She had shouted in his face, "You'd go off abroad and leave us on our own?"

"A year or two and I'll be back with lots of money."

"That's what everyone says and they never come back."

"So you like being poor? We're living day to day. Are we going to go our whole lives borrowing money?"

"Soon enough the little one will be grown up."

"Only in this country! Here everything's backward! Here it's the old who go on living and the young who die. Money begets money and poverty begets poverty."

He spoke with the calm of one who has made up his mind. How she regrets now that she obeyed him! If only she'd fought him to the last, if only she'd walked out on him, he would have given in and dropped the idea of traveling—he had loved her and couldn't bear to be far away from her. But she had surrendered easily and let him go. Everything is fated and decreed. Masoud had gone away and never come back. She was sure he had died in the war and that they had buried him over there, and everyone had written him off as vanished. It had happened like that to many families that she knew in Alexandria. It wasn't possible that Masoud would have abandoned them and left his son. Impossible! It could only be that he'd died and gone to God and left her to bear her bitter lot alone.

The time of love and passion and shame and beauty had ended. She'd endured hardship and gone hungry to raise her son and though men all had different faces, bodies, and clothes, their look was always the same—violating her, undressing her, and promising her everything if she'd say yes. She had resisted fiercely and with difficulty and feared that one day she might get tired and give in. Her job at Hannaux's was exhausting. The wages were poor, the child's expenses grew, and the burden was as heavy as a mountain. All her relatives—even her brother Hamidu—were poor, living like her from one day to the next, or creeps who would help her out with nice words and excuse themselves with spurious arguments from lending her money.

She lived through years so hard that she almost lost faith in God and more than once weakened and was on the verge of falling into sin out of an excess of despair and need. And when Hagg Azzam asked for her hand in legal marriage, she worked things out minutely. She would give the Hagg her body in return for her son's expenses. She never touched the dowry that Hagg Azzam gave her but deposited it in Tamir's name in the bank so that it would triple in ten years. The days of emotion were over and the whole thing was now calculated—one thing in return for another, by agreement and mutual consent. She would sleep with this old man for two hours everyday, leave her son in Alexandria, and collect her wages.

True, she's rent with longing for Tamir and at night often feels his place next to her in the bed and cries scalding tears. The other morning when she walked in front of an elementary school and saw the children in their school uniforms, she thought of him and cried and was wracked by sorrow and longing for days. She saw herself carrying his warm little body from the bed and washing his face for him in the bathroom and dressing him in his school clothes and getting his breakfast ready and playing tricks on him to make him drink up all his milk. Then she would leave with him and they would ride the tram to school.

Where is he now? How she worries about him! He's on his own and far away and she's in this large, cold, detestable city where she knows no one, living on her own in a large apartment in which she owns nothing, hiding from people like a thief or a loose woman. Her sole function is to sleep with this old man who every day lies down on top of her and suffocates her with his exhausted, dangling impotence and the touch of his smooth, disgusting body. He doesn't want her to go to Tamir, and when she speaks to him about it, his face darkens and he appears jealous, while she longs for her son at every second and wants to see him now and hug him hard and smell his smell and stroke his smooth, black hair. If only she could bring him to live with her in Cairo! But Hagg Azzam will never agree to that and has made it a condition from the beginning that she leave the boy behind. He said to her clearly, "I'm marrying you on your own without children. Are we agreed?" She recalls his cold, cruel face at that moment and hates him from the depths of her heart but convinces herself once more that everything she's doing is for the sake of Tamir and his future. What use would it be to him to live in his mother's arms while both of them begged from friends and strangers?

She ought to thank Azzam and be grateful to him, not hate him. At least he has married her properly and taken her expenses in charge. This direct, practical idea governs her relations with the Hagg. He has rights over her body as per the legal agreement. He has the right to come to her whenever and however he wishes, and it is her obligation always to be ready, waiting for him every day after having made herself up and put on perfume. It is his right to remain unaware of her coldness toward him and that she should never make him feel his impotence or his shortcomings in bed.

Consequently she now had recourse to a trick that she had learned by instinct to save him embarrassment. Gasping and scratching his back with her nails and pretending to reach climax, she hugged his ruined body and threw her head on his chest as though drugged by the orgasm. Soon afterward she opened her eyes and started kissing him on his beard and neck and massaging his chest with her fingers. Then she whispered in an insinuating voice, "By the way . . . where's my treat for your success in the elections?"

"Of course, my dear. A nice big present."

"God preserve you for me, my darling! Look, I'm going to ask you a question and you have to answer me frankly."

The Hagg propped his back against the end of the bed and looked at her with interest, keeping his hand on her bare shoulder. She said, "Do you love me?"

"Lots, Souad, and Our Lord knows that for a fact."

"So if I asked for anything in the world you'd do it for me?"

"Of course."

"Okay, don't forget to keep your word."

He looked at her uncertainly, but she had decided not to confront him this evening, so she said, "I'm going to tell you about something important. Next week, God willing."

"Go on. Tell me this evening."

"No, my darling. Let me make sure first."

The Hagg laughed and said, "It's a riddle?"

She kissed him and whispered in a seductive voice, "Yes . . . a riddle."

Homosexuals, it is said, often excel in professions that depend on contact with other people, such as public relations, acting, brokering, and the law. Their success in these fields is attributable to their lack of that sense of shame that costs others opportunities, while their sexual lives, filled as they are with diverse and unusual encounters, give them deeper insight into human nature and make them more capable of influencing others. Homosexuals also excel in professions associated with taste and beauty, such as interior decoration and clothing design; it is well known that the most famous clothes designers in the world are homosexuals, perhaps because their dual sexual nature enables them to design women's clothes that are attractive to men and vice versa.

Those who know Hatim Rasheed may differ about him but are bound to acknowledge his refined taste and his authentic talent in choosing colors and clothes. Even in his bedroom with his lovers, Hatim deems himself too good for the camp taste that many homosexuals affect. He tries rather, with practiced touches, to bring out the feminine side of his beauty. He wears transparent gallabiyas embroidered with beautiful colors over his naked body, is clean-shaven, applies an appropriate and carefully calculated amount of eye pencil to his eyebrows, and uses a small amount of eye shadow. Then he brushes his smooth hair back or leaves stray locks over his forehead. By these means he always attempts, in making himself attractive, to realize the model of the beautiful youth of ancient times.

Hatim applied the same sensitive taste when he bought new clothes for his friend Abduh—tight pants that showed off the strength of his muscles, shirts and undershirts in light colors to illuminate his dark face, and collars that were always open to reveal the muscles of his neck and the thick hair on his chest. Hatim was generous with Abduh. He gave him lots of money, which Abduh sent to his family, and got him a recommendation to the camp commander so that his treatment improved and they granted him holidays one after another, all of which he spent with Hatim, as though they were newlyweds on their honeymoon. They would wake up in the middle of the morning and enjoy having nothing to do and being lazy, eating in the best restaurants, watching movies at the cinema, and shopping. Late at night they would go to bed together and, after satisfying their bodies, would lie in each other's arms in the dim light of the lamp, sometimes talking until the morning—moments of tenderness that Hatim would never forget. His thirst for love quenched, he would cling like a frightened child to Abduh's strong body, nuzzling his coarse brown skin like a cat and telling him about everything: his childhood, his father and his French mother, and his first beloved, Idris. The amazing thing was that Abduh, despite his youth and his ignorance, was capable of sympathizing with Hatim's feelings and became more accepting of their relationship. The first aversion disappeared, to be replaced by a deliciously sinful craving, plus the money and the respect and the new clothes and fine food, and the high-class places that Abduh had not dreamed he would one day enter; and, at night, in the street, when he was coming back in Hatim's company, Abduh loved to pass by the privates of the Central Security forces with his elegant appearance and greet them from a distance, as though proving to himself that he had become for a time something different from those poor wretches standing long hours, for no good reason or purpose, in the sun and the cold.

The two friends lived days of pure bliss. Then came Abduh's birthday, an occasion which Abduh assured Hatim was of no importance to him since, in Upper Egypt, they celebrated only weddings and circumcisions but which Hatim insisted on celebrating all the same. Taking him out in the car and smiling, he said, "I've got a surprise for you tonight."

"What kind of surprise?"

"Be patient. You'll know soon," murmured Hatim, his face wearing an expression of childlike playfulness as he drove the car in an unaccustomed direction. He proceeded along Salah Salim and entered Medinet Nasr, then turned off and took a small side street. The shops were closed and the street almost completely dark but a metal kiosk, newly painted and gleaming in the dark, appeared. The two got out of the car and stood in front of the kiosk. Then Abduh heard a jingling and saw Hatim take out a small chain of keys. He held these out to Abdah and said lovingly, "Here. *Joyeux anniversaire*, happy birthday. This is my present for you. I'm praying you'll like it."

"I don't understand."

Hatim let out a raucous laugh and said, "You Sa'idis! You're thick as planks. This kiosk belongs to you. I used a lot of influence and got it from the governorate for you. As soon as you finish your army service, I'll buy you some stock and you can just stand here and sell it."

Then he drew closer and whispered, "This way, my darling, you can work, make money, and support your children, and at the same time I make sure that you'll stay with me forever."

Abduh let out a loud shout and started laughing and hugging Hatim and mumbling thanks. It was a beautiful night. They dined together in a fish restaurant in El Mohandiseen. Abduh on his own ate more than a kilo of shrimp with rice, and while eating they drank a whole bottle of Swiss wine. The bill came to more than seven hundred pounds, which Hatim paid with his credit card. When they were together that evening in bed, Hatim almost wept with the delicious pain. He felt as though he was hovering in the clouds and wished time would stop, right there. After the lovemaking they remained as usual clinging to each other in bed, the dim light from the tall candle dancing and throwing its shadows on the wall opposite, which was covered in decorative wallpaper.

Hatim spoke at length of his feelings toward Abduh, who stayed silent, looking ahead, his face suddenly serious. Hatim asked him anxiously, "What's wrong, Abduh? . . . What is it?"

"I'm afraid, Hatim Bey."

"Afraid of what?"

"Of Our Lord, Almighty and Glorious."

"What did you say?"

"Our Lord, Almighty and Glorious. I'm afraid He'll punish us for what we do."

Hatim said nothing and gazed at him in the dark. It seemed odd to him. The last thing he would have expected his lover to talk to him about was religion.

"What kind of talk is that, Abduh?"

"Sir, all my life I've been God-fearing. In the village they used to call me 'Sheikh Abduh.' I always prayed the proper prayers at the proper time in the mosque and I fasted in Ramadan and all the other times I'm supposed to . . . till I met you and I changed."

"You want to pray, Abduh? Go ahead."

"How can I pray when every night I drink alcohol and sleep with you? I feel as though Our Lord is angry with me and will punish me."

"You think Our Lord will punish us because we love one another?"

"Our Lord has forbidden us that kind of love. It's a very big sin. In the village there was a prayer leader called Sheikh Darawi, God have mercy on his soul, who was a righteous, holy man, and he used to say to us in the Friday sermon, 'Beware sodomy, for it is a great sin and makes the throne of heaven shake in anger.'"

Hatim could no longer contain himself and he got out of bed, turned on the light, and lit a cigarette, looking with his handsome face and the flimsy nightgown over his naked body somewhat like an angry woman. He blew out cigarette smoke, then suddenly cried, "Really, Abduh, I don't know what to do with you. What can I do for you more than this? I love you and I'm concerned for you and I try always to make you happy—and instead of thanking me, you, you go and make life miserable for me like this."

Abduh continued to lie on his back in silence staring at the ceiling with his arm under his head. Hatim finished his cigarette and poured himself a glass of whisky, which he tossed off in a single gulp. Then he went back and sat next to Abduh and said quietly, "Listen, my darling. Our Lord is big and He has true mercy, nothing to do with what the ignorant sheikhs in your village say. There are lots of people who pray and fast and steal and do harm. Those are the ones Our Lord punishes. But us, I'm sure that Our Lord will forgive us because we don't do anyone any harm. We just love one another. Abduh, please, don't make things miserable. Tonight's your birthday and we're supposed to be happy."

On this Sunday evening Busayna had spent two weeks in her new job, during which Zaki el Dessouki had taken all the preparatory steps: he

had put her in charge, first of all, of certain chores—making a new telephone list, paying the electricity bill, and sorting out some old papers;
then he had started to talk to her about himself and how lonely he felt
and how sometimes he regretted not being married; he had complained to her about his sister Dawlat and said that he was sad at the
way she'd behaved with him; he had started asking her about her family and her younger brothers and sisters; and from time to time he would
flirt with her, complimenting her on her smart dress and her hairdo,
which showed the beauty of her face to advantage, looking for a long
time at her body—all in all a lot like a skilled player of billiards who
directs his shots with confidence and calculation. She would receive his
signals with a complicit smile (the contrast between her large salary
and her trivial duties was enough to make her expected role quite
clear). The hinting back and forth had gone on for several days, until he
had said to her once as she was preparing to leave, "I feel so comfortable with you, Busayna. I do hope we can stay together forever."

"I'm at your service," said Busayna without hesitation, to clear the
way for him. Then he took her hand and asked, "If I asked you to do
something, would you do it for me?"

"If I could, certainly."

He raised her hands to his lips and kissed them, to confirm what he
meant, and then whispered, "Tomorrow, come later in the day . . . so we
won't be disturbed."

The next day, while Busayna was in the bathroom removing the
unwanted hair from her body, polishing her heels with pumice, and
putting moisturizer on her hands and face, she thought about what had
happened and it occurred to her that bodily contact with an old man
like Zaki el Dessouki would be a bit strange and peculiar. She recalled
that sometimes, when she came close to him, she would smell, along
with the penetrating smell of cigarettes that his clothes gave off,
another smell, coarse and ancient, that reminded her of the one that

used to fill her nostrils when she was small and would hide in her mother's old wooden clothes chest. She thought too that she felt some affection for him because he was well mannered and treated her with a certain *délicatesse*, and that he was indeed to be pitied, living alone at his age without wife or children.

In the evening, she went to him in the office and found that he had sent Abaskharon away early and had sat down on his own to wait for her. In front of him, there were a bottle of whisky, a glass, and a container of ice. His eyes were a little red and the smell of alcohol filled the room. He rose to greet her, then sat down and emptied what was left in the glass into his mouth and said sadly, "Have you heard what happened?"

"No, what?"

"Dawlat is bringing a case to have me declared legally incompetent."

"What does that mean?"

"It means that she's asked the court to prevent me from disposing of my property."

"Oh no! Why?"

"So that she can inherit from me while I'm still alive."

Zaki said this bitterly, pouring himself another glass. Busayna felt sorry for him.

"Brothers and sisters often get angry with one another, but they never stop caring for one another," she said.

"That's what you think. All Dawlat can think of is money."

"Perhaps if you spoke to her, sir?"

Zaki shook his head, meaning "There's no point" and to change the subject asked her, "What will you drink?"

"Nothing, thank you."

"You've never had a drink?"

"Never."

"Just try one glass. It tastes bitter at first and then you feel good."

"No thanks."

"A pity. Drinking is very nice. Foreigners understand the importance of drinking more than we do."

"I've noticed that you live just like a foreigner, sir."

He smiled and gazed at her with love and tenderness, as though she were a precocious little girl. "Please, don't call me 'sir.' I know I'm old, but you don't have to keep reminding me. It's true, I've spent my whole life with foreigners. I was educated in French schools and most of my friends were foreigners. I studied in France and lived there for years. I know Paris as well as I do Cairo."

"They say Paris is beautiful."

"Beautiful? The whole world's to be found in Paris!"

"So why didn't you go on living there?"

"That's a long story."

"Tell me. It's not as though we've got any appointments to keep."

She laughed to lighten his mood and he laughed too, for the first time. Then she moved closer and asked him affectionately, "Go on. Why didn't you live in France?"

"There are lots of things I should have done with my life that I didn't."

"Why?"

"I don't know. When I was your age, I used to think that I could do whatever I wanted. I used to make plans for my life and I was sure about everything. When I got older, I discovered that man controls almost nothing. Everything is fate."

He felt himself getting melancholy so he sighed and asked her with a smile, "Would you like to travel?"

"Of course."

"Where would you like to go?"

"Any place far away from this hole!"

"You hate Egypt?"

"Of course."

"How can that be? Is there anyone who hates his own country?"

"I never got anything good from it to make me love it."

She averted her face as she said this sentence. Zaki responded excitedly, "A person has to love his country because his country is his mother. Does anyone hate his mother?"

"That's all songs and movies. Zaki Bey, people are suffering."

"Being poor doesn't mean you can't be patriotic. Most of Egypt's nationalist leaders were poor."

"All that was in your day. Now people are really fed up."

"Which people?"

"Everyone. For example, all the girls who were with me at commercial school wanted to get out of the country any way they could."

"It's that bad?"

"Of course."

"If you can't find good in your own country, you won't find it anywhere else."

The words slipped out from Zaki Bey, but he felt that they were ungracious so he smiled to lessen their impact on Busayna, who had stood up and was saying bitterly, "You don't understand because you're well-off. When you've stood for two hours at the bus stop or taken three different buses and had to go through hell every day just to get home, when your house has collapsed and the government has left you sitting with your children in a tent on the street, when the police officer has insulted you and beaten you just because you're on a minibus at night, when you've spent the whole day going around the shops looking for work and there isn't any, when you're a fine sturdy young man with an education and all you have in your pockets is a pound, or sometimes nothing at all, then you'll know why we hate Egypt."

A heavy silence reigned between them and Zaki decided to change the subject, so he rose from his seat, went over to the tape recorder, and said gaily, "I'm going to play you the most beautiful voice in the world.

A French singer called Edith Piaf, the most important singer in the history of France. Have you heard of her?"

"I don't know French to start with."

Zaki made a gesture with his hand indicating that that didn't matter and pressed the button of the recorder. Lilting piano music emerged and Piaf's voice, warm, powerful, and pure, rose up as Zaki nodded his head to the rhythm and said, "This song reminds me of beautiful times."

"What do the words say?"

"They speak of a girl standing in the midst of a crowd and then the people push her against her will in the direction of a man she doesn't know, and as soon as she sees him she feels a beautiful feeling for him and wishes she could stay with him all her life, but suddenly the people push her far away from him. In the end she finds herself on her own and the person she loved is lost forever."

"How sad!"

"Of course it's got another meaning, which is that one can spend his whole life looking for the right person and, when he finds them, lose them."

They were standing next to the desk, and as he spoke he moved toward her and placed his hands on her cheeks. Her nose filled with his coarse, ancient smell and he said, gazing into her eyes, "Did you like the song?"

"It's beautiful."

"You know, Busayna, I really needed to meet a woman like you."

Busayna said nothing.

"You have very beautiful eyes."

"Thank you."

She whispered this, her face burning, and she let him come close enough to feel his lips on her face. Then he folded her in his arms and very soon she felt the acrid taste of the whisky in her mouth.

"Where are you off to, doll?" Malak asked her impertinently as he crossed her path in the morning in front of the elevator. Avoiding his eyes, she answered, "I'm going to work."

Malak let out a loud laugh and said, "It looks like the work agrees with you."

"Zaki Bey is a good man."

"We're all good people. What have you done about that other thing?"

"Nothing yet."

"What do you mean?"

"I haven't had a chance yet."

Malak knitted his brow, looked at her with something like anger, grabbed her hand hard, and said, "Listen, princess. This isn't a game. He has to sign the contract this week. Got it?"

"All right."

Freeing her hand from his grip, she got into the elevator.

The student protests had been going on in most faculties since early morning. They interrupted studies, closed the lecture halls, and then started moving around in large numbers shouting and carrying banners condemning the war in the Gulf. When the call to the noon prayer sounded, about five thousand male and female students lined up to perform the prayer in the forecourt in front of the auditorium (boys in front, girls behind), led by Brother Tahir, emir of the Gamaa Islamiya. Then the congregation said the prayer for the dead for the souls of the Muslim martyrs in Iraq. Shortly afterward Tahir climbed to the top of the stairs facing the auditorium and stood there in his white gallabiya and impressive black beard, his voice emerging loud from the PA system.

"Brothers and sisters, we have come today to stop the killing of Muslims in our sister country Iraq. Our Islamic nation is not yet dead, as its enemies would wish. The Messenger of God—God bless him and give him peace—has said in a sound hadith, 'Good fortune will remain with my nation till the Day of Resurrection.' So, brothers and sisters, let us say our word, loud and clear, so that those who have placed their hands in the filthy hands of our enemies, polluted with the blood of Muslims, may hear. Youth of Islam, as we speak, the rockets of the unbelievers are pounding our sister Iraq. They pride themselves that they have devastated Baghdad and turned it into ruins, saying that they have sent Baghdad back to the Stone Age by destroying the generating stations and water plants. Now, brothers and sisters, at this very moment, Iraqi Muslims are being martyred, their skins shredded by American bombs. The tragedy was made complete when our rulers submitted to the orders of America and Israel and instead of the armies of the Muslims turning their weapons on the Zionists who have usurped Palestine and befouled the el Aqsa Mosque, our rulers have issued orders to Egyptian troops to kill their Muslim brothers and sisters in Iraq. My brothers and sisters in Islam, raise high your voices with the word of Truth. Speak it loud and clear, so that those who have sold the blood of the Muslims and piled up their looted wealth in the banks of Switzerland may hear it."

The slogans rang out from all sides, chanted by students carried on others' shoulders and taken up with huge enthusiasm by thousands of throats: *"Islamic, Islamic! Not socialist and not democratic!"*

"Khaybar, Khaybar, all you Jews! Muhammad's army will return!"

"Rulers, traitors, men of straw! How much did you sell the Muslims' blood for?"

Tahir made a sign and they fell silent, his voice rising, thundering with anger, "Yesterday television screens around the world showed an American soldier as he was preparing to fire a rocket to kill our people in Iraq. Do you know what the American pig wrote on the rocket before he fired it? He wrote 'Greetings to Allah'! Muslims, they mock your God. What then will you do? They murder you and violate your women. They ridicule your Lord, Almighty and Glorious. Do your self-respect and your manhood count for so little with you? Gihad! Gihad! Gihad! Let everyone hear what we say! No to this dirty war! No to the killing of Muslims by Muslims! By God, we shall die before we let the nation of Islam become a tasty morsel in the mouths of its enemies! We will not be shoes that the Americans can put on and off as they please!"

Then in a voice choking with emotion Tahir chanted, "God is Most Great! God is Most Great! Down with Zionism! Death to America! Down with the traitors! Islamic, Islamic. . . ."

The students raised Tahir onto their shoulders and the huge throng turned toward the main gate of the university. It was the demonstrators' goal to get out onto the street so that other people could join the demonstration, but the Central Security forces were waiting for them in front of the university and the moment the students went out into the square, the soldiers, armed with huge sticks, helmets, and metal shields, attacked them and started beating them savagely. The screams of the female students rose and many students fell and were beaten, their blood flowing over the asphalt, but the masses of students kept pouring in huge numbers through the gate and many got away, bursting out and running far from the soldiers, who chased after them. These students managed to get past the square in front of the university and reformed at the bridge. Additional platoons of Central Security soldiers fell on them, but they charged in their hundreds toward the Israeli embassy and there large numbers of Special Forces troops started firing tear gas grenades at the students, the pall of gas rising till it covered the whole scene. Then the sound of heavy gunfire rang out.

Taha el Shazli took part in the demonstrations throughout the day and at the last minute was able to escape as the Security forces at the Israeli embassy started seizing students. Following the plan Taha went to the Auberge Café in Sayeda Zeinab Square where he met up with some of the brothers, among them Emir Tahir, who presented a review and evaluation of the day's events. Then he said in a sad voice, "The criminals used tear gas grenades as camouflage and then fired live ammunition at the students. Your brother Khalid Harbi from the Law Faculty achieved martyrdom. We resign ourselves to God's will for him and ask Him to forgive him all his sins, enfold him in His mercy, and reward him generously in Paradise, God willing."

Those present recited the Fatiha for the martyr's soul, all feeling fearful and oppressed. Brother Tahir then explained the tasks required of them for the following day—contacting the foreign news agencies to confirm the martyrdom of Khalid Harbi, tracking down the families of the detainees, and organizing new demonstrations, to start from a place the Security forces did not expect. Taha was charged with the task of writing wall posters and putting them up early in the morning on the walls of the faculty. He had bought for this purpose a number of colored pens and sheets of sturdy paper, and he shut himself into his room on the roof and devoted himself to his work, not coming down to the prayer area to pray the sunset or evening prayers, which he performed on his own. He designed ten posters, wrote them out, and did the drawings for them, finishing after midnight, at which point he felt extremely tired. He told himself that he had a few hours ahead of him in which to sleep, since he was supposed to go to the faculty before seven in the morning. He prayed the two superrogatory prostrations then turned off the light, lay down on his right side, and recited his customary prayer before sleeping: "O God, I have raised my face to You, placed my back under Your protection, and entrusted my affairs to You, in desire for You and in awe of You. There is no refuge from You or escape from You but through submission to You. O God, I believe in Your Book that You sent down and in Your Prophet that You sent." Then he fell into a deep sleep.

After a little, thinking he was dreaming, he awoke to confused noises, and, opening his eyes, could distinguish shapes moving in the darkness of the room. Suddenly the light was turned on and he saw three huge men standing by the bed. One of them approached and hit him hard across the face. Then the man seized his head and turned it violently to the right and Taha saw for the first time a young officer, who asked him jeeringly, "Are you Taha el Shazli?"

He didn't respond, so the goon struck him hard on his head and face. The officer repeated his question and Taha said to him in a low voice, "Yes."

The officer smiled challengingly and said, "Playing at being the big leader are you, you son of a bitch?"

This was a signal and the blows rained down on Taha. The strange thing was that he didn't protest or scream or even protect his face with his hands. His face remained expressionless under the impact of all these surprises, and he submitted totally to the blows of the goons, who took a firm grip on him and pulled him out of the room.

Of the dozens of customers who fill the Oriental Restaurant of the Gezira Sheraton, you will find very few who are ordinary citizens such as might accompany their fiancées or wives and children on their day off to eat some delicious kebab. Most of the patrons are well-known faces—leading businessmen, ministers, and present and former governors who come to the restaurant to eat and meet, far from the eyes of the press and the curious. As a result, police details were everywhere, as well as the private guards who come along with any important personage.

The kebab restaurant at the Sheraton has come to play the same role in Egyptian politics as that played by the Royal Automobile Club before the Revolution. How many policies, deals, and laws that have left their mark on the life of millions of Egyptians have been prepared and agreed to here, in the Sheraton's kebab restaurant, at the tables groaning beneath the weight of grilled meats! The difference between the Automobile Club and the Sheraton's kebab restaurant accurately embodies the change that the Egyptian ruling elites underwent between, before, and after the Revolution. Thus, the Automobile Club perfectly suited the aristocratic ministers of the bygone epoch with their pure Western education and manners, and there they would spend the evenings accompanied by their wives in revealing evening gowns, sipping whisky and playing poker and bridge. The great men of the present era, however, with their largely plebeian origins, their stern adherence to the outward forms of religion, and their voracious appetite for good food, find the Sheraton's kebab restaurant suits them, since they can eat the best kinds of kebab, kofta, and stuffed vegetables and then drink cups of tea and smoke molasses-soaked tobacco in the waterpipes that the restaurant's management has introduced in response to their requests. And during all the eating, drinking, and smoking, the talk of money and business never ceases.

Kamal el Fouli had asked for a meeting with Hagg Azzam at the Sheraton kebab restaurant. The latter came a little early with his son Fawzi and they sat and smoked waterpipes and drank tea until Kamal el Fouli arrived with his son Yasser and three bodyguards, who looked the place over. One of them then said something urgently to El Fouli, who nodded his head in agreement and said to Hagg Azzam, after embracing him in a warm welcoming hug, "Excuse me, Hagg. We have to move. The guards object because the place is too exposed."

Hagg Azzam agreed and he and his son rose with El Fouli and they all moved to a distant table picked out by the guards in the farthest part of the restaurant closest to the fountain. They sat down and the bodyguards settled at a nearby table at a distance calculated to permit them to protect the other table without allowing them to hear what was said at it. The conversation started with generalities—mutual inquiries as to each other's health and children and the usual complaints about how exhausted they were from work and increasing responsibilities. Then El Fouli said to Hagg Azzam in an affectionate tone of voice, "By the way, your campaign in the People's Assembly against indecent television advertising is excellent and has struck a chord with people."

"All credit to you, Kamal Bey—it was your idea."

"I wanted people to get to know you as a new member of parliament. Praise God, all the newspapers have written about you."

"God grant us the capacity to repay your favors!"

"Think nothing of it, Hagg. You are a dear brother to us, God knows."

"Do you think, Kamal Bey, that the television will respond to the campaign and forbid these disgusting advertisements?"

With "parliamentarian eloquence," El Fouli roared, "They will respond whether they like it or not! I told the minister of information at the meeting of the Political Bureau, 'This outrage cannot go on! It is our duty to protect family values in this country! Who can accept his daughter or sister watching the dancing and shamelessness that go on on television? And where? In the land of el Azhar!'"

"Those girls who appear half-naked on television, I wonder what their parents think they're doing? Where is the father or the brother of a girl like that, that they allow her to appear in that filthy way?"

"I don't know whatever happened to self-respect. Anyone who lets his womenfolk go about naked is a complacent husband and the Messenger of God—God bless him and grant him peace—has cursed the complacent husband."

Hagg Azzam nodded his head sagely and said, "The complacent

husband, above all, is destined to go to Hell—*a dreadful fate*, God save us!"

This conversation acted as a kind of overture, pulse-taking, and sharpening of the faculties, like the warm-up exercises that soccer players perform before a match. Now that any shyness had disappeared and the company was in good fettle, Kamal el Fouli leaned forward, smiled, and said in a meaningful tone, twiddling the mouthpiece of the water-pipe between his fat fingers, "By the way, I forgot to congratulate you."

"Thank you. On what?"

"On getting the Japanese Tasso car agency."

"Ah."

Azzam responded in a low voice, his eyes gleaming with a sudden attentiveness. Then he hung his head and took a slow pull on the water-pipe to give himself a chance to think. Weighing each word carefully, he said, "But the matter isn't settled yet, Kamal Bey. I've just recently put forward a request for the agency and the Japanese are making inquiries about me. They may agree and give me the agency or they may refuse. Just say 'O Lord!' and pray for us, for the Prophet's sake."

El Fouli let out a loud laugh and slapping the Hagg's knee with his hand he said, "Get on with you, old timer! Do you think I'm going to fall for that stuff? My dear fellow, you got the agency this week and you got the fax with the agreement on Thursday, to be precise. What do you say?"

He looked at Azzam in silence, then went on in a serious tone, "Look, Hagg Azzam. My name's Kamal el Fouli and I'm as straight as a sword." (He made a gesture indicating straightness with his hand.) "I don't go back on my word. I think you've tried me out."

"May Our Lord preserve your favors!"

"Shall I tell you the bottom line? That agency, Hagg, has profits of three hundred million a year. Of course, God knows I wish you well, but a mouthful like that is a bit much for you to swallow all on your own."

"Meaning what?" exclaimed Azzam with a touch of sharpness in his voice.

El Fouli answered, looking at him hard, "It means it won't do for you to eat it all, Hagg. We want a quarter."

"A quarter of what?"

"A quarter of the profits."

"Who's 'we'?"

El Fouli laughed loudly and said, "What kind of a question is that, Hagg? You were born and bred here and you know the score."

"What are you trying to say?"

"I'm trying to say that I'm speaking for the Big Man. The Big Man wants to be your partner in the agency and take a quarter of the profits. And as you know very well . . . what the Big Man wants, he has to get."

"Troubles never come singly" is what goes through Hagg Azzam's head whenever he thinks of that day.

He left the Sheraton at around ten o'clock that evening having agreed to Kamal el Fouli's demand. He'd had no choice but to agree, since he knew the power of the Big Man, even if he was still seething with rage at the idea of giving him a quarter of the takings. There he was, exhausting himself and slaving over and spending millions on big profits and along comes the Big Man and expects a quarter of the profits on a plate? Foul play and thuggery, he told himself rancorously, making up his mind that he'd do his best to find a solution that would put an end to this injustice.

The car was making its way back to his home in El Mohandiseen when Hagg Azzam turned to his son Fawzi and said, "Go up to the apartment and tell your mother that I'll be spending the night out. I have to talk to people about the Fouli business."

Fawzi nodded in silence and got down at the apartment after kissing his father's hand. Hagg Azzam patted him on the shoulder and said, "Tomorrow we'll meet early, God willing, at the office."

Hagg Azzam leaned back on the car seat and felt more comfortable. He asked the driver to take him to the Yacoubian Building. He hadn't seen Souad for days because he'd been busy with the Japanese agency. He smiled as he pictured her surprise at seeing him. How would he find her? What would she be doing on her own? How he needed a night with her, a night when he could rid himself of worry and wake up refreshed! It occurred to him to call her on the car phone so she could get ready for him but decided in the end to drop in on her without warning to see how she would receive him.

The driver changed his route, and Hagg Azzam went up to the apartment, quietly turned the key, and entered the reception room, where he heard a voice coming from the direction of the living room. He approached slowly, and there he found her, stretched out on the couch, wearing red pajamas and with her hair up in curlers and her face covered with cream. She was watching television, and as soon as she saw him, she cried out a welcome, jumped up, and embraced him, saying reproachfully, "Is this any way to treat me, Hagg? You might at least have called me so I could get myself ready, or do you like to see me looking dreadful?"

"You look great," whispered the Hagg. He glued himself to her and gave her a hard hug. She felt the jab of his desire and pulled her head back, saying in a saucy voice as she slipped out of his grasp, "My oh my, Hagg, what a grabby boy we are! Wait till I've been to the bathroom, and I've made you something to eat."

They spent the night as usual. She prepared the charcoal and the waterpipe for him and he smoked a number of pipes of hashish while she got herself ready in the bathroom. Then he undressed, took a shower, put his white gallabiya on over his bare body, and slept with her. He was one of those men who rid themselves of their anxieties through sex and his performance with her that night was unaccustomedly ardent and lavish—so much so that, when they had finished, she kissed him and whispered, rubbing her nose against his, "It's the old chickens that've got the fat!"

Then she let out a loud laugh, leaned her back against the end of the bed, and said merrily, "I've got a riddle for you."

"What kind of a riddle?"

"Ouff! You've forgotten already? The riddle, Hagg. The thing you're going to do to prove that you love me."

"Oh yes, right. Sorry. My mind's full of things tonight. Go on, my dear. Ask me the riddle."

Souad turned to face him and looked at him without saying anything. Then a broad grin appeared on her face and she said, "On Friday I went to the doctor."

"The doctor? Is everything all right?"

"I wasn't feeling well."

"I'm sorry."

She laughed loudly and said, "No. It turned out to be a good sickness."

"I don't understand."

"Congratulations, my darling. I'm two months pregnant."

The big van stopped in front of the Yacoubian Building. It was completely closed apart from a few small wire-covered openings. The soldiers led Taha out, beating him and kicking him with their huge boots, and before pushing him inside the van, they put a tight blindfold over his eyes. They pulled his hands behind his back and put them in handcuffs, and he felt his skin break under the pressure of the steel. The van was crowded to the utmost with detainees, who throughout the journey kept up a constant chant of "There is no god but God! Islamic . . . Islamic. . . !" as though through their cries they might get the better of their fear and tension.

The soldiers let them chant, but the van drove at top speed so that more than once the students fell down on top of one another. Then it stopped suddenly and they heard the grating of an ancient iron gate and the van moved forward slowly for a little. Then it stopped again, the back door was opened, and a troupe of soldiers shouting insults burst in on them. They had taken off their boots and used these to beat the students, who fell from the van screaming. Next, they heard the barking of police dogs, which quickly fell upon them. Taha tried to get away by running, but a huge dog pounced on him, pulled him to the ground, and started snapping at his chest and neck with its teeth. Taha turned over where he lay to protect his face from the dog's fangs. It occurred to him that they wouldn't let the dogs kill them but that if he did die he would go to Paradise. He hung on and started reciting verses from the Qur'an under his breath and thinking of bits from the sermons of Sheikh Shakir. He discovered that his bodily pain would reach a certain peak, which was terrible, but that after that his awareness of it would slowly diminish.

The dogs suddenly went away as though at a signal and they remained lying in the courtyard for a few minutes. Then the soldiers launched a new round of vicious beating, after which they started to lead them away one by one. Taha felt that he was being pushed down a long corridor. A door opened and he went into a large room full of cigarette smoke. He could make out the voices of seated officers, talking and laughing normally among themselves. One of them came up to him, struck him hard on the back of his neck, and shouted in his face, "What's your name, momma's boy?"

"Taha Muhammad el Shazli."

"What? I can't hear you."

"Taha Muhammad el Shazli."

"Louder, you son of a bitch!"

Taha shouted at the top of his voice, but the officer slapped him and asked him again. This was repeated three times. Then blows and kicks poured down on him till he fell to the ground. They pulled him up and for the first time a deep, quiet voice arose, speaking confidently and slowly—a voice that Taha would never forget.

"Enough, boys. That's enough beating. The lad looks sensible and intelligent. Come here, lad. Come closer."

They pushed him in the direction of the source of the voice, who Taha was sure must be their boss and must be sitting at a desk in the middle of the place.

"What's your name, lad?"

"Taha Muhammad el Shazli."

He spoke with difficulty and could feel the acrid taste of blood in his mouth. The boss said, "Taha, you look like a good kid and from a decent family. Why are you doing this to yourself, son? See what's happened to you? And that's nothing. You still haven't seen a thing. You know those soldiers? They'll keep beating up on you till nighttime, then they'll go home to eat and sleep and other soldiers will beat you till the morning. And in the morning, the soldiers who went home will come back and beat you again till nighttime. You'll go on that way forever, and if you die from the beating, we'll bury you here, right where you're standing. It makes no difference to us. You're not a match for us, Taha. We're the government. Are you a match for the government, Taha? See what a mess you've got yourself into, Taha? Listen, kid. Would you like me to let you out right now? Would you like to go home to your folks? Your mum and dad must be worried by now."

He spoke the last sentence as though he was genuinely upset. Taha felt a great shudder go through his whole body. He tried hard to hang tough but failed and a high-pitched sound like the howl of an animal escaped from him. Then he abandoned himself to a hot, uninterrupted bout of weeping. The officer came over to him and patted his shoulder, saying, "No, Taha. No lad, don't cry. I swear to God I really feel sorry for you. Listen, there's a good boy. Just give us some information about your organization, and I swear on my honor I'll let you go right now. What do you say?"

Taha shouted, "I don't have an organization!"

"So why do you keep a copy of the Islamic Action Charter?"

"I was reading it."

"Son, that's organization literature. Out with it, Taha, like a sensible lad. Tell us what your responsibilities are in the organization."

"I don't know any organizations!"

The blows rained down anew and Taha felt that his pain had gone beyond its terrible peak once more, turning into something more like an idea that he grasped from the outside. The officer's voice came to him, as quiet as ever, "What are you trying to do to yourself, sonny? Just say what you know and get yourself out of this."

"I swear to Almighty God, sir, I don't know anything."

"It's up to you. I can't help you if you won't help yourself. Just remember I'm the only good one here. Those other officers are unbelievers and criminals and they don't just beat, those guys do really nasty things. Do you want to talk or not?"

"I swear to Mighty God, I don't know anything."

"Okay. It's up to you."

As though this were a secret signal, no sooner had the officer finished saying the words than the blows rained down on Taha from all sides. Then they threw him facedown on the ground and several hands started to remove his gallabiya and pull off his underclothes. He resisted with all his might, but they set upon him and held his body down with their hands and feet. Two thick hands reached down, grabbed his buttocks, and pulled them apart. He felt a solid object being stuck into his rear and breaking the tendons inside and he started screaming. He screamed at the top of his voice. He screamed until he felt that his larynx was being ripped open.

With the coming of winter Abduh started his new life.

His national service term with Central Security came to an end and he took off his military uniform, forever swapping it for Western clothes, and he started work at the new kiosk. It wasn't long before he sent for his wife Hidiya and his son Wael, who was still a babe in arms, to come from Upper Egypt. They lived together in a room on the roof of the Yacoubian Building that Hatim Rasheed rented for them. Abduh's health improved, he put on weight, and he seemed settled. Having lost the miserable, underfed appearance of the conscript, he looked more like a successful young Cairo shopkeeper full of self-confidence and energy (even though he kept his heavy Sa'idi accent, his nails remained long and dirty, and his teeth—which he never brushed—continued to be stained yellow with cigarette smoke and the accumulated effects of food). He made a reasonable income selling cigarettes, candy, and soft drinks and the people of the roof accepted him and his family just as they did any new neighbor, with a welcome shrouded in reserve and curiosity. As the days passed, however, they came to like Abduh's wife Hidiya with her trim, slim figure, her black gallabiya, her dark complexion, the dark tattoo beneath her chin, her Sa'idi dishes (millet bread and okra), and her Aswan accent that they loved to imitate.

Abduh told his neighbors that he worked as Hatim Rasheed's cook, but they didn't believe him because they knew about Hatim's homosexuality and because he would spend the night with him at least twice a week. Among themselves, they would joke about these "midnight feasts" that Abduh would prepare for his master, knowing the truth and accepting it. In general their behavior with any deviant person depended on how much they liked him. If they disliked him, they would rise up against him in defense of virtue, quarrel bitterly with him, and prevent their children from having anything to do with him. If, on the other hand, they liked him, as they did Abduh, they would forgive him and deal with him on the basis that he was misled and to be pitied, telling one another that everything in the end was fate and that it was not unlikely that God, Almighty and Glorious, would set him on the straight path—and "How many others have been worse than that but Our Lord set them straight and inspired them and they became saints." They would say this smacking their lips and nodding their heads in sympathy.

Abd Rabbuh's life proceeded virtually without problems, but his relationship with his wife Hidiya remained tense. She was happy with her cosseted new life, but something deep and sharp continued to smolder between them—it would flare up, then die down and sometimes disappear from sight, but it was always there. When he came to her after a night spent with Hatim, he would be shamefaced and irritable, avoiding her eyes and rounding on her furiously for the least mistake. She would meet his outbursts with a sad smile that provoked him even more, so that he'd scream, "Say something, you dumb cow!"

"God forgive you," Hidiya would answer him in a soft voice and leave him alone till he had calmed down. When they were together in bed, at a moment of passion, Abduh would often think of his lover Hatim and then feel as though she were reading his thoughts and bury his worries in her body, making love to her extremely violently, as though he were trying to stop her thoughts or assaulting her to punish her for knowing about his homosexuality. When he had finished, he would lie on his back and light a cigarette and stare at the ceiling of the room and she would lie at his side, the sharp thing suspended between them, impossible either to ignore or to acknowledge.

Once Abduh responded to a mysterious inner urging. He was sick of the pretense of ignorance and the oppressive weight of the matter on his heart, and in the depths of his soul he wanted a confrontation with

Hidiya instead of this painful equivocation. If she would just burst out in his face and accuse him of being a sodomite, he would be freed of the burden and tell her everything and point out to her quite simply that he couldn't do without Hatim because he needed the money; so he said to her suddenly, "You know, Hidiya, Hatim Bey is a very kindhearted man. . . . Why don't you say something?"

"Because he isn't kindhearted or anything of the sort. It's just that you're honest and he depends on your work."

This was the argument she always used in front of the neighbors, and she spoke sharply because he had violated that pretense of ignorance that allowed her to avoid embarrassment. He repented a bit of his outburst and said to her calmingly, "All the same, wife, he's to be thanked because he did us all these favors."

"There are no favors. Everyone does what's in his best interest. You understand and I understand. God forgive us for Hatim and for Hatim's job and for every day we've spent with him."

Her words hurt him so he took refuge in silence and turned his face toward the wall, which made her pity him. She moved close to him and took his hand between hers, kissed it, and whispered tenderly, "Abu Wael, may Our Lord preserve you for us and send you our daily bread by honest means. I wish you'd put aside a little money that we could use so you could open your own kiosk and wouldn't owe anybody anything. Not Hatim or anybody."

Like some great colonial power, Malak Khilla's objective is extension and control. An insistent inner force drives him to take possession of whatever is to hand regardless of its value and by any means.

Since arriving on the roof he hasn't stopped expanding in all directions. It started with a small abandoned latrine that lay to the right of the entrance. As soon as Malak saw it, he started to take it over. He put empty cardboard boxes in front of it, then started storing some of them inside the bathroom, and eventually locked it with a big padlock whose key he put in his pocket with the excuse that the items inside were liable to be stolen if the latrine remained open.

Following the latrine, he took over a large area of the roof that he filled with old, broken tailoring machines, informing the residents (who were naturally upset at this development) that these machines were waiting for someone or other to take them at the first opportunity and fix them. However, this person would always miss his appointment and contact Malak at the last moment by telephone that something or other had cropped up and assure him that he was definitely coming after a week, or two weeks at the most, to take the machines. By this means, Malak kept delaying until he was able to impose a *fait accompli*. The big bay formed by the wall of the roof, on the other hand, he took at one fell swoop, bringing in three carpenters who in less than an hour had made a wooden door that covered the bay and put a padlock on it whose key he kept. This way he acquired out of thin air an extra cupboard for storing his stock.

During these battles Malak, like a seasoned politico, would absorb the anger and objections of the residents by any means possible, from appeasement, through playing down the issue, all the way if necessary (though this was seldom) to violent fights. He was assisted in this by the fact that, to his good fortune, Mr. Hamid Hawwas had eventually succeeded, after sending complaints to virtually every official in the government, in having his arbitrary transfer to Cairo annulled and had returned to his home in El Mansoura. This relieved Malak of a stubborn foe capable of thwarting his expansionist plans on the roof.

However, the small victories, such as the bathroom and the cupboard, could only satisfy Malak's lust for real estate in the manner that a victory at chess might satisfy a great military leader. He was dreaming of a major coup that would earn him a huge sum: a nice piece of land, for example, that he could get hold of by force of possession, or a large apartment whose occupant had died that he could take over. This last situation was widespread in Downtown: an aged foreigner would often die single and without family and the closest Egyptian to him—his laundryman or his cook or his maid's husband—would take over his apartment. This person would rush to take up residence in the apartment and make a report asserting that he was resident there; he would change the locks, send himself registered letters as supporting evidence, and arrange for false witnesses to affirm before the court that he'd been living there all along with the deceased foreigner. Then he would commission a lawyer to followup the long, slow court case against the owner of the building, who usually in the end would be forced to accept a settlement that was much less than the apartment's real worth.

The hope of some such stroke of luck kept playing with Malak's dreams as the breeze plays with the branches of the trees. He reviewed the apartments in the Yacoubian Building that might be possessable and found that the one most within his reach was Zaki el Dessouki's (six rooms plus reception, two bathrooms, and a large balcony looking out onto Suleiman Basha). Zaki was an old single man who might die at any moment, and the apartment was rented and rented property could not be passed on to one's heirs. Likewise the presence of his brother Abaskharon in the apartment would facilitate Malak's taking possession of it at the critical moment.

After much thought and extensive legal consultations, Malak settled on his plan—a contract with a nonexistent company that he would sign along with Zaki el Dessouki and register at the public notary's office. Then he would hide it away until Zaki died, when Malak would produce the contract. This would make it impossible for him to be thrown out of the apartment, given his status as a commercial partner of the deceased. But how to get Zaki to sign the contract?

This was when he started to think of Busayna el Sayed. Zaki el Dessouki was helpless before a woman and a clever one could sucker him into signing the contract without realizing. Malak had offered Busayna five thousand pounds to get Zaki el Dessouki to sign and given her two days to think about it. He suffered no doubts that Busayna would agree, but he didn't want to appear too eager for her agreement. As he had expected, she had agreed, but she had asked him directly and clearly, "If I bring you the contract with Zaki el Dessouki's signature on it, what guarantee do I have that you'll pay?"

Malak had his answer ready and said quickly, "It's on a give-and-get basis. Keep the contract with you until you get the amount in full."

Busayna smiled and said, "Then we're agreed. If there's no money, there's no contract."

"Of course."

Why did Busayna agree?

Why should she refuse? Five thousand pounds is an excellent sum, with which she can cover the needs of her brothers and sisters and buy what she needs to get her trousseau ready. Likewise Malak will get the apartment after Zaki el Dessouki is dead, and he will know nothing about what she has done and she won't be doing him any harm because he will be dead. And even if it did harm him, why should she pity him? In the end, he's just a doting old man with a roving eye and deserves whatever he gets.

She had lost her compassion for people and a thick crust of indifference had formed around her feelings—that disgust that afflicts the exhausted, the frustrated, and the perverted and prevents them from sympathizing with others. She had succeeded, after repeated attempts, in ridding herself of feelings of remorse and buried forever the guilt that had afflicted her when she took off her dress in front of Talal and washed off his defilement, then put her hand out to him to collect ten pounds. She had become crueler, and more bitter and daring, and she no longer even cared what the residents of the roof told one another about her reputation. She knew enough of their own shameful acts and scandals to make their pretense of virtue something to laugh at. If she had got into a relationship with Talal because of her need for money, she knew other women on the roof who cheated on their husbands just to get some pleasure. And at the end of the day she was still a virgin and could marry any respectable man and would cut out the tongue of anyone who spoke ill of her.

Busayna had started working on Zaki el Dessouki, waiting for the right time to trick him into signing the contract, but it wasn't an easy matter because he wasn't the hateful old man that she'd imagined. On the contrary, he was kind and well mannered and treated her with respect. She never felt with him that she was performing a job that she'd been paid for as she did with Talal, who would strip her of her clothes and play around with her body without addressing a single word to her. Zaki was sensitive with her. He had got to know her family and loved her little brother and sisters and bought them lots of expensive presents. He respected her feelings, listened to what she said with interest, and told her engrossing stories about the old days.

Even their encounters in bed didn't leave her with the feeling of disgust that Talal did. Zaki would caress her gently, as though he feared that the touch of his fingers might hurt her and as though he were toying with a rose whose petals might tear under the least pressure. He would kiss her hands a lot (and it had never occurred to her that a man might kiss her hands), and on the first night, when their bodies met, she had whispered gently in his ear as she held him tight, "Be careful. I'm a virgin."

He had laughed softly and whispered, "I know."

Then he kissed her and she felt her body melt completely in his arms.

He had his own magical way of making love. He substituted experience for vigor, as though he were an old player who made use of his exceptional skills to compensate for his lack of suppleness. In herself, Busayna wanted the husband to whom she would one day be tied to be as gentle as he was. However, her growing admiration for him irritated her somewhat because it called up inside her feelings of guilt. He was kind to her and she was betraying him and hurting him. This good man, who was tender to her and made a fuss of her and told her the secrets of his life, could not for a moment imagine that she was preparing to take over his apartment after his death. When she thought of it, she despised and hated herself and she felt as sorry for him as a surgeon would for his wife or children if he were to perform an operation on them. She had set about getting his signature on the contract more than once when he was under the influence of alcohol but had drawn back at the last moment. She would be unable to go through with it and then later, to her amazement, would blame herself greatly and feel exasperated with herself for her feebleness. The fact is that her pity for the old man Zaki and her feelings of guilt on the one side and her implacable desire for money on the other continued to struggle with one another inside her with equal force, until eventually she summoned up all her will and decided to settle the matter and trick him into signing at the earliest opportunity.

"See how all my suits are winter suits. I used to attend parties in the winter and in the summer I would go to Europe."

They were sitting in Maxim's after eating dinner. It was around midnight and the place had emptied of customers. Busayna had put on a new blue dress that revealed her shining throat and cleavage, and Zaki was sitting next to her sipping whisky and showing her a collection of old photographs. He appeared in the pictures as a smart, handsome young man, smiling and holding a glass in a group of men wearing evening dress and beautiful women wearing revealing evening gowns; in front of them were tables crammed with food and bottles of superb wine. Busayna looked at the pictures with passionate interest, then pointed to one of them and burst out laughing, saying, "What's that? That's a very weird-looking suit!"

"That's evening dress. In the past every occasion had its special costume: morning dress was different from afternoon dress, which was different from evening dress."

"You know, you looked nice. Like Anwar Wagdi."

Zaki guffawed loudly. He was quiet for a moment, then said, "I lived through beautiful times, Busayna. It was a different age. Cairo was like Europe. It was clean and smart and the people were well mannered and respectable and everyone knew his place exactly. I was different too. I had my station in life, my money, all my friends were of a certain *niveau*, I had my special places where I would spend the evening—the Automobile Club, the Club Muhammad Ali, the Gezira Club. What times! Every night was filled with laughter and parties and drinking and singing. There were lots of foreigners in Cairo. Most of the people living downtown were foreigners, until Abd el Nasser threw them out in 1956."

"Why did he throw them out?"

"He threw the Jews out first, then the rest of the foreigners got scared and left. By the way, what's your opinion of Abd el Nasser?"

"I was born after he died. I don't know. Some people say he was a hero and others say he was a criminal."

"Abd el Nasser was the worst ruler in the whole history of Egypt. He ruined the country and brought us defeat and poverty. The damage he did to the Egyptian character will take years to repair. Abd el Nasser taught the Egyptians to be cowards, opportunists, and hypocrites."

"So why do people love him?"

"Who says people love him?"

"Lots of people that I know love him."

"Anyone who loves Abd el Nasser is either an ignoramus or did well out of him. The Free Officers were a bunch of kids from the dregs of society, destitutes and sons of destitutes. Nahhas Basha was a good man and he cared about the poor. He allowed them to join the Military College and the result was that they made the coup of 1952. They ruled Egypt and they robbed it and looted it and made millions. Of course they have to love Abd el Nasser; he was the boss of their gang."

He spoke bitterly, his voice rising in excitement. Realizing this, he forced a smile and said, "What did you do wrong that I should be haranguing you on politics? How about listening to something nice? Christine, *viens s'il te plaît.*"

Christine was sitting at her small desk next to the bar. She had put on her glasses and was absorbed in going over the accounts, purposely leaving them alone together. Now she came over wearing a wide smile. She loved Zaki so much that she was genuinely overjoyed whenever she saw him happy, and she had taken a liking to Busayna. Zaki cried out in drunken French, holding his arms out to her, "Christine, we're old friends, *n'est-ce pas?*"

"Of course."

"So . . . you have to do anything I say right away, right?"

Christine laughed and said, "That depends on the nature of the request."

"No matter what the request, you have to carry it out!"

"When you've drunk half a bottle of whisky as you have tonight, I have to beware of your requests!"

"I want you to sing for us, now."

"Sing? Now? Out of the question!"

This conversation of theirs always followed the same pattern, as though it were a necessary rite. He would ask her to sing, she would excuse herself; he would insist, she would protest and make excuses; and then in the end she would accept.

After a few minutes, Christine sat down in front of the piano and began stroking the keys with her fingers, scraps of tunes emerging. Then all of a sudden she raised her head as if she had heard some inner voice for which she had been waiting and she closed her eyes, her face tensed, and she started playing. The music rang out through the place and her voice rose loud and pure as she sang, exquisitely, Edith Piaf's song:

Non, rien de rien. Non, je ne regrette rien
Ni le bien qu'on m'a fait, ni le mal
Tout ça m'est bien égal...
Avec mes souvenirs j'ai allumé le feu
Mes chagrins, mes plaisirs,
Je n'ai plus besoin d'eux...
Je répars à zéro...
Car ma vie, car mes joies
Aujourd'hui ça commence avec toi.

At the end of the evening they crossed Suleiman Basha Street on their way to the office. Zaki was completely inebriated so Busayna put her arm around his waist to hold him up as he described to her, his speech slurred, what the square had looked like in the old days. He stopped in front of the closed-up shops and said, "There used to be a lovely bar here with a Greek owner. Next to it there was a hairdresser's and a restaurant, and here was the leather shop La Bursa Nova. The stores were all fantastically clean and had goods from London and Paris on display."

Busayna listened to him and watched his steps anxiously in case he should fall down in the street. They proceeded slowly until they got to the Yacoubian Building, when Zaki stopped and shouted, "See the wonderful architecture! This building was copied to the last detail from a building I saw in le Quartier latin in Paris."

Busayna tried pushing him gently so they could cross the street, but he went on, "You know, Busayna, I feel as though I owned the Yacoubian Building. I'm the longest resident in it. I know the history of every individual and every square meter in the building. I've spent most of my life in it. I lived my best days in it and I feel as though it's a part of me. The day this building's demolished or something happens to it, that'll be the day I die."

Slowly and with difficulty, they managed to cross the street and climb the stairs and eventually they reached the apartment.

"Lie down on the couch," said Busayna. He looked at her, smiled, and sat down slowly. He was breathing noisily and it seemed to take him a lot of effort to focus. Busayna forced herself to stop hesitating and, pushing her body against him, said in a seductive voice, "I have a service to ask of you. Do you think you could do it for me?"

He tried to reply but was too drunk to say anything. Instead he stared ahead and sighed, and the thought came to Busayna that he might die then and there. However, she pulled herself together and said, "I'm applying to the Ahli Bank for a small loan, ten thousand pounds. I have to pay it off over five years, plus interest. They need a guarantor. Could you please be my guarantor?"

She had put her hand on his leg and spoke in such a seductive and thrilling voice that, drunk as he was, he stuck his face to her cheek and kissed her. She took this as an expression of consent and cried out joyfully, "Thank you! The Lord preserve you!"

She rose and got the papers quickly from her bag and handed him the pen.

"Sign here, please."

She had got real loan application papers ready and stuck Malak's contract in the middle. Zaki started signing, while she held his hand to help him, but suddenly he stopped and mumbled in a slurred voice, his face looking sick, "The bathroom . . ."

She didn't say anything for a moment as though she hadn't understood. He waved his hand and said with an effort, "I want the bathroom!"

Busayna put the papers aside and helped him stand up with difficulty and supported him on her arm until he got into the bathroom. She had closed the door, turned round to go back and was halfway across the hall when she heard a loud crash behind her.

That night Groppi's tea garden on Adly Street was full to overflowing with customers, most of them the kind of young lovers who feel comfortable in the dim lighting of the garden lamps that hides their faces so that they can exchange sweet nothings undisturbed and without attracting curiosity.

A man in his fifties entered, well built and sturdy and wearing a dark baggy suit and white shirt without a tie, his clothes seeming too large and not well matched to his body, as though they didn't belong to him. The man sat down at the table next to the door, ordered a cup of Turkish coffee without sugar, and sat in silence, observing the place and looking anxiously from time to time at his watch. After about half an hour a thin, dark-skinned young man arrived wearing a track suit and directed himself toward the large man. The two embraced warmly, then sat talking in low voices.

"Praise God you're all right, Taha. When did you get out?"

"Two weeks ago."

"You're being watched for sure. Did you do as Hassan told you when you were on your way here?"

Taha nodded his head and Sheikh Shakir continued, "Brother Hassan is completely secure. Use him to contact me and he'll tell you where and when to meet. Usually we choose places that don't arouse suspicion. Like here, for example. It's crowded and dark, which makes it suitable. We meet in parks too and restaurants and sometimes in bars. But . . . don't get used to sitting in bars!"

Sheikh Shakir laughed, but Taha remained unsmiling and a heavy silence took over. The sheikh continued bitterly, "The National Security Investigation Bureau is now launching a criminal campaign against all Islamists. Detentions, torture, murder. They open fire on our unarmed brothers while arresting them, then accuse us of resisting the authorities. Real massacres are committed every day. Verily, they will come back on the Day of Resurrection with the blood of these innocents on their hands. I've been compelled to leave my residence and stop going to the mosque and I've changed the way I look, as you can see. Speaking of which, what do you think of Sheikh Shakir in his Western getup?"

The sheikh let out a loud laugh, attempting to create an atmosphere of good humor, but in vain. An unbudgeable, dark shadow stretched between them, to which the sheikh soon submitted, sighing and saying "God forgive me!" Then he said, "Cheer up, Taha. I know what you've been through and appreciate your pain, my son. I wish you to think of everything the unbelievers did to you as going to your account with Our Lord, Almighty and Glorious. Verily, He will reward you for it with the best of rewards, God willing. Know that Paradise is the reward of those who are tortured for God's cause. Everything that happened to you is but a paltry tax that those who struggle pay gladly for the sake of raising high the word of the Truth, Sublime and Magnificent. Our rulers are fighting for their interests and their ill-gotten wealth, but we are fighting for God's religion. Their stock in trade finds no buyers and is of no worth, but God has promised us His aid and He will never betray His promise."

As though he had been waiting for the sheikh's words to unburden himself of his sorrows, Taha said in a husky voice, "They humiliated me, Master. They humiliated me till I felt the dogs in the street had more self-respect than me. I was subjected to things I never imagined a Muslim could do."

"They are no Muslims. Nay, they are unbelievers, according to the consensus of the jurists."

"Even if they were unbelievers, wouldn't they have an atom of mercy? Don't they have sons and daughters and wives that they care for and have pity on? Had I been held in Israel, the Jews wouldn't have done to me as they did. Had I been a spy and a traitor to my country, they wouldn't have done those things to me. I ask myself what offense could merit that horrible punishment. Has the observance of God's Law become a major crime? Sometimes in detention I'd think what was happening before me wasn't real, that it was a nightmare that I'd wake up from to find it was all over. Were it not for my faith in God, Sublime and Magnificent, I would have killed myself to escape from that torment."

The sheikh's face registered his pain and he remained silent. Taha made a fist and said, "They blindfolded me so that I wouldn't know who they were. But I have made an oath and committed myself before God to hunt them down. I will find out who they were and take revenge on them one by one."

"I advise you, my son, to put this painful experience behind you. I know what I ask is difficult, but it's the only thing to do in your situation. What happened to you in detention is not something peculiar to you. It is the destiny of all those who speak the truth openly in our unfortunate country. Those responsible are not just a few officers but the criminal and unbelieving regime that rules us. You must direct your anger against the whole regime and not particular individuals. The Almighty has said in His Noble Book, *You have had a good example in God's Messenger* (God has spoken truly). The Chosen One—God bless him and give him peace—was fought against in Mecca and abused and hurt so much that he complained to his Lord of his weakness and the contempt with which people treated him. Yet despite this he did not consider his struggle to be a personal feud with the unbelievers. On the contrary he directed his energy to spreading the Call and in the end, when God's religion was victorious, the Messenger pardoned all the unbelievers and freed them. This is a lesson you have to learn and act upon."

"That was the Messenger—God bless him and grant him peace—and the best of His creation, but I'm not a prophet and I'm not capable of forgetting what those criminals did to me. What happened to me pursues me without rest. I'm unable to sleep. I haven't been to the mosque since I got out and I don't think that I shall go. I spend all day alone in my room speaking to no one, and sometimes I think I'm losing my mind."

"Don't give in, Taha! Thousands of Muslim youth have suffered detention and been subjected to ugly tortures but left detention more determined than ever to resist injustice. The regime's true objective in torturing Islamists isn't just to hurt them physically. What they want is to destroy them psychologically so that they lose their capacity to struggle. If you surrender to melancholy, you will have realized the objectives of these unbelievers."

The sheikh looked at him for a moment, then grasped his hand on the table and said, "When will you return to the mosque?"

"I will never return."

"No, you must return. You are an outstanding student who is committed to the struggle and a glorious future awaits you, God willing. Trust in God, forget what happened, and go back to your studies and your faculty."

"I cannot. How can I face people after . . . ?"

Taha suddenly fell silent. His face crumpled and he groaned out loud.

"They violated my honor, Master."

"Stop!"

"They violated my honor ten times, Master. Ten times."

"I told you to stop, Taha!"

The sheikh shouted these words vehemently, but Taha struck the table with his fist, shaking and rattling the cups. The sheikh rose quickly from his place and whispered agitatedly, "Pull yourself together, Taha! Everyone's looking at us. We must leave immediately. Listen, I'll be waiting for you in front of Cinema Metro in an hour. Take precautions and make sure no one's watching you."

Over two months Hagg Azzam used persuasion, temptation, intimidation, and violence. He tried every method on Souad, but she adamantly refused the very idea of an abortion. Soon their shared life came to a complete standstill—no endearments, no tasty food, no pipes of hashish, and no times in bed. The only thing they had left was the subject of abortion. He would come every day and sit in front of her. He would talk to her gently and calmly. Then little by little he would lose his temper and they would fight. He would shout, "You made an agreement and you went back on it."

"So hang me."

"From the start we said no pregnancy."

"You think you're God, so you can allow things and forbid things?"

"Be sensible and get me out of this fix, for God's sake."

"No."

"I'll divorce you."

"Divorce me."

He said "divorce" with feigned casualness because deep down inside he wanted to keep hold of her, but the idea of having a child at his age was impossible. Even if he allowed it himself, his sons would never allow it, and even though Hagga Salha, his first wife, didn't even know about his second marriage, how would he keep it from her if he had a child?

When Hagg Azzam gave up on persuading Souad, he left her and went to Alexandria where he met with her brother Hamidu and told him what had happened. Hamidu hesitated and bowed his head in thought for a while. Then he said, "Listen to me, Hagg. We're both decent people and doing the right thing shouldn't upset anyone. It's true I'm her brother, but I can't ask her to have an abortion. Abortion is forbidden by religion and I'm a God-fearing man."

"But we made an agreement, Rayyis Hamidu."

"We made an agreement and we broke it. We're in the wrong, my friend. We started things on a friendly basis and we should finish them on a friendly basis. Give her her rights according to God's Law and divorce her, Hagg."

Hamidu's face at that moment looked to him ignoble, mendacious, and hateful and he wanted in fact to slap him and hit him, but in the end his good sense prevailed and he left, boiling with rage. On the way back to Cairo an idea suddenly came to him and he said to himself, "There's only one person left I can trust to save me."

The war in the Gulf was keeping Sheikh el Samman extremely busy.

Every day he organized lectures and seminars and wrote lengthy articles in the press to explain the legal justification for the war to liberate Kuwait. The government brought him to speak on television numerous times and called on him to deliver the Friday sermon in the largest mosques in Cairo, and the sheikh set about presenting to the people all the legal reasons for the correctness of the Arab rulers' position in inviting American troops to liberate Kuwait from the Iraqi invasion.

Hagg Azzam spent three whole days searching for Sheikh el

Samman before he was finally able to meet with him at his office in El Salam mosque in Medinet Nasr. The first thing he said to him as he anxiously scrutinized his face was, "What's wrong with you, Master? You look exhausted."

"I've hardly slept since the war began. Every day seminars and meetings and in a few days I leave, God willing, for Saudi Arabia to attend the emergency conference of Muslim scholars."

"It's too much, Master. You must look after your health."

The sheikh sighed and muttered, "Whatever I do is less than I should. I ask God, Sublime and Magnificent, to accept my work and place it in the scale among my good deeds."

"Can you postpone going to Saudi Arabia and rest a little?"

"God forbid that I should fall short in my efforts! It was Sheikh el Ghamidi, an outstanding scholar—we give precedence over God to none—who contacted me. I shall participate with my brother scholars there in issuing a legal ruling that will silence the arguments of the strife-makers and demonstrate to everyone the incoherence of their arguments. We shall mention in the ruling, God willing, the legal reasons for the permissibility of seeking the help of the Western Christian armies to save the Muslims from the criminal unbeliever Saddam Hussein."

Hagg Azzam nodded his head in agreement with the sheikh's words and there was a moment of silence. Then the sheikh patted him on his shoulder and asked him affectionately, "And how are you? I think you came to me to discuss something."

"I don't want to add to your worries."

The sheikh smiled and leaned his well-padded body back in the comfortably upholstered chair, saying, "You are the last person who could cause me worry. Please, tell me."

When Hagg Azzam and Sheikh el Samman got to Souad's apartment in the Yacoubian Building, they found her wearing house clothes. She greeted Sheikh El Samman with reserve and quickly disappeared inside, returning a few minutes later with her hair covered and carrying a silver tray on which were glasses of iced lemonade. The sheikh took a sip of his drink, closed his eyes appreciatively, and, as though finding the right point of entry to the subject, turned to Hagg Azzam and said laughingly, "Wonderful lemonade! Your wife's an excellent housewife. Praise God, my dear chap, for such a blessing!"

Azzam picked up the thread and said, "A thousand praises and thanks, Master. Souad's a good housewife and a good-hearted, righteous wife, but she's obstinate and annoying."

"Obstinate?"

Sheikh el Samman asked the question with feigned astonishment and turned to Souad who seized the initiative and said to him in a serious tone of voice, "Of course, the Hagg will have told you about the problem."

"May Our Lord never bring problems! Listen, my daughter. You're a Muslim and follow God's Law, and Our Lord, Glorious and Almighty, has commanded the wife to obey her husband in all matters of this world. The Chosen One — God's blessings and peace be upon him — has even said, in a sound hadith, 'Were any of God's creatures permitted to prostrate itself to another of His creatures, I would have commanded the wife to prostrate herself to the husband' (the Messenger has spoken truly)!"

"Is the woman supposed to follow her husband's orders with regard to what is right or what is wrong?"

"God protect us from what is wrong, my daughter! There can be no obedience to a creature who disobeys the Creator."

"So tell me, Master. You want me to have an abortion?"

There was silence for a moment. Then Sheikh el Samman smiled and said calmly, "My daughter, you agreed with him from the beginning that there would be no children and Hagg Azzam is an old man and his circumstances do not allow such a thing."

"Fine. So let him divorce me according to God's Law."

"But if he divorces you while you're pregnant, he'll be responsible legally for the upkeep of the child."

"So you agree that I should abort myself?"

"God forbid! Abortion is of course a sin. However, some trustworthy jurisprudential opinions affirm that termination of the pregnancy during the first two months is not abortion because the soul enters the fetus at the beginning of the third month."

"Where does it say so?"

"In authenticated legal opinions delivered by the great scholars of religion."

Souad laughed sarcastically and said bitterly, "Those must have been American sheikhs."

"Speak politely to the reverend sheikh!" Hagg Azzam chided her.

Fixing him with a furious glance, she said challengingly, "Everyone had better be polite."

The sheikh intervened in a conciliatory tone, saying, "God protect us from His anger! Souad, my daughter, don't let your temper get the better of you. I'm not discussing the matter on the basis of my own opinion, God forbid. I'm simply passing on to you a well-regarded legal point of view. Some reliable jurisprudents have affirmed that aborting the fetus before the third month should not be considered murder, if there are extenuating circumstances."

"So if I abort myself it won't be a sin? Who could say such a thing? There's no way I could believe you even if you swore on the Qur'an!"

At this Hagg Azzam stood up, went over to her, and shouted angrily, "I'm telling you, be polite when you speak to the reverend sheikh!"

Souad rose and shouted, waving her arms, "What reverend sheikh?

Everything's clear now. You've paid him off to say a couple of stupid things. Abortion's okay in the first two months? Shame on you, Sheikh! How can you sleep at night?"

Sheikh el Samman, taken unawares by this sudden attack, assumed a glowering expression and said warningly, "Mind your manners, my daughter, and watch you don't overstep your bounds!"

"I don't give a damn for your overstepping! You're a farce! How much did he pay you to come with him?"

"You filthy bitch!" shouted Hagg Azzam and he slapped her on her face. She screamed and started wailing, but Sheikh el Samman grabbed him, dragged him away from her, and started talking to him in a low voice. Soon the two of them left, slamming the door behind them.

Souad saw them off with abuse and curses. She was shaking with anger at what Sheikh el Samman had said and at Azzam, who had struck her for the first time since they had gotten married. She could still feel the pain of the slap on her face and she made up her mind to get her own back. All the same she felt a secret relief that she had reached the point of open confrontation with him. Any tie that might have obligated her or embarrassed her had been severed. He had struck her and abused her, and from now on she would express her contempt and hatred for him in the clearest possible form. In fact, her ability to fight and use abuse was something new to her, as though the rancor that was in her had suddenly exploded. Everything she had suffered and that had tortured her had accumulated and now the time had come for a reckoning. Now she was ready to kill him or be killed by him rather than have an abortion.

When she had calmed down a little, she asked herself why she cared that much about her pregnancy. She was of course religious, and abortion was a sin, and she was also terrified of the operation itself because many women died during it. All these were genuine considerations, but they were secondary. A deep-seated, instinctive desire drove her to fight ferociously in defense of her pregnancy. She felt as though if she bore the child, she would recover her self-respect. Her life would acquire a new and decent meaning. She would no longer be the poor woman whom the millionaire Azzam had purchased to enjoy himself with for a couple of hours in the afternoon but a real wife who could not be ignored or slighted. She would be the child's mother, going in and out with the Hagg's son in her arms. Wasn't that her right?

She had gone hungry, begged, and tasted humiliation, and a hundred times refused to go astray, and in the end she had given her body to a man as old as her father, had put up with his dullness, his gloominess, his wrinkled face, his dyed hair, and his flagging manhood, had pretended that she was fulfilled and that her body was aching with desire, just for him to come to her and go away again in secret, as though she were a mistress; she had done all this only to sleep on her own in a cold bed and a huge, frightening apartment where she was forced every night to turn on the lights in order to dispel the lonesomeness and every day to weep out of yearning for her son; and then, when Azzam's appointed time came, to do herself up for him and play out the role for which she had been paid. Wasn't it her right after all that humiliation to feel that she was a wife and a mother? Wasn't it her right to bear a legitimate son who would inherit the wealth that would protect her from the horrors of poverty forever? God had granted her this pregnancy as a just reward for her long patience and she wouldn't give it up at any price.

Such were Souad's thoughts. Then she went into the bathroom and took off her clothes, and as soon as the hot water gushed over her naked body, a strange and new feeling came over her that her body, which Azzam had used and defiled and abused for so long, had suddenly been liberated and become her property alone. Her hands, her arms, her legs, and her breasts—every part of her body—breathed freely and she could feel a beautiful light pulse beating inside her, a pulse that would get bigger and grow and fill her day after day until the time came and it emerged as a beautiful child that would look like her, would inherit its father's wealth, and would restore her self-respect and her proper station. She finished her shower, dried herself, and put on her night things. Then she performed the evening prayer and the additional extra prostrations and sat in bed reading the Qur'an until drowsiness overcame her.

"Who's there?"

She woke from sleep at the sound of movement and muttering outside the room. She thought that a thief had slipped into the apartment, and, quaking with terror, decided to open the window and call to the neighbors for help.

"Who's there?"

She screamed again in a high-pitched voice and strained to hear as she sat on her bed in the dark; the sounds, however, had ceased and quiet reigned. She decided that she would investigate herself and put her feet down on the floor, but fear paralyzed her limbs. She convinced herself that it was just her imagination and got back in bed and put a pillow over her head and for a few moments tried to plunge back into sleep. Then suddenly the door of the room opened so forcefully it banged against the wall and they fell on her.

There were four or five of them. Their faces didn't show in the dark. They pounced on her and one of them smothered her mouth with the pillow while the others grabbed her hands and feet. She tried with all her strength to slip out of their clutches and to scream at the top of her voice and she bit the hand of the man who was gagging her, but her resistance failed because they had tied her up tightly, completely paralyzing her movements. They were strong and well trained and one of them rolled up the sleeve of her pajamas and she felt something like a sharp thorn being stuck into her arm. Little by little her body began to weaken and relax. Then her eyes closed and she felt everything around her moving away and dissolving into nothing, like a dream.

The newspaper *Le Caire* was established in Cairo a hundred years ago in the same old building that it still occupies in Galaa Street, and since its founding it has been published every day, in French, for residents of Cairo who speak that language.

When Hatim Rasheed graduated from the Faculty of Humanities, his French mother was able to find him work on the newspaper. He proved his aptitude for journalism and was quickly promoted till he was appointed to be editor-in-chief at the age of forty-five. He introduced sweeping changes to the newspaper and added an Arabic-language section aimed at the Egyptian reader. During his time distribution rose to thirty thousand copies daily, which was a huge number in comparison to the other small local newspapers. This success came as a natural and just result of Hatim's efficiency, his assiduity, his effective contacts with varied milieux, and his amazing capacity for work, which he had inherited from his father.

If one remembers that over seventy individuals (administrative staff, reporters, and photographers) work under his direction at the newspaper, the first question that comes to mind is, Do they know about his homosexuality? The answer, of course, is yes, because people in Egypt are interested in the personal lives of others and delve into them with persistence and focus. Homosexuality is impossible to hide and all the employees at the paper know that their boss is homosexual. Despite the revulsion and contempt this arouses, Hatim Rasheed's perversion remains merely a distant, pale shadow to his forceful, compelling professional image. They are aware of his homosexuality but do not feel it in any way in their daily dealings with him because he is serious and stern (more perhaps than is necessary) and, while he spends most of the day with them, not the slightest movement or glance that might hint at his tendencies escapes him.

A few vulgar incidents have of course occurred during his time as head of the newspaper. Once there was a lazy and unsuccessful journalist on whom Hatim made a number of negative reports in preparation for his final removal from the newspaper. The journalist knew the chief editor's intention so decided to get his revenge and exploit the presence of all the reporters at the weekly editorial meeting. He asked for the floor and when Hatim gave him permission, he addressed him, saying in a sarcastic tone, "I wish to propose to you, sir, the idea of an investigative piece on the phenomenon of homosexuality in Egypt."

There was a tense silence and the writer could not conceal a smile in his eagerness to insult Hatim, who said nothing but bowed his head and stroked his smooth hair (as was his custom when surprised or nervous). Then he leaned back in his chair and said calmly, "I don't think the subject concerns the readers."

"On the contrary, it concerns them a great deal, because there's been a major increase in the number of homosexuals and some of them now occupy leadership positions in the country, and scientific studies show that the homosexual is psychologically unfit to lead the work of any institution because of the psychological aberrations that homosexuality causes."

The attack was harsh and sweeping and Hatim determined to respond with violence, so he said firmly, "Your outmoded style of thinking is one of the reasons for your failure as a journalist."

"Has homosexuality now become a progressive behavior?"

"Neither that nor is it the national issue in our country. My dear educated gentleman, Egypt has not fallen behind because of homosexuality but because of corruption, dictatorship, and social injustice. Likewise snooping into people's private lives is a vulgar way of behaving that is inappropriate for a long-established newspaper like *Le Caire*."

The writer tried to protest, but Hatim cut him off sharply: "The discussion is closed. Kindly remain silent so that we may discuss the other topics."

Hatim thus won the first round deftly, demonstrating to all his strength of personality and refusal to bow to blackmail. On the other embarrassing occasion, which was even more vulgar, a trainee journalist harassed him. Hatim was standing among the workers in the print shop supervising the production of the paper when the journalist, on the pretense of talking to him about something, came up to him and pointing to something among the papers on the table pushed himself against him from behind. Hatim immediately understood the meaning of the act and moved away, quietly, resuming his rounds of the print shop in a normal way. When he got back to his office, he sent for the journalist, dismissed the other people in the room, and then left the man standing for several minutes while he looked through his papers in front of him without letting him sit or paying him any attention. Eventually he raised his head, looked at him for a while, and said slowly, "Listen. Either you behave decently or I throw you off the paper. Understand?"

The journalist tried to make a pretense of surprise and innocence, but Hatim said in a decisive voice before going back to his papers, "That's a final warning. No further discussion is called for. Get out. The interview's over."

Hatim Rasheed is not merely then an effeminate but also a talented and inquiring individual who has learned much from experience and whose competence and intelligence have brought him to the pinnacle of professional success. Moreover, he is an exquisite intellectual, who speaks a number of languages (English, Spanish, and French, as well as Arabic) fluently and whose wide and deep reading has introduced him to socialist thinking, which has influenced him greatly. He has made efforts to become friends with the leading Egyptian socialists and as a result at the end of the 1970s was once summoned to an interview with National Security investigators, who interrogated him; however, he was released after a few hours after they had recorded in his file that he was "a sympathizer and not an organizer." His socialism has caused his name to come up several times for enlistment in the secret communist organizations (the Workers' Party, the Egyptian Communist Party) but his known homosexuality has dissuaded those in charge from going ahead.

Such is Hatim Rasheed's genuine but public persona. His secret life, on the other hand, is a kind of locked box full of forbidden, sinful, but pleasurable, toys that he opens every evening to play with, then locks again and tries to forget. He strives to reduce the homosexual space in his life to the narrowest possible, living his daily life as a journalist and an executive and practicing his pleasure for a few hours in bed at night. He tells himself that most men in the world have some special pastime that they use to relieve life's pressures. He has known men in the most elevated positions—doctors, councelors, and university professors—who were devoted to alcohol or hashish or women or gambling and this never lessened their success or their self-respect. He convinces himself that homosexuality is the same sort of thing.

This idea appeals to him greatly because it brings him relief, balance, and respect. This is why he is always looking for a stable relationship with a permanent lover so that he can satisfy his needs safely and restrict his homosexuality to his nighttime hours in bed, for when he is alone, without a lover, temptation seizes him and his importunate lust pushes him into ignominious situations. He has had days of pain and distress when he was driven to defile himself with criminal types and the scum of society in order to pick out from among them a lover with whom to satisfy his need for just one night, never to be seen again. Again and again he has been subjected to theft, insult, and blackmail. Once they beat him horribly in a public bathhouse in the quarter of El Hussein and took his gold watch and wallet.

In the aftermath of such insane nights, Hatim Rasheed would hole up at home for a few days, seeing and speaking to no one, drinking a lot, passing his whole life in review, and remembering his father and mother with resentment and hatred. He would say to himself that if they had made a little time to look after him, he would never have sunk this low, but they were preoccupied with their professional ambitions and had devoted themselves to achieving wealth and glory so they left him and his body to the servants to play around with. He never blames Idris or doubts for one moment that he loved him truly, but he longs to see his father, Dr. Hassan Rasheed, rise from his grave just once so that he can tell him what he thinks of him. He would stand in front of him and face down his powerful glances, huge frame, and awe-inspiring pipe. He wouldn't be afraid of him at all and he would say to him, "Great scholar, since you'd dedicated your life to civil law, why did you get married and have children? You may have been a genius at law but you certainly didn't know how to be a real father. How many times in your life did you kiss me? How many times did you sit down with me so that I could tell you about my problems? You always treated me as though I were a rare art object or painting you'd acquired because it had taken your fancy; then you'd forgotten about it, and from time to time, when your crowded work schedule permitted, you'd remember it, look at it for a while, and then forget about it again."

His mother, Jeanette, he would also confront with the truth. "You were just a barmaid at a small bar in le Quartier latin. You were poor and uneducated and your marriage to my father was a bigger social leap than you'd ever dreamed of. Despite this, you spent the next thirty years despising my father and blackmailing him because he was Egyptian and you were French. You played the role of the cultured European among the savages. You kept grumbling about Egypt and the Egyptians and treating everybody coldly and haughtily. Your neglect of me was part of your hatred for Egypt. I think you were unfaithful to my father more than once; in fact, I'm sure of it, at least with Monsieur Bénard the embassy secretary, whom you used to spend hours talking to on the phone, lying on the couch, hugging the receiver, and whispering, your face contorted with desire, sending me off to play with the servants. You were just a whore like the ones anyone could catch by the dozen in the bars of Paris simply by sticking out his hand." In these black moments, despair seizes Hatim, his sense of humiliation tears at him, and he surrenders himself to weeping like a child. Sometimes he thinks about suicide, but he lacks the courage to carry it out.

Right now, however, he is in the best of form: his relationship with Abd Rabbuh has kept going and settled down and he has succeeded in linking Abduh's life to his own by means of the kiosk and the room he has rented for them on the roof. He has guaranteed his physical satisfaction and stopped going altogether to the Chez Nous and other homosexual meeting places. He is urging Abduh to complete his education so that he can become a respectable, educated person capable of appreciating his feelings and ideas and worthy of his permanent friendship.

"Abduh. You're intelligent and sensitive and you can improve your circumstances through your own efforts. You're earning money now, your family is taken care of, and your life is stable. But money isn't everything. You have to get an education and become a respectable man."

They'd finished the morning love session and Hatim got out of bed, naked, and took a dreamy, dancing step on the tips of his toes, his face full of contentment and animation as it usually was after he'd had his fill of lovemaking. He started to pour himself a drink while Abduh, stretched out on the bed, laughed and said jokingly, "Why do you want me to get an education?"

"So you can be respectable."

"You mean I'm not respectable?"

"Of course you're respectable. But you have to study and get a certificate to bear witness to that."

"'There is no god but God' is the only witnessing I'll ever do!"

Abduh laughed uproariously, but Hatim looked at him reproachfully and said, "I'm serious. You have to make an effort. Study, get the Intermediate and the Secondary, and go to a major faculty, like law, for instance."

"'You can't teach an old dog new tricks,' as the old saying goes."

"No, Abduh. Don't think that way. You're twenty-four years old. Your whole life's ahead of you."

"Everything's fate and destiny."

"That backward stuff again? You can make your destiny in this world on your own. If there were any justice in this country, someone like you would get educated at state expense. Education, medical treatment, and work are the natural rights of every citizen in the world, but the regime in Egypt is determined to abandon the poor like you to ignorance so it can rob them. Have you noticed that the government selects the Central Security troops from the poorest and most ignorant recruits? If you were educated, Abduh, you'd never agree to work for Central Security, in the worst conditions and for pennies. And at the same time the big men steal millions from the people's pockets."

"You want me to stop the big men from stealing? I couldn't stand up to the major who commanded the camp and now you want me to take on the big men?"

"Start with yourself, Abduh. Make an effort and teach yourself. It's the first step toward getting your rights."

Hatim looked at Abduh for a while, then said lovingly, "And who knows? Maybe one day you'll be Mr. Abd Rabbuh the lawyer."

Abduh got off the bed, went up to him, took hold of his shoulders, kissed him on the cheek, and said, "And who'll pay for my education? And who'll open me an office when I graduate?"

Hatim's feelings suddenly took fire and he put his face close to Abduh's and said in a whisper, "I will, my darling. I'll never leave you and I'll never be stingy with you."

Abduh hugged him and the two of them lost themselves in long, hot kisses. However, a distant sound reached them and gradually they became aware of repeated loud knocks on the door. Hatim looked at Abduh anxiously and they rushed to put on their clothes any old how. Hatim preceded him in the direction of the door, preparing his face with an annoyed and haughty expression for whomever he might find there. He peered through the peephole and said in surprise, "It's your wife, Abduh."

Abduh came forward quickly, opened the door, and shouted angrily, "What's the matter, Hidiya? Why are you here at this hour? What do you want?"

Pointing to her child, who was sleeping in her arms, she said, "Help me, Abduh! The boy's burning hot and he keeps throwing up. He's been crying all night long. Hatim Bey, I beg you, get us a doctor or take us to the hospital!"

When Busayna opened the door of the bathroom, she found Zaki el Dessouki stretched out on the floor, his clothes covered with vomit, and unable to move. Bending down, she took his hand and found it was as cold as ice.

"Zaki Bey! Are you ill?"

He muttered some incomprehensible words and continued to stare into space. She brought a chair, took him in her arms, sat him down on it (discovering at the same time how very light his body was), removed his soiled clothes, and washed his face, hands, and chest with hot water. Soon he started to come round a little. He was able to stand and walk, leaning on her, and she put him to bed and went up to her room on the roof and quickly returned with a large glass of hot mint, which Zaki drank before surrendering to a deep sleep. She spent the night next to him on the couch and examined him several times. She checked the heat of his brow with her hand and put a finger under his nose to make sure that his breathing was regular. She stayed awake and determined to call a doctor if his condition got worse. As she contemplated his aged sleeping face, he appeared to her, for the first time, in simple reality, as just a good-hearted, drunk old man, frail, mild-tempered, and deserving of compassion, like a child.

In the morning, she made him a light breakfast with a glass of warm milk. Abaskharon had arrived and discovered what had happened and he stood before his sick master with his head bent in sorrow, saying over and over in an agonized voice, "A thousand wishes for your recovery, Excellency!"

Zaki opened his eyes and made a sign for him to leave. Then he got up with difficulty, leaned against the wall, and taking his head in his hands grumbled in a low voice, "I've got a terrible headache and my stomach hurts a lot."

"Do you want me to call a doctor?"

"No. It's nothing. I drank too much. This has happened to me so many times. I drink a cup of Turkish coffee without sugar and I'm fine."

He was putting on a show of holding up and being tough and she laughed and said, "So listen. That's enough machismo. You're an old man now and your health is weak. No more drinking and staying up late. You're supposed to go to bed early like old people your age."

Zaki smiled and looking at her gratefully said, "Thank you, Busayna.

You're a good and loyal person. I don't know what I'd do without you."

She put her hands on his face and kissed his brow.

She had kissed him often before, but this time she felt the touch of his face differently. She felt as she pressed her lips to his brow that she knew him well, that she loved his old, coarse smell, and that he was no longer that Bey, who, far removed from her, told her about the old days. He wasn't any longer even that rebarbative male lover who was different from her. Now he was close to her, as though she had known him for ages, as though he was her father or her uncle, as though he carried the same smell and blood as she. She wanted to hug him hard so that she could take his weak, fragile body in her arms and fill her nostrils with that old, coarse smell of his that she loved.

She thought that what was happening between them was strange and unexpected. She remembered that only yesterday she'd tried to trick him and get hold of his signature, and she felt ashamed. It occurred to her that the trick she'd played on him yesterday had been her last try at resisting her real feelings toward him. Inside she'd wanted to flee from her love for him. She'd have been more comfortable in a way if she had limited her relationship to him to sex and money—he wanted sex and she wanted money, that was how she had pictured the relationship—but she had overstepped the bounds.

Now she is facing her true feelings and she understands them clearly. She wants to stay with him, to take care of him, and to respect him, gratefully confident that he will understand anything she may say to him. She will tell him about her life, her father and her mother, and her old love for Taha; she'll even tell him the sordid details of her relationship with Talal and she won't be ashamed with him. She will feel at peace once she's told him, as though she has relieved herself of a heavy burden. How she warms to the sight of his aged face listening attentively to her as he asks her to explain some detail of her stories, then comments on them!

She cannot describe her feelings with any other word than love. It wasn't the hot, burning love she'd felt for Taha but another different kind of love, calm and deep-seated, something closer to peace of mind, and confidence, and respect. She loved him, and having worked that out she was freed forever from her misgivings. She began to live care-free and happy and started spending most of the day and a good part of the night with Zaki Bey.

One small, sharp, pointed thing, however, pricks her conscience whenever she remembers that she had been going to betray him. She had put pressure on him to sign the contract so that Malak could get hold of his apartment. She had exploited his confidence in her to do him harm. Wasn't that what had happened? Hadn't that been her goal? To make a fool of him and get his signature while he was drunk and get five thousand pounds from Malak in payment for her betrayal? Whenever that word resounded in her mind, she would remember his kindly smile and his interest in her and his concern for her feelings. She would remember that he had always treated her gently and that he had given her his entire trust. At those moments, she would feel she was vile and treacherous and would despise herself and enter a whirlpool of self-reproach.

These feelings continued to torture her until one morning she sud-denly went to Malak. It was early and he had just opened his shop. There was a glass of tea with milk in front of him from which he was sipping in a leisurely fashion. She stood in front of him, greeted him, and said to him straight off before her courage could seep away, "Mr. Malak, I'm sorry. I won't be able to do what we agreed on."

"I don't understand."

"That business of the signature I'm supposed to get from Zaki Bey. I'm not going to do it."

"Why?"

"That's just how it is."

"Is that your last word?"

"Yes."

"Okay. Fine. Thanks."

Malak spoke calmly and sucked up a sip of tea. He turned his face away from her, and she thought as she left him that she had liberated herself from a heavy worry, though she was surprised all the same that he had accepted her apology without fuss. She'd expected him to get angry and blow up, but he'd stayed calm, as though he'd been expecting that or had something or other in mind. This thought disquieted her for a few days, but she soon rid herself of her misgivings and felt for the first time a deep contentment because she had stopped betraying Zaki and had nothing left to hide from him.

At 8 A.M., Sheikh Shakir and Taha el Shazli took the Metro in the direction of Helwan. They had been engaged over several days in long discussions during which Sheikh Shakir had tried to persuade Taha to forget what had happened and pick up his life again. However, Taha remained so vengeful and angry that he seemed more than once to be on the verge of collapse. Finally, at the end of a long debate, the sheikh shouted in his face, "What do you want then? You don't want to study and you don't want to work and you don't want to see any of your colleagues or even your family. What do you want, Taha?"

"I want to take revenge on the people who assaulted me and humiliated me."

"And how will you know them, since you didn't see their faces?"

"From their voices. I could distinguish their voices from a thousand. I beg you, Master, to tell me the name of the head officer, who supervised my torture. You told me before that you know his name."

Sheikh Shakir was silent, thinking.

"I beg you, Master. I won't be at peace till I know his name."

"I can't be certain as to his identity. But torture at National Security generally takes place under the supervision of two men—Colonel Salih Rashwan and Colonel Fathi el Wakil. They're both unbelieving criminals destined for Hell—*How evil a homecoming!* But how does it help you to know the officer's name?"

"I shall take revenge on him."

"Nonsense! Are you going to spend your life looking for someone you never set eyes on? An insane enterprise, destined to fail."

"I'll go after him to the end."

"You're going to fight on your own a whole regime, with an army and a police force and huge quantities of terrible weapons?"

"You say that, when you're the one who taught us that the true Muslim is a nation unto himself? Has not the Truth, Blessed and Almighty, said, *How often a little company has overcome a numerous company, by God's leave!* (God has spoken truly)?"

"God indeed speaks truly but your fight with the regime will cost you your life. You'll die, my son. They'll kill you the first time you confront them."

Taha was silent and looked into the sheikh's face, for the mention of death had had its effect on him. Then he said, "I'm dead now. They killed me in detention. When they trespass on your honor laughing, when they give you a woman's name and make you answer with your new name and you have to because of the savagery of the torture. . . . They called me Fawziya. Every day they used to beat me and make me say, 'I'm a woman and my name is Fawziya.' You want me to forget all that and go on living?"

He spoke bitterly and bit his lower lip with his teeth. The sheikh said, "Listen, Taha. This is my last word, to clear my conscience before Our Lord, Mighty and Glorious: getting involved in fighting this regime means certain death."

"I'm not afraid of death any longer. I've made up my mind to be a martyr. I hope with all my heart to die a martyr and enter Paradise."

There was silence between them and suddenly the sheikh got up from his place and went over to Taha and looked at him for a short while. Then he hugged him hard and smiled and said, "God bless you, my son. This is what real faith does to those who have it. Go home now and pack your bag for a journey. Tomorrow morning I'll come and go with you."

"Where to?"

The sheikh's smile broadened and he whispered, "Don't ask. Do as I say and you'll find everything out in due course."

Taha deduced that the sheikh's opposition to him at the beginning had been a stratagem to test the strength of his determination. Now, the following day, they were sitting next to each other in silence in the crowded metro car, the sheikh looking out of the window while Taha stared without seeing at the passengers, a disturbing question repeating itself in his mind: Where was the sheikh taking him? Of course, he trusted him, but fear and misgivings afflicted him all the same. He felt as though he was proceeding to some perilous point of no return that would be fundamental in his life. He felt a shudder when the sheikh said to him,

"Be ready to get out at the next station, Turah el Asmant."

The station bears the name of the cement company that the Swiss built in the twenties and which was then nationalized after the Revolution and increased its production to become one of the biggest cement factories in the Arab World. Thereafter, like the other major companies, it had been subjected to the Open Door Policy and privatization, with foreign companies buying numerous shares. The metro line goes right through its middle: on the right are the administrative buildings and the giant furnaces and on the left stretches the vast desert, bounded by mountains throughout which are scattered the quarries where the huge rocks are blasted with dynamite, then moved onto large transporters to be incinerated in the cement kilns.

Sheikh Shakir got down, Taha with him, and they crossed the metro station in the direction of the mountains and walked out into the desert. The sun was hot, the air laden with the dust that covers the whole area, and Taha felt a dryness in his throat and a low, continuous pain in the top of his stomach, followed by nausea and coughing. The sheikh said jokingly, *"Sweet patience,* champion! The air here is polluted with cement dust. You'll get used to it soon. Anyway, we're almost there."

They stopped in front of a small rocky hillock and waited a few minutes. Then the sound of an engine reached their ears. A large rock-moving truck approached and stopped in front of them. The driver was a young man dressed in workers' blue overalls that were worn and faded with use. He exchanged greetings quickly with the sheikh, who looked at him appraisingly and said, "God and Paradise," to which the driver replied with a smile, "Patience and Victory."

These were the passwords, and the sheikh took Taha's hand and climbed up with him into the driver's cabin. The three said nothing and the truck proceeded along a mountain track. Other transporters belonging to the company passed them until the driver turned off onto a narrow unmetaled sidetrack on which they drove for more than half an hour. Taha almost confessed his anxiety to the sheikh, but he saw that the latter was absorbed in reciting the Qu'ran from a small copy in his hand. Eventually, there appeared in the distance indistinct shapes that gradually became clearer and turned out to be a group of houses built of red brick. The truck stopped, Taha and the sheikh got down, and the driver bade them farewell, then turned and went back.

The streets had the look of any urban slum—conspicuous poverty, puddles of water in the dirt lanes, chickens and ducks running around outside the houses, small children playing barefoot, and veiled women sitting at the doors. The sheikh strode out with the confidence of one who knows a place well and entered one of the houses, Taha behind him. They went through the door into a spacious room empty but for a small desk and a blackboard that hung on the wall. On the floor were spread large yellow rush mats on which were sitting a group of bearded young men in white gallabiyas who all jumped up to greet Sheikh Shakir, embracing him and kissing him one after the other. The oldest among them, a huge, tall man aged around forty with a large black beard and wearing a dark green sash over his white gallabiya hung back a little. He had a scar extending from his right eyebrow to the top of his forehead like the remains of a large old wound and this prevented him from fully closing his eye. On seeing Sheikh Shakir, the man whooped with joy and said in his husky voice, "Peace be upon you! Where have you been, Master? We've been waiting for you two whole weeks."

"Only urgent necessity has kept me from you, Bilal. How are you and your brothers?"

"Praise God, we're fine, God willing."

"And how is your work?"

"As you will have read in the newspapers—from success to success, thanks be to God."

Sheikh Shakir put his arm around Taha and told the man, smiling, "This is the Taha el Shazli whom I spoke to you about, Bilal. A fine example of the courageous, pious, observant young man—and we give precedence over God to none."

He brought Taha forward to shake the man's hand and Taha felt the man's strong grip and looked at his disfigured face as Sheikh Shakir's words resounded in his ears, "Taha, God willing, I introduce you to your brother in God, Sheikh Bilal, the commander of the camp. Here with Sheikh Bilal you will learn, God willing, how to take what is yours and how to wreak vengeance on all the tyrants."

Souad woke up and opened her eyes with difficulty. She had stomach pains, nausea, and a headache, and her throat was dry and hurting her. Little by little she realized that she was in a hospital. The room was large, the ceiling high, and there were old chairs and a small table in the corner. The double doors with two round glass portholes looked like those in an operating theater in an Egyptian movie from the forties. Next to the bed stood a stout nurse with a snub nose. She bent over Souad and put her hand on her face, then smiled and said, "Praise God you're fine. God's been good to you. You hemorrhaged badly."

"Liar!" shouted Souad in a strangled voice. The nurse leaped back. "You aborted me by force. I'll see you get hell!"

The nurse left the room. An insane anger swept over Souad and she started kicking her feet and shouting in a loud voice, "Criminals! You aborted me! Get me the Emergency Response Police! I'll put you all in jail!" The door soon opened and a young doctor appeared. He came up to her, the nurse following. Souad shouted, "I was pregnant and you aborted me by force!"

The doctor smiled, obviously lying and scared. He said in an embarrassed voice, "You had a hemorrhage, Madame. Calm yourself. Excitement's not good for you."

Souad exploded again. She shouted and abused them and wept. The doctor and the nurse left. Then the door opened again and her brother Hamidu appeared, with Fawzi, Hagg Azzam's son. Hamidu hurried in and kissed her. Clinging to him, she burst into passionate tears.

Hamidu's face crumpled and he shut his mouth tight and said nothing. Fawzi calmly pulled up the chair from the end of the room and sat down beside the bed. Then he leaned back and said in measured tones, enunciating the words clearly as though he were giving a lesson to children, "Listen, Souad. Everything is fated and allotted. Hagg Azzam agreed with you about something and you broke the agreement and 'the one who begins is the more unjust.'"

"God take revenge on you and on your father, you criminals, you sons of bitches!"

"Shut your mouth!"

Fawzi shouted these words angrily, his face frowning and looking stern and cruel. Then he said nothing for a little, sighed, and resumed his lecture.

"Despite your rudeness, the Hagg has dealt with you as God's Law requires. You had a hemorrhage and you would have died, so we took you to the hospital and the doctor was forced to carry out an abortion. The hospital paperwork is on file and the doctor's report is on file. Tell her, Hamidu."

Hamidu lowered his head in silence and Fawzi's voice rose again.

"My father, Hagg Azzam, is a God-fearing man. He has divorced you and given you more than your rights, God recompense him. The deferred payment and the support money we have calculated as God's Law requires, and there's something extra as a gift from us. Your brother Hamidu has a check for twenty thousand pounds. The hospital bill is paid and we've taken all your things from the house and we'll send them to you in Alexandria."

A deep silence prevailed. Souad, broken now, was weeping quietly. Fawzi got up. At that moment, he appeared strong and decisive, as though everything in the world depended on whatever utterance he might make. He took two steps in the direction of the door. Then he turned as though remembering something and said, "Captain Hamidu. Get your sister to calm down; she's a bit unbalanced. The whole thing's over and done with and she's got what she's owed to the last cent. We started on a friendly basis and we've finished on a friendly basis. If you and your sister make problems or start talking, we know how to put you in your place. This country is ours, Hamidu. We have a long reach and we have all kinds of ways of dealing with people. Choose the kind you want."

He walked slowly and deliberately away until he exited the room, the flaps of the door slapping behind him.

As a man will flick off with his fingers a few flecks of dust that have clung to the breast of his smart suit and continue on his way as though nothing had happened, so Hagg Azzam got rid of Souad Gaber and was able to erase his affection for her. It was the memory of her delectable, hot, supple body that kept coming back to him and he made a massive and painful effort to forget her, recalling deliberately her savage, hateful face during the final scene and imagining the problems and scandals that would have plagued him if he hadn't got rid of her. He consoled himself with the thought that his marriage to her, while providing him with wonderful times, hadn't cost him a great deal. He also thought that his experience with her might be replicable. Beautiful poor women were in good supply and wedlock was holy, not something anyone could be reproached for.

By means of such thoughts he had tried to wipe the image of Souad from his memory, sometimes succeeding and sometimes failing, and he had thrown himself into the maelstrom of his work in order to forget. With the opening of the Tasso automobile agency due in a few days he had set up an operations room in his office with his sons Fawzi and Quadri. As though going to war, he had overseen the preparations for the huge party at the Hotel Semiramis, personally inviting all the big shots in the city. All had come—present and former ministers, high-ranking civil servants, and editors-in-chief of the main national news-papers, their friendship costing him dozens of cars that he gave away free or for a symbolic price. This was done with the agreement of the Japanese officials and sometimes at their suggestion.

The party went on to a late hour with the television broadcasting bits of it as paid advertisements and the newspapers giving it full coverage. A well-known economic columnist at *al-Akhbar* newspaper wrote a piece presenting the opening of the Tasso agency as a courageous, patriotic step, boldly undertaken by the authentically Egyptian businessman Hagg Azzam to break the monopoly by Western cars. The columnist urged all Egyptian businessmen to choose the same righteous, difficult path as Hagg Azzam for the sake of Egypt's rebirth and the health of its econo-my. For two whole weeks the newspapers were filled with pictures of Hagg Azzam and statements by him. The picture that was published of the signing of the contract for the agency was exceptionally expressive in that it showed Hagg Azzam with his huge body, plebeian face, and dart-ing, cunning glances and sitting next to him Mr. Yen Ki, chairman of Tasso's board with his slight Japanese build, his straightforward look, and his serious, refined face—as though the difference between the two men epitomized the vast distance between what happens in Japan and what happens in Egypt.

From the first months the agency realized incredible sales exceeding all expectations, the profits pouring down on Hagg Azzam, who received his Lord's grace with gratitude, paying out from them tens of thousands of pounds in charity. The Japanese side offered Azzam additional projects for service stations in Cairo and Alexandria and Hagg Azzam lived his most glorious days ever with only one thing to spoil them, something he had tried to ignore but in vain. El Fouli had hounded him for a meeting and Azzam kept putting him off till he could do so no longer. In the end, he agreed and went to meet El Fouli at the Sheraton, having prepared himself ahead of time for a difficult interview.

The hallway, dark in the middle of the day and crowded to overflowing, appeared more like the third-class car of a train to Upper Egypt than the reception area of a hospital: the women were standing, loaded with their sick children, the smell of sweat was stifling, the floor and walls were filthy, the few male nurses who were organizing entry to the examination room were abusing the women and shoving them, and there was endless fighting, screaming, and tumult. Hatim Rasheed and Abduh, along with Hidiya, arrived carrying the child, who never stopped crying. They stood for a while in the crowd and then Hatim went up to one of the nurses and asked to meet the director of the hospital. The nurse looked at him with annoyance and told him the director wasn't there. Abduh almost got into a fight with him when the nurse told him that he had to wait his turn for the child to be seen. Hatim then went out to the nearest public telephone and called several numbers from the small notebook that he always kept in his pocket with the result that the hospital's deputy director came out to them and received them warmly, apologizing for the absence of the director. The deputy director was a fat man with a pale complexion whose face gave an impression of good-heartedness and straightforwardness. He examined the child carefully, then said in an anxious voice, "Unfortunately, the case is advanced and critical. The boy is dehydrated and feverish."

He wrote out some papers, which he gave to Abduh, who was a nervous wreck, smoking incessantly and railing at his wife. Then he took the child in his arms and ran with the nurse, to whom the doctor's concern over the case had transmitted itself, and they put the child in the intensive care ward. Glucose tubes were put into his small arms, but his face was extremely pale, his eyes sunken, and his crying was getting softer. Everyone felt heavily despondent. In response to Abduh's question, the nurse said, "The treatment will begin to show results after at least two hours. Our Lord is merciful."

Silence reigned again and Hidiya started to cry quietly. Hatim took Abduh aside, thrust a bundle of banknotes into his pocket, and patted him on the shoulder saying, "Take these, Abduh, for the hospital charges and if you need anything, please call me. I have to go to the paper. I'll call you to find out how you're doing tonight."

"I wish I'd met you a long time ago!"

"Why?"

"My life would have been completely different."

"You're still alive. Go ahead and change it."

"Change what, Busayna? I'm sixty-five years old. 'The End,' you know."

"Who says? You could live another twenty, thirty years. It's God that decides how long people live."

"That would be nice. One would really like to live another thirty years, at least."

They laughed together, he in his husky voice, she in her repeated, melodious chirrups. They were lying naked on the bed and he was holding her in his arms enjoying the touch of her smooth, thick hair on his arm. They had freed themselves utterly from any feeling of the privacy of each other's bodies and would spend hours completely naked. She would make him coffee and prepare his glasses of whisky and *hors d'œuvres* and from time to time they would sleep together. He might make love to her, but often they would just lie like that. He would turn off the light in the room and watch her face in the low, tremulous light that came from the street. At such moments she appeared unreal to him, a beautiful apparition, a night creature that with the first light of dawn would disappear as suddenly as it had come. They would talk, her voice in the darkness sounding deep, sweet, and warm. In a serious tone she said, staring at the ceiling, "When are we leaving?"

"Leaving for where?"

"You promised me we'd go somewhere together."

Gazing at her face, he asked her, "You still hate this country?"

She nodded her head, looking at the ceiling.

"I can't fathom your generation. In my day, love for one's country was like a religion. Lots of young people died struggling against the British."

Busayna sat up and said, "You made demonstrations to throw out the British? Okay, they went. Does that mean the country's all right?"

"The reason the country's gone downhill is the absence of democracy. If there were a real democratic system, Egypt would be a great power. Egypt's curse is dictatorship and dictatorship inevitably leads to poverty, corruption, and failure in all fields."

"That's big talk. I dream in my own size. I want to live comfortably and have a family. A husband who loves me, children to raise, and a lovely, comfy little home instead of living on the roof. I'd like to go to a decent country, where there's no dirt, no poverty, and no injustice. You know, the brother of one of my friends failed the general secondary exam three years in a row. Then he went off to Holland, married a Dutch woman, and settled down there. He tells us that overseas there's no injustice and doing people out of what's theirs, like here. There everyone gets what's his and people respect one another. Even the sweeper in the street gets respect. That's why I want to go abroad. I want to live there and work and become really respectable. Earn my living from my work instead of going to the storeroom with someone like Talal so that he'll give me ten pounds. Just think—he used to give me ten pounds a time, the cost of two packs of Marlboros. I was really stupid."

"You were in need and when you're in need you don't think. Busayna, I don't want you to live in the past. Everything that happened to you is a page that's been turned and is done with. Think of the future. We have each other now and I'll never leave you."

There was silence for a moment. Then Zaki went on gaily, to dispel the gloom, "A month or two from now I'll be getting a big sum of money and I'll take you abroad."

"Honestly?"

"Honestly."

"Where will we go?"

"France."

She screamed and clapped her hands like a child. Then she said, joking slyly, "But you just pull yourself together and watch out for your health so you don't flake out on me there. That would be a real mess!"

When she laughs, the muscles of her face contract, sweat stands out on her forehead, and she looks somewhat wild and strange as though she'd been taken by surprise by happiness and decided to grab it hard so it couldn't get away. Zaki took her in his arms and whispered, "Okay? Agreed?"

"Agreed."

He started with her hands. He began kissing her fingers one by one, then moved to her palm and arms and full, smooth chest. When he reached her neck and raised her thick hair to take her lovely small ears in his mouth, he felt her body burn with desire beneath his.

It started with a whisper. "Whisper" is the right word—a very slight sound that came suddenly and then was cut off while Zaki was devouring Busayna's lips in a heated kiss. Seconds passed while they embraced, and then the sound was repeated, clearly this time. The door to the room in which they were sleeping was open and it came to Zaki's mind in a flash that someone was moving around in the reception room. He leaped up naked from the bed and Busayna let out a high-pitched scream, leaping to put her clothes on any old how over her naked body. Then followed terrifying, nightmarish scenes—tense moments that Zaki and Busayna would never forget. The light went on in the room and a uniformed police officer appeared, police goons behind him. Dawlat came forward from among them, a malign, gloating smile on her face. In a moment her voice was raised, high-pitched and hateful as death: "Scandal and shamelessness! Every day bringing a prostitute and spending the night with her. Enough filth, my good man! Shame on you!"

"Shut your mouth!"

Zaki shouted this in his first reaction. He had gotten over his astonishment and appeared extremely agitated, his whole naked body shaking and his eyes bulging with rage. Unconsciously he put out his hand to take his pants, shouting as he put them on, "What's going on? What's this farce? Who gave you permission to enter my office? Do you have a warrant from the prosecutor?"

Zaki shouted this in the face of the young officer, whose features from the start were hostile, and who replied in a calm, challenging tone, "Are you teaching me how to do my job? I don't need a warrant from the prosecutor. This lady is your sister and lives with you and she presented a complaint against you for practicing indecency in her house and requested an official inspection as she's bringing a case for sequestration against you."

"Nonsense. This is my private office and she does not live with me here."

"But she opened the door with her keys and let us in."

"Even if she has a key, it's my office, in my name."

"Then you can prove that in the report."

"Prove what? I'll see you get hell! You're going to pay the price for violating the sanctity of people's homes."

"The sanctity of prostitutes, if you want the truth!" cried Dawlat, her eyes staring, and she moved toward him warily.

"Shut your mouth, I tell you!"

"You shut your mouth, you dirty old man!"

"Silence, madame, if you please!" shouted the officer at Dawlat, faking anger to mask that he was on her side. Then he turned to Zaki and said, "Listen, mister. You're an old man and there's no need for unpleasantness."

"What exactly do you want?"

"We'll just make our inspection and take a couple of words from you."

"What's to be inspected? Tell me you've been put up to this. That lizard put you up to this."

"You seem to be a rude person. Listen, because I'm telling you for the last time. Give yourself a trouble-free evening."

"You're threatening me. I just have to talk on the telephone and I'll teach you your place."

"Is that so? Okay, I apologize," replied the officer furiously. Then he said, "Come along, momma's boy, down to the station, you and your prostitute."

"I warn you not to use words you'll be held to strict account for later. And you don't have any right to arrest us."

"I know whether I have the right or not."

The officer turned and said to his goons, "Bring them." The goons had been waiting for these words like a secret code and fell on Zaki and Busayna. Zaki resisted and started uttering threats and shouting in protest, but the men grabbed him firmly, while Busayna screamed, beat her cheeks, and pleaded with them as they dragged her outside.

In the beginning Taha felt constrained, but this went away as the days passed and as he got used to the camp's strict regime — rising at dawn, performing the prayer, reciting the Qur'an, breakfast; then three hours of nonstop, demanding exercise (physical fitness and martial arts). After this, the brothers gathered to take classes (jurisprudence, exegesis, Qur'anic sciences, hadith) given by Sheikh Bilal and other scholars. Afternoons were devoted to arms training. The brothers would board a large bus (on which was written Turah Cement Company of Egypt) and go into the heart of the mountains where they practiced shooting and making and using bombs. The camp's rhythm was exhaustingly rapid and Taha had no time to think. Even in the hour set aside for chatting, after the evening prayer, the conversation of the brothers usually turned to discussion of religious issues, during which the legal proof for the infidel nature of the regime and the necessity of fighting and destroying it would be presented.

When the time came to sleep, the brothers separated. The married ones went to the family dwellings at the foot of the mountain, while the bachelors slept in a small building set aside for them. Only then, after the lights had been extinguished and silence reigned, would Taha lie on his bed in the dark and recall with total lucidity the events of his life, as though an amazing, illuminating energy were suddenly released from his memory, and he would see Busayna el Sayed and be overwhelmed with tenderness. Sometimes he even smiled as he remembered their good times. Then anger would sweep over him as her face contemplated him for the last time and she said contemptuously, "It's over between us, Taha. Each of us goes his own way." All of a sudden memories of his detention would rain down on his head like incessant blows—the beatings and the abuse; the feeling after each occasion on which they violated him sexually that he was weak, exhausted, and broken; his breaking into tears and pleading with the soldiers to stop inserting the thick stick into his body; his soft, stammering voice when they told him to say, "I'm a woman" and then beat him again, and again asked him his name, to which he would reply, in a dead voice, "Fawziya," causing them to laugh loudly, as though they were watching a satirical film. Taha would remember all that and lose his ability to sleep. He would stay awake, re-opening his old wounds. His face in the dark would crumple, his breath speed up. He would gasp as though running and an intense hatred would possess him which would not abate until he thought of the voices of the officers, categorizing, distinguishing, and storing them away carefully in his memory. After this a desire so burning that his body almost shuddered with the pressure would sweep over him, as he hankered for revenge and pictured himself exacting exemplary punishment from those who had tortured and violated him.

This thirst for revenge took him over and drove him on, so that he made amazing strides in the camp's training exercises. Despite his youth he learned to beat many who had greater experience of physical combat than he, and within a few months he excelled at using regular rifles, semi-automatics, and automatics, and had learned how to make hand grenades easily and well. His rapid progress amazed all the brothers. Once, after he had completed a shooting exercise in which he had missed only one out of twenty shots, Sheikh Bilal came up to him, patted him on the shoulder, and said, his eyebrow scar twitching as usual when he was excited, "God bless you, Taha. You've become a crack shot."

"So when are you going to let me participate in the gihad?" Taha replied boldly, taking advantage of the opportunity to ask a question that had been occupying his mind. Sheikh Bilal was silent for a moment. Then he whispered affectionately, "Don't rush things, my son. Everything in its own time."

He left quickly, as though to cut the conversation short, leaving Taha unhappy with the ambiguous answer. He was thirsting for his revenge and felt he was totally ready to go on operations, so why all this delay? He wasn't any worse than his colleagues who went out to gihad, then returned to the camp full of what they'd done and received the congratulations of their brothers. After that Taha went to Sheikh Bilal more than once to urge him to send him out on an operation, but the latter continued to put him off with ambiguous answers until, on the final occasion, Taha got angry and shouted vehemently, "'Soon, soon.' When is this soon going to come? If you think I'm no good for gihad, why don't you tell me and I'll leave the camp."

Sheikh Bilal's smile spread, as though he was happy at Taha's enthusiasm, and he said, "Be on your way, Taha, and you'll hear good news, if God wills."

And indeed, not a week went by before one of the brothers informed him that Sheikh Bilal was asking for him. As soon as he had finished the noon prayer, he rushed to the sheikh's office—a cramped room containing an old desk, a number of worn-out chairs, and a rush mat on which the sheikh was sitting reciting the Qur'an. He was deeply absorbed in his chanting and only became aware of Taha's presence next to him a few moments later. He smiled in welcome and sat him down beside him.

"I have sent for you about an important matter."

"I'm yours to command."

"It is for God alone to command. Listen, my son, we've decided to give you a bride."

The sheikh said this suddenly and laughed, but Taha didn't laugh. His dark face grew stern and he said warily, "I don't understand."

"You're going to get married, my son. Don't you know what marriage is?"

At this, Taha's voice rose: "No, Master, I don't understand. I don't understand how I can beg you to give me permission for gihad, and you talk to me of marriage! Did I come here to get married? I don't understand it at all, unless you just brought me here to make fun of me."

For the first time, the sheikh's face contracted with anger and he shouted, "It is inappropriate for you, Taha, to talk to me in that fashion, and I would be grateful if you would keep a hold on yourself in the future or I shall lose my temper with you. You are not the only one whom they have tortured at National Security. They have tortured thousands of brothers. I myself bear the traces of torture on my face as you see, but I don't go out of my mind and scream every day in the faces of my sheikhs. Do you think that I am stopping you from going to gihad? As God knows, my son, the matter is not in my hands. I do not have decision-making power over operations. In fact, I don't even know about them till the very last minute. I am a camp commander, Taha, and I am not even a member of the Gamaa's Consultative Council. Please take that in and give us both a rest. I am not the one who will make the decision. All I can do is put your name forward to the brothers on the Gamaa Council. I have been persistent in doing that and I have written a number of reports on your courage and your progress in training, but they have not decided to send you yet. So it's not my fault as you think, even though on the basis of my experience I believe that they will send you soon, God willing."

Taha said nothing and bowed his head for a little. Then he said in a low voice, "I apologize, Master, for my excitable manner. God knows how I love and respect you, Sheikh Bilal."

"Don't worry about it, my son," muttered Sheikh Bilal, who went on telling his prayer beads. Taha continued in an affectionate tone, as though he wanted to wipe out the traces of the tiff, "But I really do find the marriage business strange."

"What's strange about it? Marriage is one of God's customs for His creatures. He, Glorious and Almighty, made it lawful for the sake of the righteousness of the individual and of Islam. You are a young man and have natural needs. Your marriage is an act of obedience to God and His Messenger for which you will be rewarded, God willing. The Chosen One—God bless him and give him peace—said in a sound hadith, 'He among you who is capable of marriage, let him marry.' And he has commanded us—God bless him and give him peace—to facilitate and expedite marriage in order to protect the Muslims from abomination. Here we live and die according to the path laid down by God and His Messenger and we do not deviate from it one jot, God willing. I propose for you a righteous, virtuous sister —we give precedence over God to none."

"I have to marry a woman I don't know?" responded Taha without thinking.

Sheikh Bilal smiled and said, "You'll get to meet her, God willing. She is Sister Radwa Abu el Alaa, an outstanding example of the Muslim woman. She was married to Brother Hassan Nur el Din from Asyiut. When he achieved martyrdom, God have mercy on him, she was pregnant with her small son and she came to live the life of Islam here with us."

Taha said nothing and seemed unconvinced, so Sheikh Bilal went on, "God forbid, my son, that I should impose anything on you. You'll meet Radwa and see her face and talk with her, as the Pure Law requires. Then you may take your decision with complete freedom. I hope, Taha, that you will review the book *Marriage in Islam* that we distributed to you in class. You should know too, my son, that marriage to the widow of a martyr and taking care of his orphan son will double your reward, with God's permission."

Close to midnight, the child's condition got worse and the indicators on the screens in intensive care started to register disturbances in the breathing and pulse. The doctor on duty was called and she quickly came and prescribed an intravenous injection. The nurse gave this to the child and his condition improved a little, but after less than an hour it deteriorated again and he soon departed this life. The nurse burst into tears, covered his little face with the sheet, and came out of the room.

As soon as Hidiya saw her, she let out an agonized, high-pitched scream that resounded throughout the hospital. Then she squatted on the ground, covered her head with her hands, and started wailing. As for Abd Rabbuh, his dark face crumpled and he ground his teeth so hard that they made an audible sound. He crushed the pack of cigarettes in his hand and ripped it to shreds, so that the tobacco scattered between his fingers like dust. He made a superhuman effort not to cry, but the tears flowed from his eyes in spite of himself; then he surrendered completely and sobbed out loud. Everyone there wept—cleaners and nurses and patients' families. Even the doctor took off her glasses to wipe away her tears. Abd Rabbuh and his wife Hidiya were obliged to keep the child's corpse in the hospital's mortuary till it could be buried in the morning and this created another painful scene, for when the small body was placed in the midst of the adult corpses, the aged mortuary operator (who by virtue of the nature of his work was accustomed to the sight of death) could not contain himself and started repeating in a trembling, agitated voice "There is no god but God" and "We are from Him and to Him we shall return."

The residents of the Yacoubian Building roof had heard the news somehow and all stayed up. They opened the doors of their rooms and waited in silence with bowed heads as though at a wake. Some of them (those who owned tape recorders) played recordings of the Noble Qur'an at high volume, so that it echoed around the roof.

A little before the dawn prayer, Abd Rabbuh and Hidiya appeared on the roof, worn-out with pain and exhaustion, and all the residents rushed to give them their condolences, the sorrow rekindled. The men embraced Abduh and squeezed his hand (they were all sincere in their reaction, including even the most ferocious and aggressive among them such as Ali the Driver, from whose mouth the smell of cheap alcohol wafted as usual but who cried as hard as a lost child). As soon as El Shazli, the old doorkeeper, with his white mustaches and tall, emaciated figure, approached the grieving father and shook his hand—the two were bound by a special affection—Abduh embraced him hard, buried his face in his white gallabiya, and said with his Sa'idi accent, "My boy's gone, Uncle!"

The women knew how to give expression to disaster. Their high-pitched cries broke out, shattering the peace, and many beat their cheeks hard till they fell to the ground. Little by little, the outpouring of grief grew quiet, and as usually happens on these occasions the men insisted to Abduh that he take his wife to rest a little as they had a hard day ahead of them, and in the end the two complied and went into their room. Their light remained lit, however, till the morning, as they did not sleep. In fact, they became wrapped in a long conversation that soon turned angry and eventually became a bitter and violent fight whose echoes could be heard all over the roof. Hidiya's voice could be heard raised in reproach and challenge, while Abduh's voice grew lower and lower until it became completely silent. On the following day, once the burial and mourning procedures were over, the roof people were taken aback to find a large truck pull up at night in front of the building. Then they saw Abduh helping the workers to move the furniture from their room. The residents inquired anxiously and Abduh informed them that they were moving to another room, in Imbaba. His face was dejected and his manner so off-putting as to stop them from showing their surprise or even from bidding him farewell with appropriate warmth.

"You've got off to a bad start, Azzam."

"God forbid, Kamal Bey! I stand by my word, but the matter needs time."

They were sitting in the Sheraton restaurant and the atmosphere was tense. Azzam started by talking about something else, but Kamal el Fouli frowned and said sharply, "Don't try to distract me with other things! I'm not a child. You made an agreement and you went back on your agreement. I gave you the contract three months ago for you to sign with the Big Man and you're playing for time."

"Kamal Bey, shame on you to say so! I have to pass the matter by the Japanese partner and I'm waiting for the right moment."

"What have the Japanese got to do with it? The contract's between you and the Big Man for a percentage of the profits."

"My dear sir, the Japanese have to know everything. If I did anything behind their back, they might cancel the agency agreement."

Kamal el Fouli took a long draw on the waterpipe, then placed the big mouthpiece on the table and stood up suddenly. His son and the guards at the neighboring table rose too. He said resolutely, as he adjusted his clothes prior to leaving, "You're playing with fire, Azzam, and I'm surprised, because you're an intelligent man. You have to understand that the ones who put you into the People's Council can take you out of it."

"Are you threatening me, Kamal Bey?"

"Take it any way you like."

Hagg Azzam rose and held out his arms to grasp El Fouli's shoulder in an attempted embrace, saying, "My dear sir, please, don't make a big thing of this."

"Goodbye."

El Fouli turned to leave, but Hagg Azzam held on to his shoulder and said, "My dear sir, everything's give and take. I swear to Almighty God, I'm going to keep my promise."

El Fouli shook his arm off angrily, but Azzam moved closer and whispered almost pleadingly, "Kamal Bey, listen to me, please. I have a request that will make things easier for both of us."

El Fouli looked at him questioningly, the anger still on his face. Azzam said, "I want to meet the Big Man."

"The Big Man doesn't meet anyone."

"Kamal Bey, please help me. I'd like to meet His Excellency and explain the situation myself. By the bread and salt we've eaten together, old fellow, don't refuse my request."

El Fouli stared at him with a deep, searching look, as though probing his depths for the last time. Then he said as he left, "We'll see."

It wasn't easy for Hagg Azzam to just give up a quarter of the agency's profits, but at the same time it wasn't in his power to refuse outright. His assessment was that they would not start to attack him as long as they had a hope, even if it was small, that he would pay. He had requested a meeting with the Big Man and insisted, firstly to gain time, and secondly because he had a strange but firm feeling that if he could meet the Big Man face to face, he would succeed in persuading him to lower the percentage. He also had a final, important objective: he wanted to be sure that there really was a Big Man. Wasn't it a possibility that El Fouli was using the Big Man's name without his knowledge? Only a slight possibility, of course, but it was there.

It took a few months and a number of telephone calls in which Azzam put pressure on El Fouli to fix an appointment for him with the Big Man and then one morning the telephone rang in Azzam's office and he heard the secretary's smooth voice saying, "Hagg Azzam? Greetings. Kamal Bey will speak to you."

He heard El Fouli's terse voice saying, "Your appointment with the Big Man is Thursday at ten in the morning. Be ready in your office and we'll send you a car to take you."

Dawlat had laid her plan carefully and been able by means of influence and bribes to get all the officers on her side. As a result, they

treated Zaki el Dessouki with the utmost boorishness and imperti-
nence. They prevented him from using the telephone and exchanged
comments at his expense: "He fancies himself a Valentino!"

"So you must be the famous Drinking Sheikh then!"

"I bet the equipment's kaput and you have to do it by hand!"

They let out loud laughs, followed by a clearing of throats and
bursts of coughing, Dawlat joining in the laughter to flatter and
encourage them, and to gloat. Zaki said nothing. He didn't reply to
them. The wall that he had tried to maintain around himself had fallen
and it was all over, and he realized that if he resisted, it would only
increase their vile behavior. He also felt extremely sorry for Busayna,
who never stopped sobbing. The officer who had arrested them said to
him spitefully, "What do you say, Mr. La-di-da? Are you going to mend
your ways?"

Zaki answered him in a low voice, "Your conduct is unlawful and I
shall make a complaint against you."

The officer shouted, "Still playing the big shot? You're a real big-
mouth. Have some shame, man! One foot in this world and the other
in the next! Someone your age ought to be spending all his time at the
mosque, not being brought in naked from on top of a prostitute—and
still you have the gall to talk back?"

Busayna tried to plead with the officer, but he rebuked her sharply,
saying "Shut your mouth, whore, or do you want me to make you out a
morals charge right away?"

The two gave up completely and answered the officer's questions.
Zaki affirmed in his statement that the complaint was deceitful and that
Dawlat was not living with him in the office. He explained Busayna's
being with him by saying that she was the daughter of a friend of his,
that she'd quarreled with her family, and that he'd invited her to his
apartment so that he could make peace between them. Then he signed
the police report, as did Busayna and Dawlat (the plaintiff), who left

after thanking the officers and satisfying herself that things were going properly. After all these insults Zaki swallowed his pride and started pleading with the officer until in the end the latter permitted him, grudgingly, to use the telephone. He called a friend of his who was a former Appeals Court judge and asked for help. The judge came quickly, his face still showing traces of sleep, and went to the office of the station head. The latter summoned Zaki, invited him to sit down, insisted on ordering him a cup of coffee, and gave him a cigarette (he had left his behind in the office during the brouhaha). Then the station head looked at him and said smilingly, in a quiet voice, "Naturally, I apologize for any affronts that my colleagues may have committed, but as you know the incident touches on morality and it's a tricky thing. The officers here are jealous of our traditions and we're all religious people, praise God."

Zaki didn't say a word. He smoked, staring at the officer, while the judge broke in to say, "I do hope, sir, we can clear all this up. I'd be very grateful."

"Your Excellency's requests are my command, but unfortunately the report has been entered already with a serial number and it can't be deleted. Your Excellency knows the procedures as well as I do. All we can do is let him and the girl go tonight, and when they turn up tomorrow morning to go before the magistrate, I'll talk to him and have him suspend the investigation, God willing."

Zaki and Busayna signed an undertaking to appear before the magistrate, and when they left the station Zaki shook his friend the judge's hand and thanked him. The other said, "Zaki Bey, we're brothers. You don't have to thank me. By the way, it's clear your sister Dawlat has influence and all the officers are in her pocket. The head of the station could have torn up the report in front of us if he'd wanted to."

Zaki smiled sadly and the judge said to comfort him, "Don't worry about it. First thing tomorrow I'll call the District Chief of Police's office and hopefully everything'll be okay."

Zaki thanked him again and walked beside Busayna in the direction of the Yacoubian Building. The light of morning had started to seep into Suleiman Basha, which was empty but for the municipal workers sluggishly sweeping and a few people who either had risen early for some reason or were returning from a long night out. Zaki felt extremely tired, dizzy, and nauseous. He was neither inclined to action nor angry. All he felt was that his stomach hurt, his mind was empty, and his thoughts were scattered. Slowly he became seized by the notion that heavy sorrows were bearing down on him, like the clouds that gather swiftly before a storm. Later he will go over a hundred times the insults and abuse that they directed at him; he will never forgive himself for having meekly submitted to them; he will make a comparison—so as to hurt himself cruelly—between the respect he had known all his life and the bruising contempt with which he had been treated at the police station, where they had treated him as though he were a pickpocket or a pimp. What really wrung his heart was that he had surrendered totally. He wouldn't have protested if they had beaten him. Why had he given up and turned into a limp rag in their hands? How had it come about that he had lost his willpower, and his self-respect had collapsed to such a degree? He ought to have resisted to the end, come what may, if not in defense of his honor, then in defense of Busayna's reputation, which they had ruined. What would she think of him now and how would he be able to meet her eyes, after he had failed to protect her or even defend her with a word?

He turned to look at her. She was walking silently next to him. Suddenly he heard himself saying in a hoarse voice, "Come on. Let's have breakfast at the Excelsior. You must be hungry."

She didn't say a word but followed him in silence into the large restaurant that faced the Yacoubian Building. It was totally empty at that time in the morning except for the cleaners, who were absorbed in washing the floor with soap and water, and a single elderly foreigner in the farthest part of the place, who was drinking coffee and reading a French newspaper. They sat facing each other at a table next to the window that looks out onto the intersection of Suleiman Basha and Adly streets. Zaki ordered two *thés complets* (with cake), and a heavy, painful silence hung over them until, having taken a sip from his cup of tea, he started speaking slowly, feeling his way: "Busayna, I beg you not to be upset. In life, one is subjected to many stupid situations and it would be wrong to dwell on them. Police officers in Egypt are like rabid dogs. Unfortunately, their powers are great because the Emergency Law. . . ."

What he was saying seemed ridiculous and inappropriate and Busayna continued to hang her head. The cup of tea and cake remained untouched in front of her and Zaki grasped just how downcast she was. He said, "I'd just like to know where Dawlat got a key to the office. She planned the whole filthy move to get me declared incompetent, but she'll lose the case. The lawyer assures me she'll lose."

He was using his chatter to hold his emotions at bay, trying to turn the painful situation into mere words, possibilities, and suppositions, in the hope that this would succeed in getting them out of the misery that oppressed them.

"The lawyer explained to me the legal conditions for incompetence. It's a complicated area and the courts don't make decisions lightly. Dawlat in her ignorance thinks it's easy."

His attempt failed and Busayna remained silent and didn't utter a word, as though she'd lost her capacity to hear or speak. Zaki leaned toward her across the table and for the first time, in the light, noticed her drawn, pallid color, her reddened eyes, and some scattered scratch marks on her face and neck that were the result of her struggle with the police. He smiled lovingly, took her hands in his, and whispered, "Busayna, if you love me, forget the whole stupid affair."

His tenderness was more than she could bear, as though it were the last light touch that the mountain, cracked and barely holding together, was waiting for before crumbling. She began to cry and said in a low voice, "All my life I've had bad luck in everything."

Taha met with Radwa in the presence of the sisters. He saw her without her veil and talked to her at length. He learned that she was three years older than he, and her deep knowledge of religion and her mild, calm way of talking pleased him. She told him about herself and her former husband, Nur el Din, and how they had killed him. She said, "In the papers they wrote that he fired at the officers and they'd been obliged to kill him, but God knows that that night he didn't fire a single shot. They knocked on the door and as soon as he opened it they fired several rounds with automatics. He was martyred immediately and three brothers with him. They killed them deliberately, and if they'd wanted they could have taken them alive."

Taha's face registered sorrow and he commented bitterly, "The new instructions are for them to kill as many Islamists as they can. They call it the 'blow to the heart' policy. If this infidel regime had dealt with the Jews that brutally, Jerusalem would have been liberated long ago."

Radwa hung her head and a heavy silence prevailed. Then she went on, as though she wanted to narrate everything that had happened in her life, "After the martyrdom of my late husband, my family tried to marry me to someone else and I found out that the groom they had in mind was a rich engineer, but he'd given up praying. My family tried to convince me that he would become observant once we got married, but I refused. I explained to them that a man who has abandoned prayer is an unbeliever in the eyes of the Law and it is not permitted for him to marry a Muslim woman, but they pressured me so hard my life became hell. The problem is my family isn't observant. They are good people, but unfortunately they are still in the Age of Ignorance.

I feared I would face discord over my religion and I wanted my son Abd el Rahman to grow up in obedience to God, so I contacted Sheikh Bilal and begged him to allow me to live in the camp."

"And what did your family do?"

"I sent someone to tell them I was all right and I'll go and visit them as soon as possible, God willing. I pray God to forgive me if I've done them harm."

Listening to her, he felt she was truthful and he liked a certain serious, sincere expression that appeared on her beautiful face while she was talking, as though she were a guilty child confessing frankly. He noted too that her body was full and well proportioned and her breasts swelling and firm (after which he reproached himself for the thought and asked God's forgiveness).

A few days later, Sheikh Bilal summoned him to his office and shook his hand in welcome. Then he looked at him for a moment with a mysterious smile on his face and said in a deep voice, as though resuming a conversation in which they had been engaged, "So . . . what do you think?"

"About what?"

The sheikh let out a loud laugh and said, "You don't know what I'm talking about, Sheikh Taha? I'm talking about Radwa, man."

Taha said nothing and smiled in embarrassment. The sheikh patted him on his shoulder and said, "Congratulations, my boy."

As soon as the evening prayer was over on Thursday, the brothers hovered around Taha congratulating him, while joyful ululations rang out from the room set aside for the women. For two days the women had exhausted themselves getting the bride ready and putting together her trousseau. After a quarter of an hour of ululations and congratulations, Sheikh Bilal sat down to perform the marriage ceremony. Radwa deputized Brother Hamza (like her, from Asyut) to conclude the marriage contract and other brothers volunteered themselves as witnesses. Sheikh Bilal made the normal short speech about marriage in God's Law, then placed Taha's hand in Hamza's and pronounced the words of the contract, which they repeated after him. When they had finished, Sheikh Bilal murmured "O God, make their union blessed, guide them in obedience to You, and provide them with righteous offspring!" Then he placed his hand on Taha's head, saying, "God bless you and your marriage and join you and your wife in good fortune!"

The brothers then all rushed to embrace the groom and congratulate him and the ululations rang out loud and the sisters started singing, while beating on tambourines,

We've come to you, we've come to you
So you greet us and we'll greet you.
If it weren't for the red red gold
She'd have stopped at some other wold.
If it weren't for the brown brown wheat
Your girls wouldn't be nice and sleek.

Taha was seeing the Islamic style of wedding celebration for the first time and was much affected by the joy of the sisters and their songs and by the enthusiasm of the brothers in their congratulations. Next the sisters accompanied the bride to her new home—a single spacious room leading to a small separate bathroom in the large building set aside for married couples (and which originally, in the days of the Swiss, had been a dwelling for the cement company's quarry workers; it had been left abandoned and completely forgotten about until some of the Islamist workers in the company took it and made it into a secret camp for the Gamaa). The women left and the mosque was quiet. The brothers sat with the groom and there was merry conversation interspersed with loud laughter. Then Sheikh Bilal stood up, saying, "Off with us then, brothers."

Taha tried to detain him, but the sheikh laughed and said, "On your wedding night you mustn't dissipate your energy in conversation!"

Laughing comments showered down from the brothers as they left the mosque. Taha bade them farewell and they departed. Left on his own, he began to feel terrified. He had imagined what he would do on the wedding night in numerous ways, then in the end he'd gone ahead and decided to let things proceed as God ordained, though the idea that he had no experience of women while his wife did have previous experience, perhaps making her hard to please, continued to make him anxious. As though reading his thoughts, Sheikh Bilal had taken him aside the day before the wedding and spoken to him of marriage and his wife's rights in the Law, stressing to him that there was nothing for a Muslim to feel shy about in marrying a woman who was not a virgin and that a Muslim woman's previous marriage ought not to be a weak point that her new husband could exploit against her. He said sarcastically, "The secularists accuse us of puritanism and rigidity, even while they suffer from innumerable neuroses. You'll find that if one of them marries a woman who was previously married, the thought of her first husband will haunt him and he may treat her badly, as though punishing her for her legitimate marriage. Islam has no such complexes."

These were all indirect messages, as Taha understood, about how he should treat Radwa. The sheikh reviewed with him what takes places between a man and a woman and explained to him the verse from The Cow chapter, *Your women are a tillage for you; so come unto your tillage as you wish, and forward for your souls*, expounding at length on the Qur'anic expression "and forward for your souls" through which the Lord, Sublime and Glorious, teaches us how to have intercourse with women in a gentle and humane fashion. The sheikh had an ability to talk about even the most precise details of sex in a serious and respectable way that did not offend one's modesty. Taha benefited from what he said and learned many things that he had not known before, which made him love the man even more, so that he thought to himself, "Even if my father himself were with me, he would not have done more for me than Sheikh Bilal has."

Now the wedding ceremonies were over and the brothers had left him on his own to face the critical moment. He climbed the stairs and knocked on the door and then entered the bride's room, where he found her sitting on the edge of the bed. She had taken her headscarf off. Her hair was black and smooth and reached her shoulders, and its blackness, next to the rosy whiteness of her skin, was fascinating. For the first time, Taha noticed her beautiful neck, her small hands, and her delicate fingertips. With his heart beating hard, he cleared his throat and said in an embarrassed voice, "Peace be upon you."

Radwa smiled, bowed her head, and whispered gently, blushing, "And upon you be peace and the mercy of God and His blessings."

Hatim Rasheed heard the news the next day. He had stayed late at the paper until the first edition was out and returned exhausted to the house about 4 A.M., telling himself, "I'll sleep, then check on Abduh in the morning." He woke late, showered, put on his clothes, and left to go to the hospital. In the lobby of the building he met El Shazli the doorkeeper, who said to him tersely, "Abduh's left you the keys of the room and the kiosk."

"What?" exclaimed Hatim, taken aback. The doorkeeper informed him of the death of the child and what had happened afterward. Hatim lit a cigarette and asked, making an effort to appear calm, "Did he tell you where he was going?"

"He said he was going to live in Imbaba and he refused to leave a new address."

Hatim went back, climbed up to the roof, and started asking the residents for Abduh's new address. He put up with their insolent looks and hostile responses (whose hidden message was "Leave Abduh alone. You've done enough to him.") but in the end got nowhere. In the evening he sat in his car in front of the locked kiosk on the off chance that Abduh might have forgotten something and come back to get it with the spare key that he kept. He went to the kiosk three days running but Abduh never showed up.

Hatim did not give up. He went on searching for him everywhere and with everyone who knew him but in vain. After a long week of searching, it became clear to him that Abduh had gone forever and a raging wave of sorrow and despair swept over him. Painful and conflicting feelings engulfed him: he missed Abduh—his ardor, his strong hard body, his good nature and purity, his husky voice and Sa'idi accent. He brimmed with compassion for him too because he knew how much he had loved his son and how much his death would grieve him. He felt regret that he had left him that day at the hospital and gone to the paper, telling himself, "I could have postponed the work to be with him at that difficult time. He needed me beside him but was ashamed to ask."

Day by day Hatim's agony increased. A sense of being truly unlucky possessed him. He had spent many years in misery and suffering before finding a biddable and sensitive companion who didn't cause problems, and as soon as his life had begun to settle down, the child had died and Abd Rabbuh had disappeared, leaving Hatim to start his wretched journey over again. He would have to cruise the streets of Downtown every night to pick up a Central Security recruit who might turn out to be a thief or a criminal who would beat him up or rob him, as had happened many times before. He would have to return to the Chez Nous in search of a barghal and to the Gebelawi baths in El Hussein to pick up some adolescent with whom to satisfy his lust, only to have to put up in return with his vulgarity and greediness. Why had he lost Abduh after he had loved him, and grown to feel at ease with him and planned their life together? Was it really so difficult for him to enjoy happiness with a lover

over time? If he were religious, he might have believed that his tribulations were a punishment for his homosexuality, but he knew at least ten homosexuals who lived quiet, carefree lives with their lovers. Why should he, specifically, lose Abduh?

Bit by bit his mood deteriorated. He lost his appetite for food, started drinking a lot, and kept to the house. He stopped going to the paper except for the most pressing of emergencies, which he would resolve and then hurry back home, where everything was silence, sorrow, and memories: Abduh used to sit here, and eat here, and put out his cigarette here, and . . . here he used to lie next to him, while Hatim stroked his black body, kissing every part of it and whispering in a voice trembling with the heat of desire, "You're mine, only mine, Abduh. You're my beautiful black stallion."

Hatim spent entire nights wallowing in his memories and going over his relationship with Abduh minute by minute till one night from amid the clouds of drunkenness and despair, an idea emerged that flashed in his mind like lightning. He recalled that Abduh had said once jokingly, "A Sa'idi can't live without other Sa'idis. You know, if I go any place I have to ask where's the café that the Sa'idis hang out."

Hatim pulled himself together and looked impatiently at his watch. It was past 1 A.M. He dressed hurriedly and in half an hour he was asking people on the street in Imbaba where the Sa'idi café was. In another half hour, he'd found it. In the short distance he traversed between the car and the entrance to the café, he felt the sweat pouring off his brow, and his heart was beating so hard it almost stopped.

The café was cramped and filthy. Hatim hurried in and looked around him impatiently. Later he would ponder the relation between our extreme desire for something and our ability to realize it—was what we wanted inevitably brought about if we wanted it enough? He longed so much to find Abduh that he did in fact find him. He was sitting in the farthest part of the café smoking a waterpipe, wearing a capacious, dark-colored gallabiya and had a large Sa'idi turban on his head. At that moment he looked enormous and imposing, like a magic dark-skinned jinni that had materialized from the world of the imagination. He looked too as though he had returned to his true self, to his origin and his roots; as though he had taken off along with his Western clothes his whole contingent and exceptional history with Hatim Rasheed. The latter stood before him for a moment in silence, looking at him closely as though confirming, verifying, laying hold of, his presence, lest he disappear again. An instant later he rushed toward him and exclaimed in a gasping voice that made the customers turn their heads in his direction, "Abduh. At last."

Their intercourse on the first night was simple and spontaneous, as though she had been his wife for years. The rose opened to the touch of his fingers and he watered it more than once till it was quenched. This amazed him and he took to asking himself as he recalled the details of their wedding night how was it that he had succeeded easily with Radwa when he had never touched a woman before? Where had his apprehension, hesitation, and fear of failure gone? Perhaps it was because he felt at ease emotionally with Radwa, or because he had applied all Sheikh Bilal's advice, or because his wife had encouraged him with her experience and shown him the secret sources of pleasure. This she had done skillfully and adeptly, though without abandoning her natural modesty as a Muslim woman.

Taha thought about all this and came to the conclusion that his marriage to this woman was a great benison from Our Lord, Glorious and Mighty, because she was a woman who was refined, honest, and sincere in her Islam. He loved her and felt at ease with their daily routine. He would leave her in the morning and spend the whole day at the camp. Then he would return after the last prayer of the day to find the room tidy and clean and delicious hot food waiting for him. How he loved to sit with her at the low round table to eat their dinner! He would tell her what had happened during the day and she would recount to him her conversations with her sister Muslims and give him a summary of what she had read in the newspapers (which he didn't have time to read). They would laugh together at the antics of little Abd el Rahman and his mischief, which would only be put to a stop when he fell all of a sudden into the clutches of sleepiness, at which point Radwa would carry him to the bed she had prepared for him on the floor, returning to remove the remains of the food and carefully wash the dishes.

Then she would excuse herself to go into the bathroom and Taha would get straight into their old iron bed to wait for her, stretched out on his back, gazing at the ceiling, his heart brimming with that delicious, nervy passion that he had come to know and love and to which he looked forward every night—his implacable longing for her; her enchanting body, refreshed by the hot water, naked but for a large towel that enveloped her as she emerged from the bathroom; the tense, thrilling, silent moments, gravid with desire, while she turned her back to him and prettied herself before the mirror; and the confused words, empty of meaning, that she spoke in a hushed, gasping voice as she made a pretense of conversing on any subject, as though to conceal her desire for him. He would understand the signal and grant her no delay, crushing to himself her supple, tall, slender body and tickling her with his kisses and his burning breath till his sweetness overflowed and he emptied himself in her embrace of all his feelings—his sorrows, his memories, his frustrated hopes, his unstilled desire for revenge and his savage hatred for his torturers; even those blazing, obscure sexual yearnings that had so often swept over him and made him ache in his room on the roof—all this he would empty into Radwa's body, to emerge liberated, at rest, the fire damped and replaced by a calm, steady affection that grew more firmly rooted every night.

Once they had made love he would gaze at her with genuine gratitude and cover her hands, face, and hair with kisses. He had become an expert in the topography of her body and learned its language so well that their lovemaking would last for hours, during which Radwa's face would light up at times with intoxication.

Months passed in his life with her in which he tasted happiness. Then one night he was with her in bed when his performance unexpectedly faltered and he grew confused and finally desisted. Silence reigned and suddenly he jumped up, shaking the bed beneath them, and rushed over to switch on the light. She gathered together her clothes to cover her naked body and asked him anxiously, "What's the matter?"

He stayed silent and seated himself on the couch. Then he slowly doubled over and put his head in his hands, his faced creasing as though something was hurting him. Greatly distressed, she hurried over to him and asked, "What's wrong with you, Taha?"

Affected perhaps by her genuine concern for him, he moved restlessly, heaved a great sigh, and then said, avoiding her eyes, "Please don't misunderstand me, Radwa. I'm happy of course with our marriage and I thank God a thousand times over for having provided me with a godly wife like you. But I didn't join the camp to get married. I came with Sheikh Shakir for a particular purpose, to struggle for God's cause. I've been here for a year, I've finished all the different types of training, and till now they haven't entrusted me with a single mission. I'm scared that my determination will weaken as time passes."

He was speaking in a soft, sad voice. Then he struck his leg with his hand and cried bitterly, "If it were all about getting married, I would have married you anywhere but in the camp. Every day I ask myself a hundred times, 'Why am I here?' Why, Radwa? I'm sure that Sheikh Bilal married me to you to distract my mind from the struggle."

Radwa smiled like a wise, understanding mother and putting her arm around his shoulder said affectionately, "Seek refuge with God and chase these thoughts from your head because they're the whisperings of Satan. Sheikh Bilal is an honest man and never lies. If he thought you weren't worthy of gihad, he would have expelled you from the camp, just as he would never marry you to a corrupt woman who would divert you from your religion" (and here her voice took on a reproachful tone). "I'm your wife, Taha, and I'm the first to encourage you in gihad and I'll be the first to feel proud of you if you attain martyrdom, which I pray God I may attain alongside you. But I know from my experience with the late martyr Hassan that military operations are not a game and that they are governed by precise considerations that are known only to the brothers on the Gamaa Council."

Taha opened his mouth to object, but she quickly and gently laid her hand on it as though to stop him speaking and whispered, "Be patient, Taha, be patient. *Surely God is with the patient*."

At exactly ten o'clock on Thursday morning, a black "Phantom" Mercedes pulled up in front of the Yacoubian Building. A smartly dressed man in his forties descended and made inquiries until he was conducted to Hagg Azzam's office, where he greeted the latter and haughtily presented himself, saying, "Gamal Barakat, from the Basha's office."

Hagg Azzam sat next to him in the car, but throughout the journey they exchanged no more than a few compliments, after which Azzam busied himself with telling his prayer beads and saying prayers. He knew that the Big Man lived on the Mariyut Canal, but he'd never imagined that his house would look the way it did—a vast palace, reminiscent of the royal palaces he'd seen as a child, set on a high hill which made it look like an impregnable citadel, and surrounded by not less than fifty acres of land, all of it under cultivation.

To cover the distance between the outer gate and the door of the palace, it took the car about half an hour, during which it traveled along a long highway amid gardens and trees. Three times it came to a halt in front of a security barrier where it was inspected by security men. They were enormous and dressed in three-piece suits with matching ties. Large pistols hung from their belts and in their hands they held electrically operated batons that whistled and which they carefully examined the car with, proceeding thereafter to scrutinize Hagg Azzam's identity card, comparing its details with the permit that the secretary presented to them. This happened three times and annoyed Hagg Azzam so much that on the last occasion he came close to objecting. However, he suppressed his anger and kept silent and eventually the car mounted a broad, winding driveway that took it to the door of the palace. There the security procedures were repeated with the same care and thoroughness, and this time they opened and went through Hagg Azzam's briefcase and then asked him to go through a metal detector. The annoyance showed clearly on his face and the secretary came up to him and said rudely, "The security procedures are essential."

The secretary then asked him to wait in the lobby and disappeared. Hagg Azzam remained waiting for a while, during which he looked at the marble columns, the Persian designs on the luxurious carpets, and the giant crystal chandeliers that hung from the high ceiling. Slowly he started to feel annoyed and insulted and thought that they must be using this long wait and the exaggerated security procedures deliberately to humiliate him. "They treat me with contempt at the same time that they rob me of my money. They want to get a quarter of the profits on a platter and don't utter a word of thanks, the impudent thugs!" Azzam's resentment grew, his face darkened, and he felt a strong urge to pull out of the meeting; he felt like summoning the secretary then and there, and telling him that he was leaving, come what may, but in his heart he knew that that was impossible; even if they left him waiting the whole morning, he wouldn't dare say a word in protest. He was swimming with the big fish now and one mistake could be the end of him. It was his responsibility to prepare his gambit and draw on all his experience so as to ensure that the Big Man felt sorry for him and to convince him to reduce the percentage to less than a quarter. That was the utmost he could do and any stupidity he might commit he would pay for dearly and immediately.

Finally he heard footsteps behind him and was seized by such terror that he found himself bereft of the strength to turn around. One of the guards appeared and made a sign to him to follow him. They walked down a long corridor, their footsteps ringing on the polished marble floor, and ended up in a spacious hall, with, facing the door, a large oak desk and a large conference table around which ten chairs were lined up. The guard signaled to Azzam to sit and said insolently as he departed, "Wait here till the Basha calls you."

Azzam was perturbed by the use of the word "call." Did that mean that perhaps the Big Man was not actually there? Why hadn't he contacted him to cancel the appointment and save him all this trouble and why had they left him waiting so long? Suddenly, he heard a voice echoing loudly throughout the hall saying, "Welcome, Azzam!"

Seized by terror, he leaped to his feet and looked around, searching for the source of the voice, which uttered a gentle laugh and continued, "Don't be scared! I'm somewhere else, but I'm calling you and I can see you. Unfortunately, I don't have a lot of time. Let's get to the point. Why did you ask to meet me?"

The Hagg pulled his wits together and made an effort to raise his voice and say the things that he'd prepared over the past two weeks, but he was so rattled that the ideas evaporated in his head. After a few moments he was just able to get out, "I'm at your service, sir, and Your Excellency's to command. Your graciousness overwhelms me and your goodness embraces the whole nation. May Our Lord keep you for us and preserve you for Egypt! I live in expectation that Your Excellency will regard my case with mercy, sir. I have many responsibilities and I've got households to support, God knows. Twenty-five percent's a great burden for me, sir, really."

The Big Man said nothing, so Azzam was encouraged and he went on, "I am covetous of your Excellency's generosity. For the sake of the Prophet, don't send me away brokenhearted! If Your Excellency could lower the percentage to an eighth, for example, I'd be most grateful."

Another moment of silence passed. Then the voice of the Big Man rang out irritably, "Listen, Azzam. I don't have time to waste on you. That's the set rate and it's the same for everyone. We go into any big business like your agency as partners for a quarter of the profits. We get that percentage in return for our work. We protect you from the tax office, the insurance office, the safety standards office, the audit office, and a thousand other offices that could bring your project to a halt and destroy you in a flash. And anyway, you especially should thank God that we're willing to work with you at all, because you're in a dirty trade."

"Dirty?"

Azzam repeated the word in a loud voice and a murmur of denial escaped from him that provoked the Big Man even more, for his voice rose warningly as he said, "Are you really an idiot or are you just pretending to be one? Your basic profit comes from a dirty trade that has nothing to do with the Japanese agency. Bottom line is, you deal in hard drugs and we know all about it. Sit at the desk and open the file with your name on it. You'll find copies of the reports on your activities—investigations by National Security, the Narcotics Squad, and Central Criminal Investigations. We have everything. We're the ones who have put a hold on them and we're the ones who can activate them at a moment's notice to destroy you. Sit down, Azzam, and don't be silly—read the file. Study it and learn it well, and at the end, you'll find a copy of our partnership contract. If you feel like signing it, sign it. It's up to you."

The Big Man let out a derisive laugh and the voice was cut off.

Abduh greeted him with distaste. He shook hands with him coldly without rising, then averted his face and occupied himself with his waterpipe. Hatim smiled and said affectionately, "What kind of a way to greet someone is this? At least order me some tea!"

Without looking at him Abduh clapped his hands and ordered a glass of tea from the waiter. Hatim began the conversation by saying, "My condolences, Abduh. You believe in Our Lord and His power. But does grieving over your son have to stop you from seeing me?"

Abduh suddenly exploded, "Stop it, Hatim Bey! God forgive us, my son died because of me."

"Meaning what?"

"Meaning Our Lord punished me for sinning with you."

"So everyone whose son dies is being punished by God?"

"Yes. Our Lord, Glorious and Mighty, 'delays but does not forget.' I offended greatly with you and I deserve to be punished."

"Who made you believe that? Your wife Hidiya?"

"What business is it of yours if it was Hidiya or anyone else? I'm telling you it's over between us. Each one goes his own way. I don't see you and you don't see me ever again."

His voice was agitated and strangled and he was shouting and waving his hands as though to push himself past the point of no return. Hatim said nothing for a while, then started to talk calmly with a changed plan in mind.

"Okay, old chap. We're agreed. You've left the roof and the kiosk and you want to end our relationship, and I agree. But where are you going to find the money for yourself and your wife?"

"God provides."

"Of course God provides. But it's my duty to help you, even if our relationship is over. Despite your ill treatment, Abduh, I still care about you. . . . Listen. I've found you a great job so you'll remember me kindly."

Abduh remained silent and seemed to be hesitating. He took a long draw on the waterpipe as though to hide his confusion.

"Aren't you going to ask me what the job is? . . . I've recommended you for the post of doorkeeper at the French Cultural Center in El Mounira. It's a decent and easy job and the pay is five hundred pounds a month."

Abduh remained silent, neither accepting nor objecting. Hatim, sensing his success, went on, "You deserve the best, Abduh. Here."

He took a pen and a checkbook from his purse, put on his glasses, wrote a check, and said, smiling, "This is a check for a thousand pounds to cover your expenses till you take over the new job."

His hand remained extended for a moment until Abduh slowly stretched out his hand and took the check, saying in a low voice, "Thank you."

"Abduh, I never forced our relationship on you. If you've decided to leave me, leave me. But I have one last request to make of you."

"What request?"

Hatim leaned toward him until they were touching, put his hand on Abduh's leg, and whispered in a passionate voice, "Stay with me tonight. Just tonight, and it'll be our last. I promise, Abduh, if you come with me tonight, you'll never see me again after that. I'm begging you."

They sat next to each other in the car wrapped in a tense silence. Hatim was putting his plan into effect with precision and reckoned that in the end he would be able to keep Abduh, who would be incapable of resisting the attractions of the money and the new job, just as he would resume their relationship as soon as he had tasted the plea-

sure once again. Abduh for his part had justified his acceptance of
Hatim's invitation as something unavoidable imposed on him by his
circumstances: since leaving the kiosk, he'd been unable to find the
money to support himself and his wife, taking even his tea and
tobacco on credit from the owner of the café, who was from his home
village. He had borrowed three hundred pounds in less than two
months from his Sa'idi acquaintances and he was fed up with his fruit-
less search for suitable work. He had worked as a day laborer, but he
couldn't stand it and left after a few days. It was no longer in his power
to endure that kind of hard work, carrying the heavy basin of mortar
on his back up and down all day long for a few pounds, half of which
were stolen by the contractor, to say nothing of the insults and indig-
nities. What was he to do, then? The job that Hatim was offering him
was respectable and decent and would keep the wolf from the door
forever. So why shouldn't he sleep with him just tonight, do what he
wanted just this once, and then cash the check, pay off his debts, cover
his immediate needs and the moment he started his new job break off
the relationship and close this dirty chapter in his life? He was
confident that God would forgive him and accept his repentance and
he would go at the first opportunity once this was over and make the
pilgrimage so that he could return purified of all sin, just as his mother
had borne him. It would be the last night for him to commit the sin
and the next day he would announce his repentance and sin no more.
Abduh decided privately that he would not inform Hidiya that he had
seen Hatim because if she knew she would make his life hell. In fact,
she hadn't gone a day since the death of the child without fighting
with him and abusing him and calling God's wrath down upon him.
The sorrow had caused her to lose her mind and she had become a
heavy burden on his nerves, treating him as though he had murdered
his son with his own hands. The sad thing was that the feeling of guilt
had seeped into him from her and taken him over, often preventing

him from sleeping. All that would come to an end tonight. He would satisfy Hatim's body one last time, get the position, and stop sinning.

They entered the apartment without speaking and Hatim turned on the lights, saying cheerfully, "The house is horrible without you."

Abduh suddenly drew close to him, embraced him, and tried to take off his clothes so that he could make love to him. He was in a hurry to get the job done but Hatim understood his haste as a sign of his longing for him and laughing a happy coquettish laugh whispered, "Be patient, Abduh!"

He hurried into the inner rooms while Abduh opened the bar, took out a bottle of whisky, and poured himself a large glass, which he polished off at one gulp without water or ice. He felt an urgent need to get drunk and, in the short time that it took Hatim to pretty himself up, had emptied a number of glasses into his belly. The alcohol took immediate effect. He could sense the blood surging passionate and hot through his veins, and the feeling took possession of him that he was strong and capable and that nothing could stop him from doing what he wanted. Hatim came out of the bathroom wearing rose silk pajamas over his naked body and walked slinkily to the kitchen, returning with hot food, which he placed on the table, and poured himself a glass of whisky, which he slowly sipped, provocatively licking the edge of the glass with his tongue. Then he put his hand on Abduh's strong arm, and sighed, "I've missed you so much."

Abduh removed his hand and said in a drunken voice, "Hatim Bey, we made a deal. Tonight's our last night. Tomorrow morn, each goes his own way, roight."

Hatim smiled and, passing his fingers over Abduh's thick lips, said, in playful imitation of his accent, "Roight, you Sa'idi you."

This time Abduh could not contain himself, pounced on Hatim, and picking him up like a child despite his laughing protests and provocative cries, threw him down on the bed, pulled off his pants, and

234

threw himself on top of him. He made love to him violently, ravishing him in a way he had never done before and causing Hatim to scream out loud more than once from the pleasure and the pain. Abduh slaked his lust in Hatim's body three times in less than an hour without uttering a single word, as though he were enthusiastically performing an unwelcome task in order to be quit of it. When they were done, Hatim lay stretched out naked on his stomach and closed his eyes in an ecstatic swoon, like one who was drugged or asleep and wanting never to awake from his delicious dream. Abduh meanwhile remained stretched out staring at the ceiling and smoked two cigarettes without saying a word. Then he jumped up and started putting on his clothes. Hatim, becoming aware of what he was doing, pulled himself up into a sitting position on the bed and asked him anxiously, "Where are you going?"

"I'm leaving."

Abduh said this with indifference, as though the matter was closed. Hatim got up, stood in front of him, and said, "Stay here tonight and go tomorrow."

"I'm not staying one minute."

Hatim hugged his naked body to him and whispered, "Stay the night, for me."

All of a sudden, Abduh pushed him so hard that Hatim fell into the chair next to the bed. His face turned red and he shouted furiously, "Have you gone crazy? What do you think you're doing, pushing me?"

Abduh replied defiantly, "Each goes his own way now."

Abduh's clear statement, which proved that his plan had failed, angered Hatim. He said, "We agreed you'd spend the night."

"What we agreed to I've done and I owe you nothing."

"Who exactly do you think you are?"

Abduh didn't answer and finished dressing in silence so Hatim went on with even greater rancor, "Answer me! Who do you think you are?"

"A human being, just like you."

"You're just a barefoot, ignorant Sa'idi. I picked you up from the street, I cleaned you up, and I made you a human being."

Abduh took a slow step toward him, looked at him for a while with his drink-reddened eyes, and then said threateningly, "Look. Watch out you don't get rude with me. Got it?"

But Hatim had lost control of himself and as though touched by some satanic urge that was pushing him to the limit, he looked Abduh up and down contemptuously and said, "Have you taken leave of your senses, Abduh? With one telephone call I can send you to hell."

"You can't."

"I'll show you whether I can or not. If you go now, I'll call the police and tell them you robbed me."

Abduh almost answered him but instead shook his head and moved toward the door to leave. He felt he was the stronger and that Hatim could do nothing to implement his threat. He stretched out his hand to open the door of the apartment, but Hatim grabbed onto his gallabiya and shouted, "You're not going!"

"Let go of me, I'm warning you!"

"When I tell you to stay, it means stay!"

As Hatim cried out these words, he clung tenaciously to the neck of the gallabiya from behind. Abduh turned around, easily pulling away his hands, and slapped him hard on the face. Hatim stared at him for a moment, eyes bulging madly. Then he shouted, "You'd strike your master, you dog of a servant? I swear by your mother's life, no job and no money! First thing, I'll call the bank and stop the check. You can boil it and drink the water."

Abduh stood for a moment in the middle of the room while things sorted themselves out in his mind. Then he let out a hideous noise, something like the roar of an angry wild animal, and fell on Hatim, kicking him and punching him. He grabbed hold of him by the neck and started beating his head with all his might against the wall till he felt the blood spurting hot and sticky over his hands.

Later, in the police report, the neighbors mentioned that around four o'clock in the morning they had heard shouts and screams issuing from Hatim's apartment but had not interfered because they were aware of the nature of his private life.

In the Name of God, the Merciful, the Compassionate.
So let them fight in the way of God
who sell the present life for the world to come;
and whosoever fights in the way of God and is slain, or conquers,
We shall bring him a mighty wage.
How is it with you,
that you do not fight in the way of God,
and for the men, women, and children, who, being abased,
say, "Our Lord, bring us forth from this city whose people are evildoers,
and appoint us a protector from Thee,
and appoint us from Thee a helper?"

Sheikh Bilal recited from the chapter called "Women" in a sweet, mellifluous voice that affected those who were praying behind him. Holy awe took possession of them and they repeated after him the Prayer of Obedience in humble submission. The dawn prayer came to an end and Sheikh Bilal sat telling his prayer beads as the brothers came to him one by one to shake his hand with love and respect. When Taha el Shazli bent down over him, he pulled him gently toward him and whispered, "Wait for me in the office. I'll catch up with you there right away, God willing."

Taha set off straight for the office, asking himself why the sheikh wanted to see him. Radwa was always saying that she loved Sheikh Bilal like her father, but did she love him so much that she'd report to him what her husband had said about him? If she had done so she would have a painful reckoning with him. He would never forgive her; a wife had to be the faithful guardian of her husband's secrets. If the sheikh asked him about what he'd said to Radwa, he wouldn't lie. He would repeat it in front of him and take the consequences. What could the sheikh do to him? The most he could do was to throw him out of the camp. So be it. What was the point of his staying in the camp to eat, drink, sleep, and do nothing? If the sheikh was not going to let him join the gihad, it would be better to throw him out of the camp to return to where he'd come from.

Taha went on thinking along these lines until he pushed open the door of the office and warily entered. Inside he found two brothers waiting—Brother Dr. Mahgoub, who was a veterinarian of over forty, one of the pioneering generation that had founded the Gamaa Islamiya in the 1970s, and Brother Abd el Shafi, from the Fayoum, who had been a law student at Cairo University, then was repeatedly detained and hunted by Security till he abandoned his studies and came to live in the camp. Taha shook their hands affectionately and the three of them sat talking of general matters, though inwardly all of them felt anxiety and foreboding. Sheikh Bilal arrived, shook hands with them, embraced them warmly, and said as he looked at them with a smile on his face, "Youth of Islam, this is your day. The Gamaa's Consultative Council has chosen you to go out on an important operation."

A moment of silence passed. Then the brothers shouted "There is no god but God!" and embraced one another in happiness, the most joyful of all being Taha, who shouted out "Praise be to God! God is great!" The sheikh's smile widened and he said, "Bravo! God bless you and increase you in faith! This is why the enemies of Islam tremble in fear of you—because you love death as they love life!"

His face resumed its serious expression and he sat at the desk, spread a large sheet of paper out in front of him, and said, searching in the pocket of his gallabiya for a pen, "We don't have much time. The operation has to be carried out at 1 P.M. today or we'll have to wait a whole month at least. Sit down, boys, and give me all your attention."

Two hours later a small truck loaded to the brim with cylinders of cooking gas was making its way toward the Feisal area in the Pyramids district. In the driver's seat was Dr. Mahgoub and next to him Taha el Shazli. Brother Abd el Shafi had taken up position among the cylinders piled in the back of the truck. They had shaved off their beards and dressed themselves as workers distributing gas, the plan being for them to carry out a visual inspection of the site at least one hour before the operation, then stay in the street in a perfectly normal way until the National Security officer left his house. In the time between his exiting the door of the apartment block and his getting into his car, they were supposed to delay him by any means available to them, then open fire with the three automatic rifles hidden under the driver's seat. They were also provided with stern additional instructions. If the officer was able to get into his car before the plan had been implemented, they were to cut him off with their truck, then throw their whole supply of hand grenades at him at once, abandon the truck, and each run in a different direction firing into the air so that no one would pursue them. If they suspected that they were being observed, Dr. Mahgoub (as the emir of the group) had the right to call off the operation immediately, in which case they were to leave the truck in any side street and return to the camp separately using public transport.

As soon as the truck entered the Feisal area, it reduced speed and Brother Abd el Shafi started banging with his wrench on the gas cylinders to announce their arrival to the residents. A few women came to their balconies and windows and called out to the truck, which stopped more than once, Abd el Shafi carrying the cylinders to the residents, taking the money, and returning to the truck with the empties; these were the instructions of Sheikh Bilal, who was concerned that they have good cover. The truck arrived at Akif Street where the officer lived and a woman asked for a cylinder from her balcony, so Abd el Shafi took it to her. This provided an opportunity for Mahgoub and Taha to inspect the place at their leisure. The officer's car—a blue, late-seventies Mercedes—was waiting in front of the entrance to the building. Mahgoub carefully studied the distances, the neighboring shops, and the exits and entrances. When Abd el Shafi returned, the truck sped off to a point away from the site, where Dr. Mahgoub looked at his watch and said, "We have a whole hour. What do you say to a glass of tea?"

He spoke in a cheerful voice as though to instill confidence into them. The truck stopped in front of a small café in a neighboring street, where the three sat and drank mint tea. Their appearance was completely ordinary and incapable of provoking any suspicion. Mahgoub noisily sucked tea from his glass and said, "Praise God, everything's okay."

Taha and Abd el Shafi responded in a low voice, "Praise God."

"Did you know that the brothers in the Gamaa Council have been watching the target for a whole year?" he whispered.

"A whole year?" asked Taha.

"I swear, an entire year. Investigations are difficult because the high-ranking officers in National Security go to enormous lengths to conceal themselves. They use more than one name, have more than one residence, and sometimes they move with their families from one furnished apartment to another, all of which makes it almost impossible to get to them."

"What's the officer's name, Brother Mahgoub?"

"You're not supposed to know."

"I understand that it's forbidden, but I'd like to know."

"What difference would his name make to you?"

Taha fell silent, then looked at Mahgoub for a moment and said irritably, "Brother Mahgoub, we've started the gihad for real and maybe God will honor us with martyrdom and our souls will rise together to their maker. So can't you trust me a little, as we stand at death's door?"

Taha's words had an impact on Mahgoub, who was very fond of him, so he said in a low voice, "Salih Rashwan."

"Colonel Salih Rashwan?"

"A criminal, an unbeliever, and a butcher. He used to take pleasure in supervising the torture of Islamists and he's the one directly responsible for the killing of many brothers in detention. In fact, he killed with his own revolver two of the best of the youth of Islam, Brother Hassan el Shubrasi, the emir of Fayoum, and Dr. Muhammad Rafi', the Gamaa's spokesman. He boasted of killing them in front of the brothers in detention at the El 'Aqrab prison—may God have mercy on our innocent martyrs, bring them to dwell in the mansions of His paradise, and unite us with them without mishap, if God wills!"

At five minutes to one the gas truck pulled up on the other side of the street from the entrance to the apartment building. Abd el Shafi got down, went up to the driver's cabin, took a small notebook out of his pocket, and pretended to go over the accounts with Mahgoub, the driver. The two of them busied themselves with an audible discussion of the number of cylinders sold, appearing entirely natural, while Taha grasped the door handle in readiness. The entrance to the building was in clear view in front of him and he felt as though his heart was almost bursting it was beating so hard. He tried hard to focus his mind on a single point, but a roaring cataract of images swept through his mind's eye and a minute passed in which he saw his whole life scene by scene—his room on the roof of the Yacoubian Building, his memories of his childhood and his good-hearted mother and father, his old sweetheart Busayna el Sayed, his wife Radwa, the general in charge of the Police Academy condemning him for his father's profession, and the soldiers in the detention center beating him and violating his body.

He burned with longing to know whether this was the officer who had supervised his torture in detention, but he had not been frank with Mahgoub about this desire in case the latter should feel uneasy about him and exclude him from the operation. Taha kept staring at the building entrance, the memories rushing past in front of him, and then the officer appeared. He looked the way they had described him—portly, with a pale complexion, the traces of sleep and his hot bath still on his face, walking calmly and confidently, a cigarette dangling from the corner of his mouth.

Taha quickly opened the door, got out onto the street, and headed toward him. It was his job to detain him however he could till the others could fire at him. Then Taha would run and jump into the truck and throw a hand grenade to cover their flight. Taha approached the officer and asked him in a voice that he strove to make seem ordinary, "Please, sir, which way is No. Ten, Akif Street?"

The officer didn't stop but pointed haughtily and muttered, "Over there," as he continued toward his car.

It was he. He was the one who had supervised his torture, who had so often ordered the soldiers to beat him and shred his skin with their whips and force the stick into his body. It was he without the slightest doubt—the same husky voice, the same dispassionate intonation, and the familiar slight rasp due to his smoking. Taha lost all awareness of what he was doing and leaped toward him, letting out an inarticulate, high-pitched cry like an angry roar. The officer turned toward him with frightened eyes, his face pinched in terror as though he realized what was happening, and he opened his mouth to say something but couldn't because successive bursts of fire suddenly erupted from the automatic rifles, all of them striking the officer's body, and causing him to fall to the ground, the blood gushing out of him. Taha disobeyed the plan and remained where he was so that he could watch the officer as he died; then he shouted, "God is great! God is great!" and leaped to return to the truck. Something unexpected occurred, however. Sounds of glass being violently broken were heard on the first floor and two men appeared who started shooting in the direction of the truck.

Taha realized what was happening and tried to get his head down and run in a zigzag course as they had taught him during training so as to get out of the line of fire. He was getting close to the truck, the bullets flying around him like rain, but when he got to within two meters he felt a coldness in his shoulder and chest, a coldness that burned like ice and took him by surprise. He looked at his body and saw the blood spurting from his wounds and the coldness was transformed into a sharp pain that seized him in its teeth. He fell to the ground next to the rear wheel of the truck and screamed. Then it seemed to him as though the agony was diminishing little by little and he felt a strange restfulness engulfing him and taking him up into itself. A babble of distant sounds came to his ears—bells and sounds of recitation and melodious murmurs—repeating themselves and drawing close to him, as though welcoming him into a new world.

Starting in the late afternoon, Maxim's had been turned upside down.

In addition to the restaurant's own employees, ten other workers had been called in to help, and everyone was busy cleaning the floor, the walls, and the bathroom with soap and water and disinfectants. Then they moved the tables and chairs to the sides of the room so as to leave a broad corridor from the entrance to the bar and a wide space in the middle that could serve as a dance floor. They continued working tirelessly under the supervision of Christine, who had put on a baggy training suit and was helping them to move things herself (which was her way of encouraging them to work with a will), her voice ringing out from time to time in its broken Arabic that used feminine forms of Arabic words even when she was speaking to a man, saying, "You, move all that here! Clean it well! What's the matter? Are you tired or what?"

At seven o'clock the place was sparkling, with new gleaming white cloths, brought out especially for the occasion, spread on the tables. Then the flower baskets arrived and Christine oversaw their correct placement, the small bouquets untied and the flowers distributed among the vases, while she ordered the workers to place the large baskets at the entrance to the place outside, the length of the passageway. Next she took out from the drawer of her desk an elegant old sign on which was written in French and Arabic "The restaurant is reserved tonight for a private party" and hung it on the outer door. She poked her head inside for a last look and, satisfied with the restaurant's appearance, hurried to her house nearby to change her clothes.

By the time she returned an hour later in her smart blue gown, wearing restrained and expertly applied makeup and with her hair put up in a chignon after the fashion of the fifties, the band had arrived and its members were bent over tuning their instruments—mizmar, saxophone, violin, and rhythm section—the confused snatches of melody rising like the murmuring of some giant musical being.

The guests had started to arrive. A few old people who were Zaki el Dessouki's friends came, some of whom were known to Christine and with all of whom she shook hands, inviting them to visit the bar, where beer and whisky were offered free. The numbers of the guests continued to swell. Friends of Busayna's from Commercial College came, bringing their families. Ali the Driver came (and forced his way straight through to the bar) and Sabir the laundryman with his wife and children and many others from the roof. The women were wearing shiny gowns embroidered with gold thread and sequins, and the girls of marriageable age came in their best and smartest clothes, conscious of the opportunity for marriage that was implicit in the wedding. The roof people were awestruck at the poshness of the restaurant and its old European style, but little by little the women started to break through this by means of mirthful conversations on the side and loud bursts of laughter that were closer to bawdiness than the spirit of the occasion demanded.

At around nine the door opened and some people entered quickly, followed unhurriedly by Zaki el Dessouki in his smart black suit and a white shirt, a large red bowtie at his neck and his dyed hair swept back in a new cut that the hairdresser had suggested and which had secured its object, in that he appeared ten years younger than his real age. His steps were a little halting and his eyes bloodshot as a result of the two double whiskies that he had decided to start the evening with, and no sooner did he appear at the party than shouts, whistles, and applause— "Congratulations! A thousand congratulations!"—rang out on every side, with a few shy ululations. While everyone was shaking his hand and wishing him the best, Christine darted up to him, embraced him, and kissed him in her warmly affectionate way.

"You look like a movie star!" she exclaimed enthusiastically. Then she sighed, looked at him for a moment, and said, "How happy I am for you, Zaki! You've done what you should have done long ago."

This was the wedding party of Zaki Bey el Dessouki to Busayna el Sayed—who was a little late in coming from the coiffeur, as brides usually are, but who soon arrived in a white wedding dress the ends of whose long train were borne by her sisters and her little brother Mustafa. The moment the bride appeared, the sight of her touched all present and a clear and uninhibited storm of melodious, repeated ululations burst forth. Everyone was happy and as soon as the band had finished with the wedding march and the buffet had opened, Christine made a bid to preserve the European style of the occasion by playing Edith Piaf's song "La Vie en Rose" on the piano, singing in her mellifluous voice,

Quand il me prend dans ses bras
Il me parle tout bas
Je vois la vie en rose

Il me dit des mots d'amour
Des mots de tous les jours
Et ça m'fait quelque chose
Il est entré dans mon cœur.

The bride and groom danced on their own, Busayna a bit nervous and almost stumbling but guided to the right steps by the groom, who took advantage of the opportunity to pull her close to him in a move that did not escape the notice, or the laughing comments, of the guests. Zaki thought that Busayna in her wedding dress looked like some wondrous, pure, newborn creature and that she had rid herself forever of the blemishes of the past that through no fault of her own had tarnished her. When the song was over, Christine suavely tried to propose other French songs but in vain. Public opinion was so pressing that in the end it had to be accommodated and the band started playing oriental dance numbers. This was the magical moment, for the women and girls jumped up as though they had finally found themselves, clapping, singing, and swaying to the rhythm, more than one of them tying a sash around her hips and dancing. They kept insisting that the bride do the same until she gave in and allowed them to tie a sash on her and joined the dancers, while Zaki Bey el Dessouki watched her with love and admiration, clapping enthusiastically to the rhythm. Then little by little, raising his arms aloft amid the joyful laughter and cries of the others, he joined her in the dance.

Glossary

Abd el Halim Hafez: a singer and youth icon (1929–1977) who starred in many movies as the sort of character Busayna describes.

Abduh: a short form of Abd Rabbuh.

Abu Bakr: the first caliph (successor to the Prophet as ruler of the Islamic state) (died 634).

Abu el Aala el Mawdudi: a revolutionary Indian Islamist thinker (1903–1979).

Abu Hamid el Ghazali: a celebrated scholar of medieval Islam (1058–1111).

Abu Wael, i.e., Father of Wael: it is polite to address a parent by his or her child's name, preceded by "father of" or "mother of."

Age of Ignorance (*jahiliya*): this term is used in general parlance to mean the period before the announcement by the Prophet Muhammad of his mission. Radical Islamic groups, however, apply it to the (in their eyes) nonobservant mass of Muslim society today.

Ali Badawi: a leading jurist of the 1940s.

Ali ibn Abi Talib: son-in-law of the Prophet and fourth caliph (died 661).

Anwar Wagdi: dashing film star of the late 1940s and early 1950s (1904–1955).

Approval and Light Stores: the name has strong religious connotations, the "Approval" and "Light" referred to being God's.

El 'Aqrab Prison: a high-security prison in the Western Desert.

El Azhar: a mosque-university in Cairo and one of the most authoritative seats of Islamic learning.

basbusa: baked semolina soaked in syrup.

Bilharzia: a debilitating liver disease contracted by peasants from parasites in irrigation canals.

Center Platform: in 1975, following the liberalization of the economy under Anwar el Sadat, and by way of liberalizing political life, three wings or platforms were allowed within the Socialist Union—the Right, the Center, and the Left. The Center was understood to represent the ruling regime.

Central Security: a heavily armed branch of the police force used for crowd control at demonstrations or after large public events; the riot police.

Court of Cassation: Egypt's highest court of appeal.

Dar el Salam: a densely inhabited suburb of southern Cairo.

Drinking Sheikh: the logo of a brand of tea, in the form of an old man elegantly dressed in oriental clothes and holding a small cup in his hand.

Egypt Party: within a year or so of the formation of political platforms within the Socialist Union, the platforms were turned into parties. The Center Platform became the Egypt Party.

Emergency Law: in 1981, following the assassination of President Anwar el Sadat, a state of emergency was declared that suspends the constitution and gives expanded powers to the president; the Emergency Law remains in force to the present time.

emir: "commander"; a title used by Islamist groups to denote the leader of a cell or grouping.

Fatiha: the opening chapter of the Qur'an, often recited to conclude and seal a transaction.

The Fayoum: a large agricultural oasis southwest of Cairo that is said to be Egypt's poorest rural area.

feddan: a unit of land measurement equal to slightly more than an acre.

Free Officers: a clandestine organization within the Egyptian army that organized the overthrow of the monarchy in 1952.

gallabiya: a full-length gown closed in front, the traditional dress worn by many Egyptians.

Gamaa: i.e., Gamaa Islamiya (the "Islamic Group"), one of the best-known Egyptian militant Islamist groups.

Gezira Club: the oldest, best-known, and most socially desirable club in Cairo, with large grounds in Zamalek.

gihad: Muslims distinguish between the "spiritual" or "greater" gihad, which is the Muslim's effort toward moral and religious perfection, and the "physical" or "lesser" gihad, which is military action for the expansion or defense of Islam. The "paean to gihad," referred to in the text, could be any of a number of chants popular among Islamic activists. One such chant (used by the Muslim Brotherhood) goes, "Allah is our god, the Prophet our leader, and to die for Allah our dearest wish."

hadith: an act or saying of the Prophet Muhammad. Reported Traditions are graded from "weak" to "sound" on the basis of the reliablility of their chains of transmission.

Hagg: title of respect to a man who has made the pilgrimage to Mecca.

Hamas: a Palestinian Islamist political and military movement.

Hizbollah: a Lebanese Islamist political and military movement.

El Hussein: grandson of the Prophet Muhammad; a relic of El Hussein is contained in a large mosque in Cairo's old city that is the focus of intense popular piety.

Imbaba: a poor and densely populated district on the west bank of the Nile.

El Karadawi, Yusef: an influential Egyptian Islamist preacher, writer, and theorist (born 1926).

Khadra el Shareefa: a character in the traditional epic, *The*

Adventures of the Bani Hilal. The chaisty of a high-born woman, Khadra el Shareefa is unjustly impeached.

Khalid: Khalid ibn el Walid, a leading Companion of the Prophet Muhammad and a commander of the Muslim armies during the early conquests (died 642).

Khaybar: an oasis and settlement in the region of Medina, the Prophet's capital, that was inhabited by Jews. In retaliation for the latter's intrigues with local Arab tribes against the nascent Muslim state, Khaybar was attacked, besieged, and finally defeated.

Kotzika substation: located on Marouf Street (a turning off Suleiman Basha Street) and named after a Greek businessman who owned property in the area.

Liberation Organization: founded by the new revolutionary regime of Gamal Abd el Nasser in the early 1950s; the liberation alluded to was that of the Canal Zone, from British occupation.

Mahmoud Said: Egyptian painter (1897–1964) of upper-class background, many of whose paintings depict voluptuous women of the lower classes.

El Mansoura: a large town in the northeast Delta, about a hundred miles from Cairo.

modest dress: the concept of "modest dress" gained currency in Egypt in the 1970s and as usually employed means dress that covers all of a woman's body except her face and hands, conceals the outlines of her figure, and covers her hair and neck; in an extended interpretation, it may involve the covering of the face and hands as well.

Muhammad Naguib: Egypt's first president, who acceded to the position in 1953 and was deposed by Gamal Abd el Nasser in 1954.

mulukhiya: a leafy green vegetable (Jews' mallow or *Corchorus olitorius*) that is prepared as a slightly viscous soup.

Muslim Brothers: an Islamist political movement founded in Egypt in 1928.

Nahhas Basha: Prime minister at the time of the 1952 revolution by Gamal Abd el Nasser's Free Officers against the monarchy.

National Union: replaced the Liberation Union in the wake of the evacuation of foreign troops from Egypt in 1956.

Open Door Policy: introduced by president Anwar el Sadat with the aim of reversing Gamal Abd el Nasser's "Arab Socialism" and restoring capitalism to Egypt.

Patriotic Party: no party by this name exists in Egypt.

People's Assembly: the Lower House of the Egyptian parliament.

People's suit: a men's outfit made of unlined cloth and consisting of pants and a short-sleeved top. It was introduced during the Nasser era as a cheap alternative to the conventional business suit and sold at government-owned People's Stores.

Phantom Mercedes: the nickname of the Mercedes S320 (1991–1998).

rayyis: a title for lower-class men who hold positions of responsibility in traditional occupations.

Saad: Saad ibn Abi Waqqas, a leading Companion of the Prophet Mohammad, reputedly the first Muslim to fire an arrow "in God's cause," and a commander of the Muslim armies during the early conquests (died between 670 and 680).

Sa'idis: Upper Egyptians.

Sayed Kutb: Islamic writer and activist, the leading thinker of the Muslim Brothers (1906–1966).

Shibin el Kom: a medium-sized town about eighty kilometers northwest of Cairo.

Sidi Bishr: a suburb of Alexandria.

siwak: a small stick, usually of the arak tree, the tip of which is softened by beating or chewing and which is rubbed on the teeth and gums.

Socialist Union: replaced the National Union in 1961 following massive nationalizations and other measures which inaugurated the new phase of "socialist transformation."

Suleiman Basha Street: one of the main avenues of Cairo's Downtown, running between Tahrir ("Liberation") Square and Twenty-sixth July Street (formerly, King Fouad Street). The street is named after Joseph Sève (1788–1860), a French officer who following the defeat of Napoleon was hired by Muhammad Ali, viceroy of Egypt, and became commander-in-chief of the Egyptian army, having converted to Islam. In 1954, the official name was changed to Talaat Harb Street but many people still use the old name.

Taha Hussein: literary critic, author, and educator (1889–1973).

Tahrir Square: "Liberation Square," the main square in Cairo's downtown area.

Talaat Harb Street: though the author generally refers to the street by its original name of Suleiman Basha Street, its official name since 1954 has been Talaat Harb Street, after the nationalist banker and entrepreneur of that name.

Throne Verse: Qur'an II, 255; in Arberry's translation this reads "God, there is no god but He, the Living, the Everlasting. Slumber seizes Him not, neither sleep; to Him belongs all that is in the heavens and the earth. Who is there that shall intercede with Him save by His leave? He knows what lies before them and what is after them, and they comprehend not anything of His knowledge save such as He wills. His Throne comprises the heavens and the earth; the preserving of them oppresses Him not; He is the All-hearing, the All-glorious" (I, 65).

Turah el Asmant: an industrial suburb about fifteen kilometers south of Cairo and the site of a large cement factory and other major industrial plants.

Umar: Umar ibn el Khattab, the second caliph (died 644).

Vanguard Organization: created in 1964 or 1965 to act as a clandestine network within the Socialist Union to ensure the latter's fidelity to its socialist vocation.

Wafd: the largest political party during the monarchy.

Workers' seat: Under the constitution, Egyptian parliamentary constituencies are represented by two seats, one of which is reserved for workers or farmers, the other for "other categories."

Zaki Naguib Mahmoud: literary critic, translator, and essayist (1905–1993).

Qur'anic References

Had the peoples of the cities
believed and been God-fearing,
We would have opened upon them
blessings from heaven and earth.
VII, 96 (Arberry 155)

It may happen that you will hate
a thing which is better for you.
II, 216 (Arberry 29)

A monstrous word it is, issuing
from their mouths; they say nothing
but a lie.
XVIII, 5 (Arberry 288)

In the name of God, the Merciful,
the Compassionate. . . . who said of
their brothers . . .
III, 168–74 (Arberry 66-67)

You have had a good example in
God's Messenger.
XXXIII, 21 (Arberry 429)

How evil a homecoming!
II, 126 (Arberry 16)

How often a little company has
overcome a numerous company,
by God's leave!
II, 249 (Arberry 36)

Sweet patience.
LXX, 5 (Arberry 606)

Your women are a tillage for you . . .
II, 223 (Arberry 31)

Surely God is with the patient.
VIII, 46 (Arberry 174)

In the name of God, the Merciful,
the Compassionate. So let them
fight in the way of God . . .
IV, 74–75 (Arberry 83)

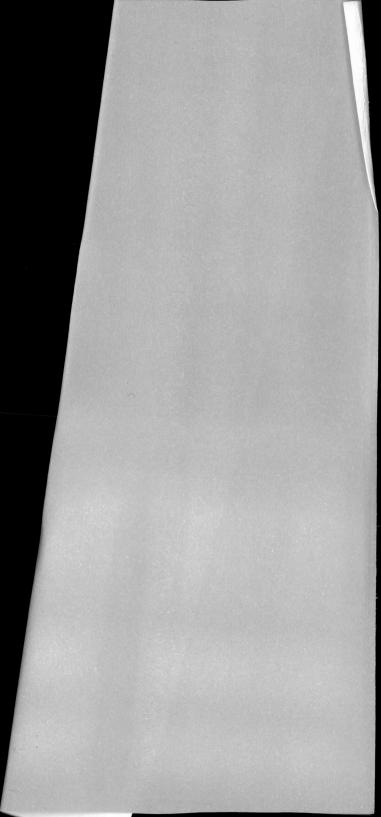

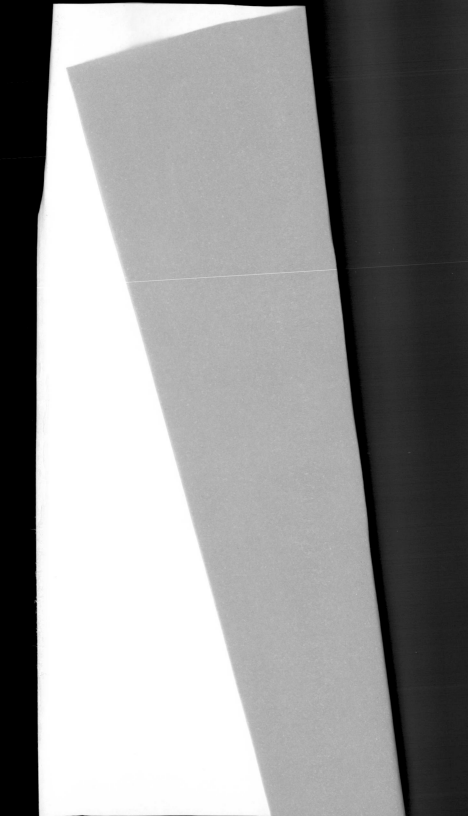